VAMPIRE BOYS

An Erotic Anthology

Edited By Mickey Erlach

STAR BOOKS PRESS

Herndon, VA

Published in the United States by STARbooks Press, PO Box 711612, Herndon, VA 20171. Printed in the United States

Many thanks to graphic artist Emma Aldous: www.arthousepublishing.co.uk

Herndon, VA

CONTENTS

MONSTER UNDER THE BED
By Logan Zachary

Logan Zachary (LoganZachary2002@yahoo.com) lives in Minneapolis, MN. His latest books are available, and his short stories can be found in many anthologies.

As a kid when I had Friday night sleepovers, we always watched scary movies and told ghost stories before we went to bed. Movies like *Carrie, Friday the 13th*, and *Prom Night 2, Hello Mary Lou* were some of the crazy ones we watched

After the movies were over, we would huddle together in our sleeping bags on the floor and tell spooky stories. There was one tale about Bloody Mary in the bathroom mirror, and the one about the girl on a car date with a crazed-hook-handed killer being dragged to death behind the car, and there was the one about the thing under the bed that licked the girl's hand when she was afraid because she heard dripping in the night. She thought it was her dog licking her hand, but it was really a monster, and the dripping she heard had been her dog's blood.

Now being a gay boy with all these straight ones, I could somehow relate but didn't understand the girls in these stories. I enjoyed sleeping in my tightie whities with the other boys. If I was lucky, I would curl up next to a cold boy and get to share a warm sleeping bag.

Sometimes, we'd play with Tarot cards, a Ouija board, or a regular deck of cards for strip poker. We didn't understand why our little dicks got hard and why each one of us was so different, bigger balls, long or thicker cocks, or a fatter butt.

These were the years before pubic hair and hormones, but even then, I knew I liked boys and wanted to marry one.

Now it was ten years later, and I was twenty-two. I had a hairy chest and balls, a huge penis, a furry ass of death, but no boyfriend in sight. What was I to do? Move into a haunted house and learn about the occult, so I could conjure up my own handsome man/ghost?

Well, my magic skills suck and no supernatural elements have come to find me. So I did buy a haunted house, and I'm still waiting to see a ghost or ghoul or anything.

On the night of the full moon during the fall solstice, I lit a few black candles and went to bed. During the midnight hour, I heard a drip, drip, drip. Did I leave the water on in the bathroom?

I stumbled out of bed bare footed and checked the bathroom sink, tub, and toilet.

Nothing.

I went downstairs and checked the dishwasher and sink.

No leaks.

I got chilled and crawled back into my bed and curled up, trying to get warm. As I rubbed my hairy legs together to warm up, my cock started to rise. I reached down and adjusted myself in my shorts. The leg loop was digging into my groin, so I slipped them off. With my balls and cock free, my erection grew to full length. I stroked it a few times but knew I had to go back to sleep. My cock felt so good, another stroke, and I tickled a ball, then the other one.

The cool sheets slid over my hairy body and sent more waves of excitement through me. Should I jack off or should I try to sleep? Jacking off would help me fall asleep, but the cold, wet spot in the sheets would wake me up.

Drip.

I stopped jacking and listened.

Drip.

Where was that noise coming from?

Drip.

My cock started to deflate, and my mood faded. I rolled over onto my back and stretched out, finally warmed up and relaxed. I closed my eyes and took a deep breath. My hand slipped out from under the covers and slowly slipped off the bed. Sleep fell over me, and I drifted, drifted off to sleep.

But as I drifted off, I swore a tongue licked my hand.

# # # # #

The next morning, I searched the whole house and didn't find a leaking faucet anywhere. I stood and listened, stood and listened.

Nothing.

No water rings or spots on the floors, or on the walls, or on the ceiling. I had better things to do, so I went around the house and did my other chores. The day flew by, and I showered before bed.

I was exhausted and walked to my bed naked. I slipped in and lay on my back, looking up at the ceiling. The shower had warmed me up and relaxed me, so as I started to drift off. My body became too hot, and I slipped a foot out from under the covers. My bare foot started to cool off as it was exposed to the night air.

Drip.

Was I dreaming as I drifted off to sleep or did something really lick my toes? I slept great, better than I ever remembered, but ...

Drip.

Being exhausted made me fall asleep quickly, but a wet warm thing licked between my toes, and I drifted off.

Drip.

# # # # #

3

I awoke and lay staring at the ceiling.

What had happened last night?

I closed my eyes and forced my mind to replay the last few seconds before I fell asleep. I could have sworn that a warm, wet tongue licked between my toes, but I may have been dreaming at that point, too.

I did remember hearing the dripping again as I fell asleep, and I got out of bed naked and looked under my bed. My bare butt was in the air, as I saw I had done an excellent job dusting under the bed the previous weekend. No dust bunnies, no wet spots, nothing. My balls swung free in the cool morning air and sent my hair to stand on end all over my body. My morning wood demanded attention, and I wasn't sure if the bathroom or my hand called louder.

My bladder won.

The bathroom tiles were cool on my bare feet. I looked at myself in the mirror as I ran my hand through my hair and pulled it back. I scratched my hairy ass as I emptied my bladder. The ball pressure went down as did my erection. I grabbed my cock and shook off the last few drips and pulled on my balls to get them from sticking to my leg. They were so full, and they needed a good jerk off session to release some pressure, but I jumped into the shower and soaped up. As I rinsed my hair, I stroked my cock back into a full hard on and thought of the last night.

What could it have been? It had happened twice now, so what was going on? Creamy foam flowed over my balls and cock as I soaped between my legs and balls. I washed along my cock, my hand slipped easily over my palm as I scrubbed. It felt great.

But, the phone rang and startled me out of the pleasure. I rinsed off quickly, jumped out of the shower, and ran to the phone wet feet slipping and slapping the wood floor as I grabbed my towel and wiped my hands and face.

"Thank you for using Walgreens automatic refill service."

I set the phone down and dried off the rest of my body. A small pool of water surrounded my feet. Once dry, I dropped the towel and soaked up the water.

The mood to jack off had passed, and I made a special note for tonight, I would make time.

# # # # #

Wrong answer. I stripped and dropped into bed, and let my whole leg hang off the bed. I couldn't bring it in. I was done. I lay there and fell asleep. As REM sleep settled over me I felt a tongue lap up my foot, around my ankle along my calf, and over my knee. At that point, my cock started to swell under the covers and grew with each beat of my heart.

The tongue continued up my leg and along the sensitive inside of my thigh. It moved closer and closer to the sheets that covered my hairy balls, but the deep crease where my leg attached to my torso was wide open and extra tender. The licking edged to the sheets, straining to go deeper to my arousal. My hips pushed toward the wonderful feeling and then sleep took over, and I was out.

Drip.

Lick.

Drip.

Lick.

Drip.

# # # # #

Then next day I knew I was either going crazy or there was someone in my house. Could ghosts touch me? Could they lick me? Did they have warm tongues? Maybe there was a portal to another world in my house and under my bed... I'd been watching too many rerun episodes of *Buffy the Vampire Slayer*.

Anyway, I planned on going to bed early and pretending to sleep and see what happened.

5

I had a raging hard on in my pants all day, just at the thought of someone licking my toes, my legs, my thigh, and my ....

I daydreamed at work, but no magic tongue found my nether region to lick. I oozed in my pants and even noticed a wet spot forming. I added toilet paper to my underwear to absorb my own juices.

The afternoon took forever, and I was depressed when I remembered I had to meet my sister for supper. I just wanted to go home, get into bed, and see what happened.

Maybe I needed the drip, drip, drip.

# # # # #

Supper went on forever, and I have no clue what my sister talked about.

But I wondered as she droned on and on was there a Hobgoblin in my house? Maybe it was an Elf? A Troll? The Boogeyman? An Incubus? A Succubus? A Vampire?

Nothing made sense.

So finally, I kissed my sister goodbye and headed home. I jumped in the shower scrubbed every inch of my body and walked naked to my room. My cock grew harder and harder the closer I got to my bed. It was a raging hard on as I crawled under the covers but remembered whatever it was couldn't get under the sheets, so I pulled them back and let my cock wave in the dark.

I closed my eyes and waited. I dropped my leg and arm over the side of the bed and waited.

Nothing.

Maybe it knew I wasn't asleep. I controlled my breathing and started a snort and a snore. Yes, I snore. Friends have threatened me with a C-PAP, but I wanted to be hose free.

Drip.

I stopped snoring and listened.

Nothing.

I snored.

Drip.

I snored louder.

Drip.

Lick.

It was happening.

Drip.

Lick.

The tongue darted between my toes and along the arch of my foot, shivers of pleasure flowed over me as I pretended to snore.

The licking became more daring and bold, longer, harder strokes along my leg and across my thigh. The warm breath gasped as it saw my cock waving in the night. Inch by inch, the tongue neared the base of my shaft. It combed through the thick hair and touched the base of my dick. It trailed along the underside to the loose foreskin at the tip. The warm mouth gasped again as it realized my cock had been oozing pre-cum. The flashy chamber was filled with liquid.

The tip slipped into the opening and quivered with delight. Slowly, it pealed back my foreskin and swallowed the fat, wet head of my dick. Soon my whole penis was down its throat.

I rocked my hips, sending a wave of joy over my nerves. I wasn't going to last long with this wonderful sensation all over me.

The mouth gagged on me and slowly drew off me, only to plunge down on my cock, again. It buried itself deep into my pubic bush and savored me. That was all it took to send me into climax. The last few days of stress and no release, exploded out of me. Hungrily, it swallowed my eruption and sucked out more and more.

My mind spun as my balls drained. I reached new heights I have never felt before. My hips plowed into the mouth and allowed the tongue to clean my cock. As the last wave of cum flowed out of me, I collapsed and fell asleep instantly.

# # # # #

I woke refreshed and glowing, no stress, no worries, no wonder. It was the best orgasm I had ever had. I needed to know what that was, who that was. It was fantastic.

The day dragged by as I prayed for night and bed.

I repeated my nightly ritual and lay perfectly still in bed. I pretended to sleep and the licking started again. But tonight I lay on my side, and as the tongue worked between my legs, it found a tight, hairy hole to lick.

OH MY GOD!

Can I say yes? It rimmed me as I had never been rimmed before. The warm tip relaxed my opening and entered me. Deeper and deeper it went, filling and probing.

Oh yes.

My prostate was discovered and explored. Pre-cum filled my fleshy foreskin chamber and flowed down my shaft. The tongue flipped inside me, triggering my orgasm. As my dick shot its first load, the tongue pulled out and caught the blob before it hit my bed. The lips wrapped around the tip and sucked me in, rope after rope of come spiraled out of me as the mouth locked onto me and sucked on me dry, using my cock as a straw.

I have never came so much at one time. My head spun as the fluids poured out of me, and I passed out.

# # # # #

Water. Water. My brain screamed for water as I woke. It felt like the mother of all hangovers. Had I been drained dry last night? I stumbled to the bathroom and couldn't even pee. Nothing came out. I grabbed the glass on the sink and drank one, two, three glasses. I jumped into the shower and let the water flow over my body, and I drank each time I brought my head back.

Was a cum-drinking vampire draining me? Was there even such a thing? I'm sure blood became boring after a while, and why wouldn't a gay vampire want semen instead or as another alternative to blood?

The water cascaded over me, and I heard how crazy I sounded. Could I Google vampires who drink cum? Was it killing me with pleasure? What a way to go. Maybe it was an incubus or a succubus. They wanted sex all night and visited men in their sleep and had sex with them as they slept. That supposedly killed their victims over time. Was I dying?

I drank more water and finished the shower. As I dried off, I realized I had never felt better in my life. More energy, more happiness, more alive, and no stress. I dressed and searched online for an hour and found nothing more than what I already knew.

So how could I find out? I had to know.

Then an idea started to form. Yes, yes, I think I can do that.

# # # # #

That night I did the same thing I did the last two nights. I spread my arms and legs wide as I lay on the bed. I placed a pillow under the small of my back to open my ass up and offered up everything as fair game.

I pretended to sleep, and a weight came onto the bed. It licked between my legs and loosened up my butt. As my cock was swallowed and stimulated, a thick hard cock slipped between my butt cheeks and pressed against my pink pucker. It oscillated side to side and slowly entered me. Once inside, it seemed to grow in girth and fill me up. It surged into me and nearly blew my head off.

9

A moan escaped from my mouth. I licked my lips and felt the warm, wet pleasure on my cock receded. A hand wrapped around my dick as the marvelous mouth came down on mine. Tongues dueled in my mouth as its dick filled my ass, and his hands worked my cock.

My hands came up and found my nipples, hard and erect. I pinched them and rolled them between my fingers. My whole body arched as the force above me loved my body, filling me with pleasure and joy. The sensation rose and rose, the pressure built, and I willed my body to relax and enjoy, but it couldn't. It wanted more, more, more.

It thrust into me deeper than before, and hot goo filled me. My cock blasted into its hands as my semen sprayed all over it and my body. I released my nipples and grabbed its head and held its mouth against mine. My legs wrapped around it, and I pulled it even deeper into me. Another tidal wave of cum crashed over us, into me and through me.

I wrapped my arms around its body and held it firmly. My lips refused to let go also, sucking him into deeper into me. Semen, sweat, saliva, and cum mixed between us, as our bodies clung to each other.

As it relaxed, I refused to let go. I wanted to see who this was or what it was. My hands explored his body, and everything felt wonderful. Perfect. Warm, hairy and hung, what more could I want? He was willing, caring and compassionate. He brought me joy and pleasure and asked nothing in return.

I let go with one hand and reached over to the bedside table to turn on the light.

As my fingers found the switch, it said, "If you turn on the lights and see me, I'll disappear, and I'll never, ever come back again."

My fingers played with the switch. Should I or shouldn't I? He was amazing. Could I lose that? Did I need to see him so badly, that I would give this all away for one peek?

The other side of my brain asked, what the hell did he look like then if he was so afraid to show me?

A blind man may never see someone, but they can still see them with their other senses. Would that be enough for me?

I remembered the last few nights of sex.

Hell, yes. I didn't care what the fuck he looked like. My hand came back to him and caressed his body. "I promise not to look, if you promise to cum on me before I fall asleep and stay with me all night, even after I fall asleep."

His warm arms wrapped around me and held me close. He kissed me and said, "Deal, I promise."

I snuggled into his arms, and we held each other in my bed. Smiling, I closed my eyes and listened.

Drip.

Lick.

Drip.

Lick ...

Ahhhh ...

INCUBUS STEAMS
By Logan Zachary

Incubus – a demon in male form who lies upon sleepers in order to have intercourse with them.

Third Young Man, Missing! – Another young man has disappeared over the weekend, Jeron Nichols, twenty-two, was last seen Friday night with his friends. His roommate hasn't seen him since ...

Detective Timothy Ryan entered the new bathhouse called Incubus Steams. Its tag line read: Meet the man of your dreams and make all your fantasies come true... Ryan smiled to himself, a bold statement for any place to make, but from a bathhouse in Toronto? He doubted it.

Damon Noir sat at the front desk in the lobby's booth, shirtless. He smiled when he saw Ryan enter. "Good morning, and welcome to Incubus Steams."

Ryan scanned Damon's hairy, twenty-two-year-old chest. He noted the black hair and a dark olive complexion, his deep, brown eyes, and an even smile under a small moustache. Ryan reached into his jacket pocket and pulled out his badge. "I'm here to ask you a few questions."

Damon stood up, revealing he was naked sitting in the booth. He had a thick bush of black hair and a thick penis that appeared to be semi-erect. It rose up and down as Ryan's eyes looked at it.

Ryan startled at the sight and brought his eyes back up to Damon's eyes. He could see the smile inside, knowing he had been caught staring.

"As you can see," Damon spread his arms wide and thrust his pelvis forward, "we have nothing to hide. What can I do for you?"

"I'm here about Jeron Nichols, a young man who disappeared over the weekend. The last place his friends saw him was here." He pulled out a picture of the man and handed it to Damon through the booth's window.

"He's a very handsome man," Damon said. "He'd be more than welcome here." His cock swelled and stood straighter. He handed the picture back to the policeman as his other hand mindless reached down and pulled up on his low hanging hairy balls. The pair swung back and forth, making his thick dick sway.

Ryan took the picture back and pulled out two more. "What about these men?" One was a yearbook picture of a husky football player, and the other was a lean swimmer in a Speedo. Both men were handsome, young, and model material.

Damon shook his head. "No. Sorry. Anything else I can do for you?" He handed the pictures back and stood up, pushing his hips forward.

Ryan swallowed hard. "I would like to take a look around, but I don't have a warrant..."

"That shouldn't be a problem. I own Incubus Steams, so, just as I said, we have nothing to hide."

Ryan nodded, surprised at how easy it had been.

Damon reached over to the peg board next to him and handed him an elastic ring with a plastic number on it and a key.

"What is this?"

"It's a locker key." Damon placed a towel on the counter and pushed it through the window.

"What's this?"

"If you want to come in and look around, you'll have to follow the rules, just like everyone else. No shoes, no shirt, no clothes. No nothing."

"I can't ... I'm on duty."

"I can't make my customers feel uncomfortable while they're here. I don't allow any street clothes past the locker room." He pressed a button on the microphone next to the cash register. "Bill, can you come up to the front desk, please." His voice echoed through the building.

"I don't understand." Ryan turned the key over in his hand. The number 13 was carved into the plastic.

"Bill will cover the front desk for me, while I take you on a tour. Anything you want to see will be revealed." He picked up the towel on the chair he had vacated and wrapped it loosely around his narrow hips. He opened the door and stepped out into the lobby. His bare feet stood next to him.

"I'm not sure…" Ryan started.

"I'm sure you have been to a Y or a health club, it's all the same thing, with a few different features and services offered. I'm sure you know what I mean." He winked at Ryan.

Ryan bit his lower lip. How did this young man know he was gay? He knew his arousal wasn't showing. Did his eyes reveal more about him than…? Did he spend too much time looking at his…?

Bill arrived with a towel wrapped around his waist and slipped into the vacated booth.

"Thanks, Bill. I'll be showing this officer around Incubus Steams. I'll be back once all of his questions have been answered."

"Take your time." Bill unwrapped his towel from his waist and set it on the chair. He bent forward showing a perfect, tight ass, smooth and white as cream. He sat down. His huge cock flopped over one leg. He adjusted himself and sat back as if he was sunning himself.

Damon motioned to the doorway that led to the locker room with an arrow painted on the wall. "After you," he said.

Ryan didn't move.

Damon reached over and took the key from his hand. "Thirteen, my lucky number." He walked through the

15

doorway and along the red carpeted hallway. Pictures of naked men in different poses covered the walls. A hollow, echoing ring could be heard at the end of the hallway, where the locker room was.

White tiled floor and wooden lockers lined the walls and made a maze in the room. A big, muscle bound black male showered in the biggest shower room ever. Thick foam flowed over his body as he washed between his cheeks. He looked over his shoulder and continued washing down his leg.

Damon walked over to number thirteen, inserted the key and opened the wooden door. He stood back to make room for Ryan to undress.

Ryan looked at him and then inside the locker. This wasn't a rusty health club locker. This one held hangers and a pull out, rolling shelves for shoes and underwear. There was even a shelf with deodorant, toothbrush, tooth paste, comb, brush, razor, shave creams, soap, and cologne, everything you would need and not think to bring.

"We have everything you could ever want or need. Just ask, and you will receive." Damon's eyes glowed as he spoke.

Ryan didn't know what to do. He stood staring into the locker.

"Well," Damon asked, "do you want the tour?"

Ryan hesitated for a second and slowly removed his jacket. He pulled out a hanger and hung it up, wrinkle free.

Damon watched his every move.

Ryan started and then stopped unbuttoning his shirt. "Are you sure this is necessary?"

"If you want to see beyond the locker room, it is." He never looked away. "Am I making you uncomfortable?"

Ryan shrugged and started to unbutton his shirt. He wouldn't give his kid the satisfaction of making him feel self conscious. He worked out four times a week. He knew he had a great body. He just didn't want to be on display. Turning his back to him, he opened the shirt and placed it over another hanger. He pulled his T-shirt over his head as he kicked off his shoes. He bent over to pick them up.

Damon took careful notice on how the dress slacks hugged his muscular ass. The seam rode deep in his crease. Boxers he thought as Ryan unbuckled his belt and open his fly. Blue striped boxer briefs cover his butt as he slipped out of the slacks, electricity snapped over the hairy legs and fabric.

Ryan tossed his pants on a sliding shelf and pulled off his socks. He looked over his shoulder and saw Damon still stared at him. He took a deep breath and pushed his boxers down. They slid down to his ankles as he reached for his towel and wrapped it around his narrow waist. He pulled the ends around his waist and tucked the end in deep. He stepped out of his boxers and kicked them up to his hand.

"See, that wasn't too bad, now was that?" Damon walked around him and handed him the key. He noticed the way his towel bulged in front of him and smiled. "Lock your stuff up, and then we can head in, unless you want to shower first?"

Ryan closed the locker and quickly locked it with the key. He stretched the elastic around his hairy wrist and let it snap closed. "I'm fine." His bare feet felt how warm the floor was.

"Everything is well heated and cleaned so no worries of infections or cold feet."

The black bodybuilder turned off the shower and walked to the entryway of the showers. He toweled the back of his head dry and showed his hairless body in all of his wet, shining glory. His massive cock started to grow and swell as the men looked at him. He smiled at the attention.

"As you can see, this is a very friendly place," Damon stroked the body builder's cock as they passed by. "If you went down the hallway to the left, you'd find private rooms. There is a loop of rooms to walk around, and on busy nights there is a lot of bed hopping going on."

17

"Is there anyone down there?" Ryan paused at the intersection.

"You're more than welcome to go down there, but I doubt you'll find anyone. It's still too early in the day."

"I would like to be the judge of that." Ryan started down the hallway and passed by room after empty room. They paused at one room where a naked man lay on his stomach, his bare ass centered in the open doorway.

"You're able to partake of anything you want to while you're here. You're my guest, free of charge, a massage, a private room, whatever." He motioned to the naked man. "I'm sure he wouldn't mind a little attention." Damon entered the room, rubbed his hand over the fleshy mounds of his perfect ass. He spread his cheeks and slid a finger down his crack. "So tight, so hot, and so available."

Ryan felt his cock swell underneath his towel, but he shook his head. "Tempting, but I'm sure there's more to see."

Damon slapped the man's butt. "He's not jumping at the first piece of ass he sees, I respect that." He left the room. "Back to the tour."

The rest of the private rooms were empty, and Damon returned to the intersection. "Which way now? To the hot tubs, saunas, steam rooms, video rooms, massage tables, glory holes, bondage a go go?" Damon looked into his eyes. "You want to see them all, don't you? Follow me."

They went to the hot tubs, which bubbled with no one inside; a row of rooms that looked like changing rooms in a clothing store lined one wall. "Glory, glory, hole-alleluia." He pushed the swinging doors open. "There are holes between the booths and," he motioned to walk around the side, "a wall of wieners over here." A few dicks poked out of holes and slipped back in, like gophers at the zoo.

On the other side of the wall, a round stage dominated the center of the room, and the stage's floor glowed. Cameras and video monitors were everywhere in the room. Not an inch of the wall space was empty.

Ryan watched as they walked to the stage. Damon dropped his towel and jumped on top.

All the video monitors suddenly showed every angle of his body. The light in the floor intensified, and the cameras missed nothing. Even a camera from beneath the stage showed his ass and hairy balls in all their beauty.

"Did you ever want to be on TV?" he asked.

Ryan handed the discarded towel up and waited.

Damon ignored it. "All our recordings are saved for six months, in case anything happens that we need to go back and review."

"I would like to see Friday, Saturday, and Sunday night's tapes."

"That can be arranged. Would you like to view them here? Or in my office?"

"Your office would be easier."

"Anything else you'd like to see, now?" Damon stepped on a button, and a dildo rose out of the floor like a microphone at an award show. There was a camera in the tip, and as it rose, Damon's balls and tight ass came into a sharp view. A line of black hair circled his pink opening. On one video monitor, his tender bud grew and grew in size. A sheen of lube flowed over the lens as it got closer to his hole.

Damon leaned forward, using the monitors to guide himself into the perfect position on stage. He lowered himself slightly over the ascending phallus, and he impaled himself on it. Images from every angle flooded the screens, even a view from deep inside Damon. His foot worked the pole that rose and fell from the stage. He rode the rod, moaning as he did.

Ryan tied his towel tighter as it threatened to slip off. He adjusted his cock as it doubled in size.

"You can join me on stage. There is another internal cam." He rocked his hips and swayed back and forth.

A naked man emerged from one of the glory hole booths. Working his raging hard-on, he took a spot next to the stage and stared up at Damon as he jacked off. He waved Ryan over.

Music started and laser lights swirled around, but Ryan stepped back into the shadows to watch. A camera zoomed in on Damon's cock and showed a pearl of pre-cum pooling at the tip. The laser light hit it, making it glow an iridescent pink then purple. Streaks of electricity sparked over his tan skin, and his eyes glowed even brighter.

The man jacked his dick harder and harder. His balls rose, and he arched his back as an arc of semen sprayed across the stage. A camera caught his action and replayed it from several different angles, over and over in a loop, making it look like a Niagara Falls of orgasms.

Ryan mused that football games and convenience stores should have as good a camera work and security. He rubbed his erection. Savoring the sensation, but not willing to release his load.

Damon groaned and shot his load across the stage at the naked man. He pumped out his cum and milked out a small pool on the floor. His bare foot stepped on the button, and the dildo cam retracted from his ass and descended into the floor. The beautiful image of his ass disappeared, too.

The naked man reached onto stage and scooped up Damon's seed and rubbed it over his lips and into his mouth. He fingered his face as he continued to work his cock.

Damon walked to him at the edge of the stage, knelt down and let him clean his dick and suck out the last few drops of cum. He stood, ruffled the man's hair and jumped down from the stage.

The man grabbed and slapped Damon's ass as he headed over to Ryan.

Damon turned and said, "I'll find you later, we can finish what you started..." and he winked and thrust his ass out to him. As he neared Ryan, he wrapped his towel around his hips. "I have to make the customers happy, give them what they want and make them beg for more. You'll see..."

Ryan worried at that last comment, but followed him out of the video area. A hallway arrow read "Sauna and Steam."

"I doubt this is what you came for. I bet you want to see the real deal." The men walked side by side down the darkened hallway.

"How did you come up with the name Incubus Steams?" Ryan broke the silence and tried to steer the tour back to the information he needed and not sex. He hoped that would help calm his arousal.

Damon smiled. "I used Incubus for the sexual content of this place pure and simple. I wanted to use Dreams, but I felt that Steam told more about the business. It rhymed with dreams, so I figured I could use it as a double entendre and make this place mysterious, sexy, and a little scary. Do you like to be scared, Ryan?" His voice was soft and smooth, caressing with each syllable.

Ryan nodded before he could stop himself.

An open door showed a naked man lying on his back with two men, one on each side, massaging every inch of him. Oil flowed over his body and off the table. The masseurs' arms glistened above the elbow. One man worked the massive cock as the other worked between his butt cheeks.

"There is always time for a four handed massage..."

Ryan inhaled deeply, the scent of man, sex, and coconuts filled the room. "I'm good."

"That you are," Damon licked his lips as he looked down at Ryan's damp towel. "I think you're gonna need a new towel, soon."

"I'm fine."

21

"That you are..." Damon opened a cabinet on the wall and pulled out a new fresh towel and handed it to him. "If you need..."

The carpeting ended, and the floor turned into heated tile. A wooden door with a window radiated heat as they neared. "SAUNA" was engraved into a sign on the door.

Damon pulled the wooden handle open and motioned for Ryan to enter. A wall of humid heat slammed into them. "Hurry, so we don't let the heat out." He pushed Ryan inside and followed close behind and slammed the door.

Two men rolled on the bottom step in each other arms, kissing and licking each others' face as their hands caressed all over.

A man on the top bench flung a ladle full of water onto the hot stones, and steam formed immediately as the water evaporated instantly. The air in the room expanded, hot and humid, with enough force to pop the door open.

Sweat broke out over Ryan and ran down his body, instantly soaking his towel.

"Told you," Damon said. He sat down on a middle bench and motioned for Ryan to join him.

Ryan reluctantly sat down, towel still tightly wrapped around his hips.

Damon flung his open and spread his legs wide. The scent of sweat, semen, and something else rose from his body and mixed with the humidity. He ran his finger up Ryan's hairy leg and pushed the towel up and open.

Ryan clamped his hand down and stopped him.

"I've seen it already."

Ryan looked nervously around the room.

Damon smiled. "Oh, I get it. Follow me." He wrapped his towel around his waist and pulled Ryan out of the sauna. "This way." He pointed to the writing on the wall: "STEAM ROOM."

They turned the corner and found a glass door with a metal frame. Damon picked up a sign and hooked it over the metal bar on the steam room's door: 'Closed For Cleaning'. "This will give us the privacy you want."

Ryan entered the steam room; a thick mist filled the tiled room, drops of water dripped from the ceiling as more steam billowed from the metal pipes. Eucalyptus hung in the humidity and cleared his sinus passages. The heat soaked into his body and made his limbs feel heavy. His new towel drooped and clung to his skin, the thin white cotton was almost see-through.

Damon sat on the tile bench and made room for Ryan.

Ryan sat down next to him and inhaled deeply. The moist heat flowed over his body as if in a tropical jungle.

Damon moved closer and guided Ryan's body to lie down on the bench. He lifted his hairy legs up and cradled his feet in his lap. He massaged his feet and ran his thumbs up the arch of each foot and sent shivers across his body.

Ryan felt his body start to relax for the first time since he entered Incubus Steams. His towel grew heavy over his waist, and slowly he relaxed his hold.

Damon gently opened the towel and allowed Ryan to finally be free. He watched as Ryan's cock flipped up and lay over his abdomen. Damon rubbed up his legs and thumbed along his inseam.

Ryan's hairy balls rose as something fluttered over them. His cock jerked, rocking up and down, pre-cum oozed out of his tip. The moist heat relaxed him. He stroked his penis once to adjust himself and then felt the pre-cum flow out of him and filled his belly button.

"Now, you get it," Damon cooed. "Let your body go, close your eyes, breathe deeply, sleep ..."

Ryan's eye grew heavy, and he exhaled deeply, drifting, floating...

Damon rose and straddled his hips. He reached back and pulled Ryan's cock up and sat on it. His butt was still lubed from the dildo cam on stage.

Ryan's dick entered him easily. He reached up and ran his hands over his torso and down to his hips. His fingers curled around his waist and pulled Damon's pelvis down on his dick. He thrust up with his hips and enjoyed the pulsating muscle as it swallowed his cock.

He combed his fingers across Ryan's hairy chest. His hand slipped easily with the sweat and humidity. He increased his speed as he rode the thick cock drilling his ass. One hand jacked himself as he bounced. Instead of relaxing, his butt sphincter tightened and increased the stimulation on Ryan's dick.

Faster and faster, their rate increased. Ryan pulled down harder and harder on Damon's hips, driving deeper inside. The pleasure grew and grew.

Damon's ass bore down on his dick, and Ryan couldn't last any longer. His cock exploded again and again with each thrust. White hot cream flowed out of him and filled Damon.

As the last drop shot into him, Damon bound off of Ryan and spread his legs. He oiled his dick and slammed it into Ryan's ass.

Ryan gasped as the sensory overload took his body. He arched his back and allowed easier access to his butt. He grabbed onto the bench and lifted his legs up and opened them wider to allow for full penetration.

Damon's hips pushed into him, and his thick cock swelled, doubling in girth. His body heat increased also.

Ryan opened his eyes and watched as Damon started to glow, his whole body swelled and pulsated with an unearthly light. The feeling was amazing, and his cop mind didn't care what happened next; he felt his body warm, then heat up. Pressure built inside him, but the pleasure was too good, he wanted more, more, more.

Damon drilled into him with all his might. He could feel the climax simmering in his balls turn into a full rapid boil. Heat, cum and light shot out of him and into Ryan.

Ryan screamed in the most intense pleasure of his life.

Damon pumped into him one more time, emptying his balls, and watched as Ryan's body exploded in a burst of steam, semen and blood.

An outline of Ryan remained on the wooden bench, but the rest of him was splattered everywhere. Damon licked the back of his hand and wiped the goo from his eyes. "Wow, that was a hot one." He stood on unsteady legs and skated over to the corner, where a hose hung on the wall. He turned on the faucet and let the cool water wash over his body.

Once he was clean, he looked around the steam room. "Why no, Officer Ryan, I have no idea where all the handsome young men have disappeared to." He looked at the gooey mess on the walls, the floor, and the ceiling. He grabbed the hose and started to wash everything down the drain. "Do you?"

Officer Ryan awoke and sat up with a gasp as the cold water splashed over his sweaty body.

"You don't mind if I rinse you off? Do you?" Damon asked, innocently as he sprayed him with the hose.

The water washed the blobs of semen off him and cooled his feverish flesh.

"Sometimes bad boys need to disappear, and good ones ..." Damon continued to hose him off, "Come clean."

"Thanks," Ryan stood and grabbed for his towel to dry off. "I need to go, and get back to work."

"You're welcome back anytime, and I hope you find those missing boys. The good turn up, and the bad ones ..."

"I'll be back, just give me some time."

"You can have all the time you need." Damon kissed him, knowing he was a good one, and he'd be back.

MERMANCHANT MARINE
By Logan Zachary

"Mayday, Mayday, is there anyone out there? Mayday, Mayday. "

I released the red button on the mic and static feedback came back at me from the speaker.

"Crap."

I flipped through the operation manual and looked for what to do next. This was my first trip along the St. Lawrence Seaway, and the freighter that I was piloting steamed straight ahead toward the convoluted waterway of the Twin Ports of Duluth and Superior. The whaleback ship was seven hundred feet long and hundred feet wide. We were carrying 30,000 tons of grain. The hull of the ship was fifty-six feet deep, and even with our heavy cargo, we still towered twenty feet over the lake's surface.

I was the new harbor pilot for the Great Lakes along the north shore of Minnesota and Wisconsin. Lake Superior was my new home, well, supposed to be my home, but after my maiden voyage, it would probably be my last.

I didn't know how to operate this ship, let alone navigate these waters. The rest of the crew was trapped in the head. An outbreak of food poisoning hit and incapacitated everyone, everyone but me.

But how could I steer this huge ship through the Twin Ports and the Aerial Lift Bridge?

"Mayday, Mayday." Sweat broke out on my palms, and the wheel slipped as the shoreline loomed closer.

The helmsman that was to train me lay on the floor, unconscious and in a fetal position. The ship was newly painted a reddish, rust color with the bridge all white. I didn't want to be the one to put in the first scratch or the first hole.

27

I wanted to kick him awake and almost did as I stood over him. How could this be happening? I pinched myself and knew I was awake. How could I slow this ship down? Could I stop it and just have us float out here until the crew was able to take over? I looked over at the Captain propped up in a corner, asleep.

The SS Edmund Fitzgerald sank many years ago, would we today? I opened the door and stepped out into the night air. The lights of Duluth lit the horizon. "Help," I yelled across the water. "Help! SOS! Mayday! Whatever the hell you're supposed to say in an emergency like this."

I ran to the bow of the ship and hung my head over the railing. The low steady drone of the engines pushed me forward into the night. My career was over before it started, and who knew if I'd survive. Any of us would survive.

My cell phone!

I fumbled with it in my pocket. I could call 9-1-1, and then the phone slipped out of my hand and tumbled into the water.

SPLASH!

"Well, that was that," I said, and rubbed my eyes in disbelief.

There was another splash from the water, but as I opened my eyes to see what it was, a large shape hurdled itself out of the water, rose, up and up along the side of the ship, and landed behind me. Cold water sprayed over me as I stepped back, slamming into the railing.

The light from the bridge revealed a naked man at my feet. Long flowing blond hair covered his head. A long spear like object was in one hand with three prongs. His skin had an odd gray color in the faint light.

I didn't see any movement and suddenly, his chest expanded as he took a deep breath. Broad muscles rippled across his back, chiseled and not an ounce of fat. Water rushed out of his nose and mouth and formed a puddle on the deck. He coughed once and gasped for a deep breath. His skin turned instantly pink.

I stepped back. Was he a terrorist? He had a weapon, but he was naked. He lay prone on the deck. His body was smooth everywhere, not a hair in sight ... and his ass. I gasped.

He held up his empty hand and said, "I'm here to help you." His voice was wet, but calming. He turned to look at the wheel.

My face burned with embarrassment. I gasped at his amazing ass, not because I was afraid, but because I had just seen the best butt in the world.

He flipped his wet hair away from his face and looked at me. He had the deepest blue eyes I had ever seen. I wanted to swim in them.

I reached down, took his hand, and helped him to his feet. The rest of his body was perfect, sculpted and ... cool to the touch.

He shifted his weight, and the lower half of his body came into the light. At first, I would have sworn he had a fish tail, but his legs were runner's legs, muscles defined and amazing. And then I saw his penis, thick and long dangling between his legs.

I was instantly hard. He was the perfect man, in every way. I couldn't pull my eyes away, but something forced me to look up into his deep blue eyes. They scanned mine, and it felt like he was reading my thoughts.

Slowly, his mouth opened, downward, more like a trout's and said, "I'm here to help you." His tone soothed me, my rising panic left, and a sense of calm descended on me. I knew everything was going to be okay. "What is the problem?"

"The crew is sick, the Twin Ports are coming up, and I don't know how to navigate the ship through the narrow waterway." I could feel the terror start to rise again, but his touch kept it at bay.

"I know these waters well. I'll show you the way." His bare feet slapped the deck as he walked to the bridge.

I watched his bubble butt flex and relax with each step. A deep dimple appeared and disappeared. I swallowed hard as I followed.

He moved as if unaware of his nudity, comfortable in his own skin. He looked at the doorknob and turned his head to the side.

I jumped forward and opened it for him.

He passed through the doorway and stood at the helm looking over the seaway. "You need to travel that way." He pointed into the dark.

I couldn't see anything. "I don't see it. You'll have to maneuver the ship."

He looked at the wheel with a blank expression.

A metallic scratching sounded along the hull of the ship.

"Hurry," he said.

I stepped in front of him and grabbed the wheel at the helm with both hands. I turned it into the direction he had indicated.

The metal scrapping stopped.

I exhaled the breath I had been holding.

"You're not done yet," he said. This time, his bare arms wrapped around mine and covered my hands. He guided me with his body. I felt his huge penis press between my butt cheeks as his chest spooned my back. "I can't feel you," he said.

"What?" I looked over my shoulder at him and before I knew it, he pulled my shirt over my head and reached around to unbuckle my belt and pants. The pants and underwear dropped to the floor, and he stepped on them and pulled them away from my body.

He returned to his position, and I swear his cock had doubled in size. This time it was standing up between my ass cheeks.

The sensation was amazing, and I forgot all about sailing this ship. I felt his body tense, and he backed up.

"It's still not right." He stepped forward and this time his dick slipped into my tight hole. How he entered me so smooth and quickly without pain was beyond me, but suddenly, we were connected. Our legs became one, and I knew what he needed me to do.

I sank back against him, allowing him to use my body.

He controlled me like a puppet, and I let him.

I looked at one of the screens on the control council and saw the ship glide through the narrow turns. I felt as if I was playing a video game, and my body was the controller.

Several times, he rocked his hips back and forth. His cock dove in deeper and pulled back out to the surface. He was thick and filled me but never hurt me. The sensation started as a cool, calming wave, but turned into a warm ripple of heat that radiated through my body.

My erection stood straight out in front of me and brushed the steering column. A thick wetness started to form at the mushroom head and slowly seeped out. How I wanted him to dive in and out of my ass, pound my butt as if there was no tomorrow.

The darkness lifted, and suddenly, I could see the waterway as clearly as if it was high noon. But the night colors and the sky changed for me. The stars twinkled above as the black water, took on new tones of blue, and green and silver. A school of fish swam in front of the bow, guiding the way. They looked as if they were racing us.

The ship sailed back and forth around the bends with ease. The horizon glowed bright and loomed nearer. A metal skeletal structure crossed the seaway ahead. I recognized the shape of the Aerial Lift Bridge.

The ships horn blew across the silent night water and slowly the cross beam rose. The whirling engine pulling the metal against gravity as it rose out of our way. The passageway narrowed as our ship seemed to widen.

"We're not going to fit." My body tensed.

But my helper rocked my hips and body as he sang into my ear. The melody was beautiful and haunting, full of longing and desire. My body tingled as he serenaded me at the helm.

"What are you?" I asked.

"The Greeks thought we had seaweed hair and beards, the Irish thought we were extremely ugly with sharp green teeth, pig-like eyes, green hair and a red nose, and the Chinese thought we were what caused storms." He continued his song.

"Mermaids?"

"Mermen. The Finnish knew us and got it right. They said we were magical, powerful, and handsome men with the tail of a fish. We could cure illness, brew portions, and lift curses."

"I thought that the mermaids lured sailors to their deaths with their songs."

"We loved to sing to men and gods. Little did we know that our songs would enchant you so easily, making some walk off the deck or run their ships ashore. That was a mistake we made. We were very curious of humans. We figured your kind were more like us and would be able to breathe under water. When we found a handsome mate that was willing to follow us, we were so excited we didn't notice until it was too late, and the person drowned. We tried to help them to breathe, but we ended up squeezing the life out of our victim as we tried to bring them to our underwater kingdom."

I seemed to be dreaming as he told of this amazing tale, and as we sailed through the water. We breezed under the lift bridge and watched as the criss-cross metal work passed over us. The concrete breakwater guarded the lake effect and made the harbor's surface as smooth as glass, just as his cock slid in and out of me. He was teasing me, he was the harbor pilot and ...

The ship held a steady course and entered Lake Superior. The lift bridge lowered its cross beam, so traffic could continue again.

We had made it to open water.

"You are safe, now." He pulled out of my ass and released his hold on my body, and I almost collapsed on the deck.

"No, don't stop," I said.

"Don't stop saving you?" He looked confused.

"No, you know, doing me?" I motioned to my ass.

"Doing you?"

"I want you inside me."

"Why?" His brow furrowed as he looked at me.

"It feels great and ..."

"Show me." He turned his body to face the wheel and spread his legs, granting me access to the most amazing butt in the world.

I stepped behind him and guided my cock to his perfect ass. I pressed into his tight opening and entered him inch by inch. I rocked back and forth gently, diving in deeper and deeper. I had never felt anything like it before.

He pushed back on me and matched my pace. He made a sound; I wasn't sure what it was. His tone changed, and he seemed to purr.

How could I be so lucky to have this man all to myself? I reached around his body and grabbed onto his cock. Stroking in time with my thrusts, my excitement grew.

His moans and music increased, too. A song of joy came from him, and I joined in on his song. Together, we harmonized and his hands grabbed a hold of the wheel. The ship followed.

The ship started to circle the harbor as the pleasure increased. A melody carried across the ship's bow with the wind. At first, I thought it was the night breeze, but as it grew louder, I could hear a chorus of men's voices singing, an ancient mariner's tune of a days gone by.

My hand worked his cock as my other hand caressed his torso. I felt every muscle in his body; sharp lines of definition helped me trace each fiber of his being. He was so powerful and strong, yet such a gentle lover.

I could feel my cock getting close to exploding inside him as he turned his head to find me, and said, "What else can you do?"

I slowly pulled out of him and spun him around to face me. Our cocks rubbed against each other as my mouth found his. I kissed him, licking his lips and entering his mouth. Our tongues touched and tasted each other.

I kissed along his neck and licked down, tasting, savoring.

He threw his head back and allowed me to ravage his body.

My tongue found his nipple and licked it. My teeth closed on it as it swelled into a point. I continued kissing over to the cleft in the center of his chest and down, down, down. I circled his naval and dove lower.

His whole body tensed as my tongue tasted the root of his shaft.

I smiled as I knew what would drive him crazy. I moved over to the crease between his ball and leg. Up and down my tongue tickled. I brushed against his smooth nut and rolled the other one between my fingers, so soft and yet firm, smooth and oh so tasty. I kissed the one and drew it into my mouth. I swallowed and tongued it over and over.

He spread his legs wider and shifted over slightly.

I took both balls into my mouth, and I sucked on them. I wanted to eat him whole.

He moaned and grabbed my hair and held my head in place. His cock ran along my nose and its tip oozed with his excitement.

I let his balls fall from my mouth, and I licked up his shaft. The fat head oozed more, and I sucked his sweet nectar away. I took his cock into my mouth and deep throated him.

He thrust into me, faster, deeper.

I felt his balls rise along side of his shaft, and I wanted him to slow down, make it last. I slipped a finger between his beautiful cheeks and entered him. I found his prostate and tickled.

He grabbed my head and held it still. He pushed into my mouth one more time, and I tasted the sweetest cream ever. Wave after wave flowed over my tonsils and down my throat. I sucked on him, applying pressure to draw more out and drain his balls.

He pulled me to my feet and turned around. I knew where he wanted me. I slipped into his ass and pounded deep into him. Three strokes and my balls exploded into him. His muscles rippled and drew more out of me, milking my dick.

As soon as I emptied into him, he pulled away from me and spun around to face me. He kissed me hard and tasted his own juices on my tongue. I didn't want him to stop. I hoped the crew would stay asleep forever, and we would circle the harbor for eternity.

"So, this is what I've heard so much about." His breathing came in short gasps. "I can see why my people come to the surface."

"You don't do this underwater?" I asked.

"We do something, but nothing like that? My body still tingles, and I want to do that again." A lazy smile curled his full lips.

I kissed him again and held his naked body close to mine. Our still sensitive dicks rubbed against each other and sent shivers over us. I felt him wrap his arms and legs around me, refusing to let go. Over his shoulder, I could see something in the distance, and it was moving in our direction.

A red light flashed on a fast moving boat that drew near. A siren cut the silent night air. I found my briefs and stepped into them. The helmsman lying on the floor, stirred slightly at the commotion. I looked over at the Captain, who remained still.

My merman bent over showing his gorgeous bottom and picked up his trident. He stepped over to the railing and looked over the edge.

The Duluth Seaway Port Authority raced up to the side of ship and pulled out a bull horn. "Throw down a ladder, we want to board. Stop your engines, and let us board. Now."

No response.

"Stop your engines now, and throw down a ladder."

The Merman brought a conch shell to his mouth and blew. A low mournful horn blasted across the water.

I peeked over the bow and saw a silver swirl in the water below. A school of fish swam in a spot, seeming to open a portal into another world. Colors and lights came from the opening, and my merman stepped up to the edge and smiled.

He kissed me, a long penetrating kiss and dove off the side of the ship. An Olympic diver looked like a beginner as my merman entered the water without a splash.

I looked down at the spot where he had stood only seconds before. My cell phone sat on the deck, dry and working. How could that be? Had he known? How could he leave?

A large fishtail waved at me from the swirl.

I grabbed an oxygen tank and mouthpiece. I stuck the tube into my mouth and dove over the side of the ship. The cold water swallowed me and the darkness descended on me. I couldn't see, and I couldn't breathe. What was wrong with the tank? I was drowning, and the tank meant to keep me alive was killing me.

I let go of the metal tank, and the rubber tube pulled from my mouth. Deeper and deeper, I sank into the depths. My last gasp was gone, and the world turned black.

Then suddenly, a warm mouth kissed me, breathed life into me, and saved me. My merman rescued me and took me to his kingdom under the sea ...

STALKING PREY
By Rob Rosen

Rob Rosen (www.therobrosen.com), award-winning author of six novels and editor of two anthologies, has had short stories featured in more than 180 anthologies.

Glenn stalked the gym, not so much for cock, which was ample and easy enough to come by, but for blood. There it was iron-rich, flowing with strength and energy, and steeped in vitality. And at the tender age of, well, four-hundred-sixty-two, vitality was a must, especially if he was to remain the strongest of his kind, the strongest the world over, in fact. This he prided himself on: the knowledge that he was the utmost branch on the evolutionary tree.

"Wait," he said, thinking it over. "Four-hundred-sixty-three." He scratched his dimpled chin and squinted at the overhead light as he finished his set. "There was that hazy year in China. Nothing but opium-infused blood for months." His stomach gurgled at the drug-clouded memory. Then he looked around, at the wide array of opportunity, and grinned. "Just the occasional tinge of GNC additives in this place." He chuckled to himself. "Yum." His shorts tightened at the crotch at the very thought of his next nearby meal, prick pulsing within.

Not that any of it mattered, really. Blood, ultimately, was blood. And as long as he drank, he'd always be the strongest, always be the branch closest to the sun, closest to God.

Still, it was nice when it tasted oh so sweet and pure and rich. And gay, suffice it to say, which was the blood of choice in this particular gym. That, of course, had its own distinct advantages. Icing on the cake, as it were.

His stalking, after all, usually ended up in the locker room, in the showers or steam room, around furtive corners, away from prying eyes. "Mmm," he purred, suddenly spying his flavor du jour, a lithe blond with worked-out arms, curly chest hair poking out of a V-neck tank-top, eyes the color of the Adriatic as she had been centuries earlier. "Don't you look tasty," he added, barely above a whisper, following the man inside the locker room a scant few minutes later.

Their eyes met, locked, a knowing nod added to the mix, a wink for flavor. The blond sat down in front of his locker, Glenn a few feet away in front of his, both men continuing the flirtation, the game underway. Clothes were removed, muscles revealed, flexed, underwear last, cocks dangling, blood already beginning its rhythmic flow within.

"Mmm," repeated Glenn, following the man to the steam room, the door opened, closed, opened again. "Mind if I join you?" he asked.

The man smiled, nodded. "Join me?" he said. "Two words, so much promise." He patted the seat across from him. "Help yourself."

Glenn returned the smile and the nod. "Help yourself," he echoed. "Two words, so much promise." So much. And certainly more than the man had intended.

They sat facing one another, the towels open now, cocks beginning their slow, steady rise upward, helmeted heads widening, blood-rich veins pulsing. The blond eyed Glenn's prick hungrily, Glenn the same in return, though hungrily in a much different way, more out of necessity than yearning, though perhaps not all that much more.

"Impressive," said the blond, voice thick, raspy, chest rapidly rising and falling.

"Tastes even better than it looks," Glenn said in reply, spreading his legs apart, heavy balls hanging over the towel and the bench, sweat already trickling down his chest as he wiped a river of it off his forehead.

The man fell to his knees, quick as a wink, slapping Glenn's thick prick against his bee-stung lips before gliding it down his throat.

Ah, thought Glenn. Appetizers before the main course. He grabbed for the man's soft, wheat-colored head and pushed down, his cock disappearing as a tendriling volt of adrenaline worked its way up his spine. Up and down the man went, in and out his cock slid, balls bouncing all the while, cum welling up. Glenn stared past the spectacle to the action further down, the man stroking his hefty rod, flesh upon flesh, all but a blur. God you look delicious. Good enough to eat, I'd say. He laughed internally, biding his time. After all, he had plenty of it to spare. Eternity, for that matter.

The blond's mouth was suddenly ground to the hilt, balls brushing against chin, a gagging tear gliding down his face, mixing with copious amounts of sweat. In an instant, his legs began to tremble, his eyes shut tight in rapturous ecstasy as Glenn shot a molten river of cum down his throat, the man's cock spewing at the exact same moment, the steam room smelling all at once both sweet and acrid.

"Nice," moaned Glenn, his head thrown back, mouth in a pant as he came and came and came some more, jizz dripping down the blond's chin, across his neck, down his throbbing jugular. "Nice," he repeated as his fangs extended, protruded, glinted in the dim light. "Nice," he whispered, a third and final time as he sprang, his mouth upon the neck so quick as to appear that time had been spliced together, a piece suddenly missing.

The razor-sharp fangs pierced in an instant, the blood rushing in, appetizer finished, entrée began. Though this was more like a four-course meal, Glenn's hunger abated within mere moments, fresh blood suffusing him, permeating him, lifting him up and over the edge, heaven on earth. How appropriate for a deity such as himself, he realized.

"Forget," commanded Glenn, softly, fangs retracted, his blood-stained mouth against the blonde's ear. "We were never here," he added, softer this time, stroking the wound marks as if they were a faithful pet. "Forget it all, young one."

The vampire rose, licked the blood off his lips, and wrapped the towel around his narrow waist, cock again flaccid. For now. He stroked the blond head as he left, the door opening and closing once more before he made his way to the locker, to his clothes, and out of the gym. Glenn breathed in the cool, early evening air and smiled blissfully as he headed for home, a spring in his step, power-infused blood coursing through his ancient veins.

Little did he know that he was being watched, though. That he had, in fact, been watched since long before entering the gym. Long before that day began, even.

Long, long before.

The knock on the door came later that night, the moon high, full, and blisteringly bright. Glenn answered it in nothing more than a pair of boxers and a curious grin on his face. "Yes?" he said, door swung open, eyes suddenly wide and alert as he gazed upon the man that stood there, a perfect specimen of humanity in every way, Adonis on a really good day.

"Lucius," said the man, a smile broadening on his impossibly handsome face.

Glenn froze, his own smile suddenly faltering. "Glenn," he corrected the man. "Sorry, you must have the wrong house." He started to close the door, his heart beating out a mile a minute now, lub-dub in double time.

"Glenn, yes," said the man. "My mistake. Lucius suited you better in Europe."

The door remained open, Glenn's hand vise-tight on the wood. He squinted at the man then frowned, looking past him to make sure he was alone. "Who are you?" he managed.

The man proffered his hand. "Mark," he said. "A pleasure."

Glenn took the hand, flesh meeting flesh in an electric spark. "We shall see about that," he replied, allowing the man inside despite his better judgment.

"Shall we?" said the man, the door closing behind him. It sounded to Glenn more of an invitation than a question, and his cock stirred upon hearing it. Or perhaps it was simply the close proximity to this divine creature.

"So then," said Glenn, walking the man to the living room and offering him a seat. "How do you know about Europe?" Again his heart raced. No one could have known about that. No one that could live to tell the tale that is.

Mark smiled, coyly. "You left a trail, Glenn."

Glenn swallowed and nodded. Suddenly, he didn't like this man all that much. Then again, at least he could dispose of him, should it come to that, so he heard him out. "A trail? Of what exactly?"

The man's smile rose northward on his face, teeth gleaming. "Well, of blood, of course."

Glenn rose and stood, arms akimbo, the smile all but vanished. "This is not funny anymore," he said. "Perhaps you should leave."

Mark also rose, slowly, moving forward, his hard instantly on the prize, the boxers tenting upon contact. "You sure about that, Glenn?" he cooed, their faces now an inch apart and then not even that, a bite on the lip, a lick quick to follow.

Glenn retracted his face, but just barely. "I could kill you, you know," he said, menace creeping into his voice.

The other man smiled and nodded. "Oh, I know," he replied, his hand now inside the flimsy fabric, the cock gripped, already leaking. "In fact, you could do one of three things to me."

Glenn remained in place and eyed the man before him. He was clearly human and not vampire, but how on earth could he know about him? It just wasn't possible. And, more importantly, why wasn't he afraid, as he well should have been? Glenn had, in fact, struck terror in countless men before this one, so why was this one different? "Gee, only three?" he replied, his hand stroking the man's scruffy cheek.

Mark chuckled and winked. "Three after you fuck me, I mean."

Glenn again gulped. This wasn't how things went. Not ever. Still, he asked, "And what three possibilities do I have at my disposal after I fuck you?" The mere thought made his belly rumble, his cock throb.

The stranger released his prick and moved to the center of the living room. He kicked off his sneakers, his eyes locked on Glenn's. Then he moved his hand to his shirt, unbuttoning it from top to bottom, parting it to reveal a muscle-dense chest, a matting of curly brown down running across his chest and etched stomach, disappearing teasingly inside the unbuttoned jeans. "First," said Mark, "you could feed on me, as you did to the man in the gym today."

Glenn flinched. Had he really been that careless? "Or?" he croaked out, mesmerized at the spectacle unfolding before him.

Mark, slid the jeans down to the carpet, stepping out of them before kicking them to the side, revealing hairy legs thick as tree trunks, calves the size of boulders, briefs tenting something fierce, containing untold riches that made Glenn's mouth water. "Or," he continued, "you could kill me outright." He grinned. "How many men have you killed in your lifetime, Glenn? Dozens? Hundreds?"

In fact, Glenn had lost count ages earlier. What was the point of keeping track? In any case, it was the third choice that interested him now. And, for that matter, what lay beneath the briefs, which he knew was somehow tied to that choice. "I've already fed today, as you somehow know, so, why not, as you say, just kill you outright?"

Mark grinned, again flashing his pearly whites as he slid down his briefs, enormous cock springing out, hairy balls dangling. Naked, he was even more stunning, more unearthly. Once again, Glenn's belly rumbled, his own cock steely stiff. "Yes," he said, "you could. Or, I hope, go with the third option."

Glenn knew the third option. It wasn't one he took lightly or, in fact, chose all that often. Perhaps only a few times over the centuries, when his heart grew lonely, eager for company more to its liking than the mere mortals it had grown accustomed to. Still, even then, he dispatched them all, in time, when he grew weary of them. Or they became too powerful, threatening to overshadow him. If that was even possible. "So much better to just fuck you and then kill you, I should think." He had slid out of his boxers and was stroking his club of a cock, Mark mirroring the action, stroke for stroke.

The stranger smiled and moved in closer. "Or teach me, be even more powerful with me by your side," he said, his face tantalizingly close now. "Look how careless you've become, Glenn. Look how easy it was for me to find you, to know all that you've done, to know who and what you are."

A pang rose in Glenn's heart, a nervous tic lifting his eyebrow. How, he wondered, had he grown so careless? And how had this man found him so easily. Maybe, he figured, he would indeed make an ideal protégée. However temporarily, that is. "So," he replied, "I fuck you and turn you?" Because, regardless of what he chose, he was certainly going to fuck him.

Mark wrapped his arms around the vampire, their lips brushing, chests pounding together. "Fuck me, change me, and then fuck me for all eternity, Master."

Ah, now that Glenn liked, the master part. That made his heart skip a beat, made his balls rise. He pressed his lips to

Mark's lips, ground his cock into Mark's cock, and sighed contentedly. "Yes," he groaned, the kiss repeated, more insistent this time, tongues snaking and coiling together.

"Yes," moaned Mark, when they'd come up for air. "Now fuck me, Master. Fuck me and make me yours."

Oh how the words swirled around Glenn's head, like a swarm of wasps jabbing at his very soul. If, in fact, he could even lay claims to one anymore. And so he grabbed the man that would soon be made immortal and led him to the bedroom. He tossed him on the bed as if he were no more than a rag doll, then looked down in awe at the sheer perfection, at the mass of muscle and hair, at a face that made him very nearly breathless. "Legs up," he commanded.

Mark smiled and did as was told, his legs up, knees out, holding his feet with one hand while pushing his cock forward with the other. Glenn sank to his knees and gazed at the holy trinity, cock and balls and hole, at the swirls of curly hair. He breathed in deeply, the smell of musk and sweat rising up his nostrils, making his cock pulse and drip in anticipation.

He then craned his neck in and took a lick, a bite at the hole. It tasted of ambrosia, of nectar, almost as perfect as the blood flowing within. He grabbed the cheeks and spread them further apart, devouring the area within, probing as far as his tongue would permit, all while Mark bucked and writhed on the bed. "Fuck me, Master," he pled, stroking his cock above Glenn's head. "Fuck me. Change me."

Again Glenn said, "Yes," hopping up to retrieve some lube before he impaled the man. The rubber was not necessary, viruses and germs incapable of infecting a being such as himself, still a little help greasing the wheel, as it were, was generally necessary.

He squeezed the bottle, his prick glimmering, and he applied the lube, a matching dollop to the hole before him, fingers slid inside, Mark's back arching with his ministrations. Then the cock was knocking at the portals

46

before entering, slow and steady, one glide, inch by steely inch, until balls were brushing flesh.

Mark pushed himself up on his elbows as Glenn leaned down, until their faces were again united, mouths joined, while the cock slid in and out, hovering mid-air before pumping in again and again and again.

"Who are you?" rasped Glenn, shocked at the realization that he'd never met a man such as this before, not in all this time.

"I am yours," replied Mark, ass meeting cock above the bed, until it was impossible to tell where one man ended and the other began.

"Mine," moaned Glenn, his mouth moving to the side before resting above the throbbing neck, blood coursing mere centimeters beneath. "All mine," he added, teeth suddenly jagged, incisors like daggers that pierced through as the cock within the hole spasmed, shook, the entire body attached rocking, consumed in lust. Both men came in torrents of cum as Glenn drank his fill, allowing Mark to experience the mix of both pain and ecstasy, to remember it in total, to change from human to immortal, human to vampire.

Satiated, Glenn retracted his teeth, his head moving away to admire his work, the marks healing quickly, as was the way of his kind, their kind now.

Only, not quite. In fact, not at all.

Glenn pulled his still rigid cock out and began to stand when he noticed with alarm the second transformation that had begun on the man below. Except, of course, that man was no longer man, nor mere vampire for that matter. The beast on the bed stared up, fangs twice as long and sharp as Glenn's, muscles that were already large to begin with now doubly so, a mass of them, each one flexed and solid as granite. And the hair, all that glorious hair that fairly covered him, now did so completely, every square inch of flesh covered in it.

"I... I don't understand," squeaked out Glenn, trembling as he stood there in shock, cock at last shriveling.

The werewolf now also vampire gazed up, grinning with row after row of teeth, saliva dripping down from his gaping maw. "No, Master?" he growled. "How do you think you were found out so easily, followed between countries? Do you think a mere human could have done so?"

Glenn's body shook in fear. "That explains it; it wasn't carelessness."

Mark jumped off the bed, so quick as to make Glenn fall back onto the floor, face shielded by his hands. "Well, perhaps a little carelessness, but mostly it takes one superhuman being to stalk yet another one, successfully at any rate." He then pointed out the window, to the full moon that hung in the sky, bathing the room in a silver glow. "Just took the right timing, Glenn." He jumped again, pinning the vampire to the floor, deadly fangs above tender flesh.

"But I am your master," Glenn whined, terror now gripping him.

Mark laughed, which sounded more like a bray, a bark. "Temporally, Glenn. And look at all I've learned from your tutelage. From mortal to immortal in the blink of an eye, in the sinking of a fang. From superhuman to supreme human." The teeth above cracked the neck below in that same blink of an eye and the blood that had been sucked out was just as rapidly returned to its rightful owner.

The werepire, the first and only of his kind, again jumped up and stared down at the crumpled remains below. "Evolution has taken a giant leap forward, Glenn," he said, head pointed up to the ceiling, a ferocious howl spewing out that made the walls rattle. "And the tree has a new branch that will cast a shadow upon all that dwell beneath it." Again he smiled, teeth glinting. "Except now that shadow will last always and forever, my friend." He leapt threw the window, rushing on all fours into his future as he shouted over his hairy shoulder, "Always and forever!"

SUCKING WOUNDS
By Landon Dixon

Dixon's writing credits include many magazine and anthologies.

Connor was sneaking a nip out of the flask he kept in the bottom drawer of his battered desk next to the boiler room, when Argue, the night editor, barged in. He had a bum with him.

"This guy's got a tip for you, Connor!" Argue bellowed. "A real hot, juicy story."

The flask jumped out of Connor's twitchy hands and crashed to the cement floor, spilling some of its precious contents. Connor sat up and wiped his mouth, nervously eyed his boss and the bum. "Yeah?"

"Yeah!" Argue grabbed the disheveled man by the raggedy arm and slammed him up against Connor's desk. "Don't be shy," he sneered at the man. "Connor here will listen to you. He's always up for a queer story." Argue leered at Connor when he made that crack, his beefy red face split wide with a grin.

"W-What story?" Connor croaked. He ran a thin, pale hand through his jet-black hair, picked up a pencil with his other shaking mitt.

"A real queer story," Argue jeered on. "Guy says he's got some inside dope on all those deaths in the Tenderloin district. An eyewitness account. Lurid details. Weird circumstances. I figured it'd be right up your alley, Connor."

The boys on the news beat never got tired of riding the rundown reporter. Just because he was built slender and boyish, spoke with a bit of a lisp and walked with a bit of a lilt.

49

Connor smiled pleasantly up at Argue, wishing his boss hemorrhoids the size and sting of wasp nests. He had to take it and hate it. He was lucky to swing even this job, or be stuck with the galley slaves in the proofreading dungeon. Tarawa and Okinawa, the hazing in the Marines, had taken it all out of him. The bottle only put so much back in.

"Sit down, won't you, Mr. ...," he said to the hapless bum cowering alongside the big strident night editor.

Argue gave a last snort of derision and then turned and strode out of the dusty box office.

"I'd rather not tell you my name," the bum said, sitting down in the one rickety chair Connor had to offer. "I don't want any trouble. Only ... I thought I should tell someone – about what I saw."

The man's eyes shot up from the soiled hat he was fidgeting with and stared into Connor's blue beams. "They shouldn't be allowed to get away with what they did to my friend!"

Connor offered him a hit off his flask. The man gulped as if he was dehydrated. His red-veined eyes went glassier, and his red nose all but glowed.

Connor licked his lips. "Tell me what you saw."

"Well, my buddy and I were sharing a jug – up against the fence in this empty lot between the McClaren and the Biltmore. In the Tenderloin, see. And then Dennis – my buddy – gets up to give a speech, and he loses his balance and grabs onto the fence and gets a real bad gash from a nail sticking right out. He was bleeding pretty good but not that bad. So I called for an ambulance from the phone in the McClaren, and it rolled up almost right away, it seemed like. Two guys in white got out and went to my buddy."

The man's rummy eyes brimmed tears one-hundred proof. "They were supposed to help Dennis. Not kill him!"

Connor was sober now, interested for a change. "What happened?"

50

"I was hiding behind the fence, in the shadows, see. 'Cause I didn't want to get run-in if any cops showed up. And ... I saw one of those ambulance attendants bend over Dennis' wound, while the other one bent over his groin. And then they started sucking!"

Connor's pencil froze in mid-scratch over his pad. "They ..."

"I seen it! One guy was sucking on Dennis' cut, while the other guy was sucking on his cock! Draining him dry, see! Dead-dry!"

# # # # #

There'd been six deaths within the last three weeks in the Tenderloin district. Three murders and three accidents. All six men had bled to death.

Connor walked out of the newspaper morgue scratching his chin. It was crazy, probably the hallucinations of delirium tremens, but it was worth following up. First, though, he walked down the hall into the washroom, checked for any occupants then slipped into the last stall in line and beat off to the bum's sensational story, while the lurid details were still fresh in his mind.

# # # # #

Connor finagled a ride-along on a meat wagon the following night. Just a routine feature on the tough job the boys in white had, especially in the Tenderloin. Topical with all the carnage going on down there; timely PR for the department with the city budget coming down.

He shook hands with the two tall, pale, dark-haired ambulance attendants who would be his escorts for the evening. Their names were Rudy and Thomas. They were even more handsome in-person than Connor's tipster had described.

51

"Where we headed first?" the reporter asked, sticking his head over the front seat in between the two attendants, crouched in the back of the ambulance with the gurney.

"A parking lot on Front Street," Rudy responded, smoothly turning the vehicle left onto Main. "We'll sit and see what happens – wait for a call."

Thomas turned his head, putting his chiseled features close-up to Connor's eager, perspiring face. "We like to be close to the action. So we can get to the scene quicker when the call comes in."

Connor nodded. There was always action down in the Tenderloin.

Except for the first hour of this particular graveyard shift.

The two ambulance attendants climbed into the back of the vehicle with Connor, starting their own action; Connor getting the intimate, human interest side of the story. He pulled Rudy's hard cock out of the man's white pants and started sucking on the long, pale appendage. As Thomas got in behind and skinned Connor's baggy pants down, started eating out the newsman's ass.

Connor had felt an instant attraction to the two men. An unspoken kinship, almost a chemical reaction forging a bond. The men's dark eyes were full of longing, their lush, red mouths salivating with hunger. Connor knew the feeling well and recognized it; the lust for a kind of loving that existed only in the twilight, due to an unforgivingly straight post-war world.

He didn't give a damn if it was unprofessional or not. He had a tough beat on a two-bit newspaper where he garnered more insults than bylines. So, he had to grab his pleasure where and however he could get it, to paper over the pain. And these men, he felt, and now knew, understood.

He was down on all-fours in the back of the meat wagon, the gurney shoved to the side. He swirled his wet, red tongue all around the beautifully bulbed tip of Rudy's long cock, making the man sprawled out with his back to the bench seat groan in appreciation. Connor pumped Rudy's shaft with his hand, as he slathered the hood with his spit, groaning himself when he felt Thomas' tongue take a swipe up his ass.

The other man was crouched down in behind, his strong, slender hands on Connor's upraised and trembling buttocks, spreading them, spearing his tongue in between. Connor gulped hood and grunted, shivering each time Thomas' wide, damp, budded tongue stroked all along his sensitive ass cleft. He clutched Rudy's taut thighs and bobbed his head, sucking more of the man's cock into his mouth, tugging on the tool with his lips, painting it with his tongue. He had to sink his teeth into the rigid shaft, though, and gasp, when Thomas corkscrewed his own tongue deep into Connor's gaped anus.

Thomas had Connor's cheeks spread wide, the man's long, cool fingers digging into the tight flesh back there, the man's long tongue writhing around in sensationalized asshole. Connor mouthed as much of Rudy's meat as he could, sucked hard and tight, pouring on the passion that throbbed electric all through him, that was plugged into his ass. Rudy slid his fingers into Connor's hair and took firm hold, as Connor bounced backwards in rhythm to his own cocksucking, impaling his anus on Thomas' incredibly thrust-out tongue.

The two ambulance attendants switched positions. Connor remained exactly where he was. He grasped Thomas' long, pale cock now and kissed the gaping slit, licked it, then greedily gobbled up half of the man's tremendous erection and sucked on it. Rudy's cock in back was slickened with more than just Connor's saliva as he grabbed some oil from a secret hiding place. The man pried Connor's reddened cheeks apart with his hood, abruptly staked Connor's chute with half of his shaft.

Connor shuddered and gulped, caught between the two men's cocks. Right where he wanted to be in all the world. Rudy's erection filled his anus, driving deep to the balls and the bowels, Thomas's cock filling Connor's mouth, plugging the back of his throat. One man gripped Connor's head while the other gripped his hips. They both pumped, fucking the fortunate reporter mouth and ass.

Connor's own cock was a solid rod of sensation jutting out from his loins, jumping to the powerful beat of the dicks inside of him. He grabbed onto his meat and jacked, pumping fast and furious to keep pace with Rudy churning his chute and Thomas fucking his face. The three men oiled together, the ambulance rocking, flesh smacking against flesh, grunts and groans and gasps filling the heated, humid interior.

Connor burst with emotion, banged to sudden, uncontrollable eruption. Semen jetted out of his hand-cranked cock and striped the floor of the ambulance. He jerked and rippled between the two fucking men, streaming out his wild ecstasy.

The men humped into his mouth and ass, but he neither felt nor tasted their own hot, salty orgasms, if they had them. The fact hardly registered on Connor's bliss-flooded mind, however, so enthralled was he by his own wicked joy.

The radio suddenly crackled to life. Report of a man bleeding in an alley off Water Street.

Rudy and Thomas pulled out of Connor and leapt back into the front seat. The ambulance wheeled out of the parking lot and raced toward the scene of the victim.

Connor lolled around in back with his pants still down and his cock and body still throbbing pleasurably, the man wallowing in the glowing after-rapture of having his holes stretched and stoked, his balls blown and emptied.

The ambulance rocked to a stop in the darkened alley. Rudy and Thomas jumped out. Connor slowly pulled up his pants and swum around and crawled out the back doors. Propping himself up against the ambulance, he peered around the side of the vehicle.

There was a young, blond-haired man with his back to the brick wall of the alley. It looked as if he was struggling with the two ambulance attendants who were supposed to be helping him. There was blood on his left wrist, as if maybe he'd cut it with the broken liquor bottle that lay discarded on the asphalt at his feet. But if he'd been hell-bent on self-destruction before, fuelled by alcoholic self-loathing, now it appeared he was fighting for his life.

Even Connor, in his blurred and dazed state, could see that. And hear it. The blond's screams rang out clear as a knell.

Rudy had hold of the man's left arm, while Thomas was gripping the man's other hand. And as Connor watched, Rudy swooped his open mouth down onto the man's open wound, while Thomas yanked the man's cock out and swooped his mouth down onto that. Both men sucked, their long, pale throats working obscenely, ferociously.

The wounded man fluttered against the brick wall like a pinned butterfly, unable to escape the other two men's powerful grasps and gulping. The stunning look of sheer fear and shocked pleasure in the man's bulging eyes shook Connor right out of his stupor, chilled him right down to his balls.

He staggered forward to help the man, whose face was rapidly draining of color, staring with horror at Rudy sucking viciously on the man's wound, Thomas on the man's cock. But he tripped over something, and stumbled sideways, scraped his hand against the sharp brick to keep from falling. A few drops of blood welled up and trickled from the cut on the heel of his hand.

Rudy and Thomas's heads snapped around, their black eyes glittering in the dim light. And whereas before Connor had experienced horror at seeing what was happening to the blond man, now he experienced terror – at what was about to happen to him.

Rudy and Thomas advanced on him, leaving the blond man to slump down to the floor of the alley, pale as a ghost.

Connor gaped from one approaching man to the other, his addled brain realizing now that the scratch he'd suffered was about to become a sucking wound. Just like with those six other men, plus one, who had all died under the strange ambulance attendants' care.

CAMP VAMP
By Landon Dixon

It was fast-approaching midnight, and I still had my thumb out, trying to hook a ride on the Southern byway for a destination unknown. I was drifting, heading anywhere the road and a ride would take me. Leaving behind two years of med school and the blood and gore and high-stress lifestyle that went with it. I just wasn't cut out for the healing and billing racket, and the college had agreed, expelling me after I'd tried to heal myself with some classroom opiates.

The moon shone down from a black, cloudless sky, the night cool despite the southern clime and summer time. The asphalt coiled out in front and in back of me like a twisted dark serpent; the road less taken. I was about ready to bed down in the thicketry alongside of the highway, when, finally, two beams of bright white light shone forth around a corner, bearing down on me. Maybe this was my lucky night, after all.

The car zoomed to a stop right alongside of me. A long, finned, midnight-black, mid-1970s Cadillac. The boat-sized vehicle throbbed quietly with power. Then the tinted front passenger window whispered down, and a deep voice intoned, "Going my way?"

The door winged open on its own. I jumped inside, shucking my backpack into the spacious backseat. "Thanks, I really appreciate the lift," I enthused, getting nice and comfortable on the padded black leather bench seat. "It's so late I was giving up hope of ..."

"I always travel at night."

The voice was rich and powerful, like the car. The man was tall and lean, dressed entirely in black, suit, shirt, shoes and tie. His dark glossy hair was slicked back in a widow's peak, and he had a thin, handsome, pale face, deep-set eyes that held mine like the twin beams of his car had first attracted my attention.

"I dig it," I said. "You're an undertaker."

He smiled, bloodlessly. "Not quite. I work with the undead. Yourself?"

The Cadillac barreled down the highway, the man's eyes still locked onto mine. I gave my Afro a rub, responded with a lie, "I'm, uh, just taking a year off from college. A break from my medical studies."

The man's nostrils flared. He licked his thin lips with a blood-red tongue. "Really? So you know human anatomy?"

"Uh, sure."

He unfolded a long arm and extended a slender hand. "I'm Al Raduc. I run a camp for lost boys about twenty miles up the road – teaching and training them, preparing for life, and death. Would you be interested in instructing a class on basic anatomy for the boys? As part of their science program."

He grasped my hand and shook it. His clasp was firm and cool, like his demeanor. "Titus Kendrick," I responded. "Well, I've never actually taught kids before ..."

"Oh, they're not kids. They're young men, just reached the age of maturity, ready to fulfill their destinies – properly equipped, of course."

He slowly released my hand, but the electric touch lingered, spreading and tingling down into my cock and balls. Al had a very persuasive way about him. And other young men always interested me, being one flagrantly gay one myself.

"The boys are eager and willing to learn – be taught by a knowledgeable man like yourself."

I licked my plush lips, the blood pumping in my veins. "Well, okay, sure, I'll do what I can." I had no other plans, after all. "Uh, what sort of pay would ..."

"Oh, you'll be richly rewarded. Rest dead-assured."

Al slewed the car off the road and rocked to a stop on the shoulder. Then he slid closer to me on the seat, unfastened my jeans with masterful speed and ease. My cock was already pitching a tent in my tightie-greyies, Al's charm and charisma, his old-school distinguished good looks and chloroform-like cologne, the thought of all those hungry-for-instruction boys, engorging my loins with excitement and making my head spin.

"Yes, I can see you're just the man for the job," Al purred, pulling my waistband down and popping my erection up and out.

My cock throbbed in the open air, a licorice-black club of lust and raw nerves. My body and mind quavered, as Al slowly lowered his head, slowly opened his mouth. He breathtakingly engulfed the bloated tip of my heated bone with his cool, dry lips.

"Yes!" I sang out, bucking shaft up into the man's red velvet-lined maw.

He closed down on my cock with startlingly speed and depth, consuming me whole, his cheeks bulging and throat expanding, his lips kissing up against my pube-pebbled balls. I jerked, jumping and shuddering, clamped vacuum-tight inside the man's face. His eyes rolled glittering up at me, his one hand snaking into my tee and onto my chest, other hand coiling around my balls. I grabbed onto the back of the seat and the door armrest, overwhelmed by the sudden deep-throat turn of events.

Al's soft fingers played with my nipples and balls, pinching and rolling my blue-black buds to pulsing rigidity, tickling and fondling my nuts to boiling elation. My cock seemed to balloon in his mouth and throat, pounding pure passion all through my dazed body and brain.

Then Al slowly brought his head back up out of my lap, his lips and tongue and mouth dragging up the surging length of my cock, my appendage squeezing out of his throat. He halted his tantalizing ascent at my beefy cap, bit into it briefly and playfully; then slowly, at the same precise so-sensual speed that he'd sucked up my dong, he swallowed me whole again, flowing his mouth down my shaft and opening his throat up to my meat. He bobbed up and down, blowing my every veined, pulsating inch with a controlled pneumatic suction and intensity.

I dug my fingers into the deep leather on either side, gloriously flooding with a languorous ecstasy of soul-shimmering depth. I couldn't move, couldn't resist, brimming dong immersed in the man's face, stroked and stoked tight by the man's mouth and throat, bathed by the man's tongue. I could only watch wide-eyed, feel wondrously, as Al sucked on my cock.

His teeth lightly scraped my shaft on the sides. Not his front teeth, strangely enough, more like his canines. But that only added to the wicked eroticism of the awesome blowjob.

My mouth hung open and my tongue lolled out. Al sucked me past the point of all self-control. I gasped, and shivered, and shot sizzling semen deep into his throat, my body burning and mind bending.

It was utter, blinding bliss. Silently, searingly, spasmodically, I spurted burst after burst of wild joy into Al's mouth. His teeth bit in, and his mouth and throat clamped tight. He sucked every line and drop of heated jizz out of my cock and balls. Leaving me drained and limp and weak; insanely desirous for more.

# # # # #

There were six boys in all at the camp. Young men, actually, as Al said, just a couple of years younger than I. Al introduced them as he gave me a tour of the camp. The facility consisted of little more than a two-story stone house with a stone workshop attached, set in the middle of a lonely field, shielded from the road and surrounding land by a thick screen of evergreens.

The boys did woodworking in the workshop – there were a number of pine boxes stacked up in one corner. And sewing – there was a long rack of suits and capes in another corner. "Busy hands are the devil's workshop," Al put it.

"They also take flying lessons," he explained, taking an obvious pride in the industry of his boys, the camp he'd established for them. "And some rudimentary dentistry – sharpening and shaping and such. And we go on nature hikes, of course, cave spelunking mainly."

I nodded my admiration, at the boys and their programs. They really were a fine-looking bunch, younger versions of Al himself for the most part. "The boys are, uh, juvenile delinquents, then? I mean, young offenders?"

"They're an offence to conventional society, yes. They've been persecuted. I've taken them in and am training them for a successful after-life."

"Most commendable," I stated, not totally sure what he was talking about.

Al clamped a hand onto my shoulder. "Shall you impart your wisdom to them? Teach them about anatomy – the major veins tonight, if you don't mind."

It was two o'clock in the morning, but no one showed any signs of being tired, or going to bed. Al escorted me down into the stone cellar of the workshop that served as a darkened classroom. The boys gathered in a semicircle around me and another man.

"This is Stuart McFarlane," Al said. "I found him hitchhiking along the road, like you. He's been helping the boys out with locksmithing – bedroom windows and boudoir and bathhouse doors and such."

I shook hands with the short, freckled, curly-haired redhead. He was around my age, appeared rather nervous. It was cool down there in the cellar and dank.

Al stared into Stuart's pale blue eyes and intoned, "Stuart will assist you with your lesson, Titus, acting as a model. Won't you, Stuart?"

The guy gulped and bobbed his head. Then he undressed, completely. His smooth, compact, ivory body glowed in the muted lamplight Al shone on him. His pink cock hung thick and long, semi-erect, out of a nest of ginger pubes. Al handed me a laser pointer and told me to commence.

I cleared my throat and focused a shaky red dot on Stuart's left thigh. "Well, uh, this is the femoral vein. Just below the skin's surface here." I darted the red beam over to Stuart's right thigh. "And here."

The low-ceilinged room was unnaturally quiet, the boys seemingly holding their breath, no one taking any notes. The darkness shrouded everything except Stuart's ethereally illuminated body. The man's pubes twinkled in the light, his puffy nipples shining brilliantly pink, his meaty cock making my dry mouth water. I did note a throbbing swell in my jeans. There was just something about the whole atmosphere, the beautiful boys and Stuart's naked body so close. Eroticism hung heavy in the air.

"And, uh, here's where the iliac vein is located," I rasped, jogging the dot up to Stuart's flat stomach. Then I moved the red light over to his left arm. "And the brachial vein."

Suddenly, I heard the unmistakable rustling of black clothes being discarded. My cock bulged my zipper with pulsing emotion, my heart racing.

I pointed at Stuart's clean-shaven neck. "And this is the jugular vein, here in the neck."

All bloody hell broke loose, the tension snapping with a vengeance.

The boys rushed Stuart as a group, bowling him over onto the stone floor and piling on top of him, burying his naked body under their naked bodies. In the wavering light of the lamp, I could see them pinning the squirming man down, then slamming and sinking their teeth into the veins I'd just identified. And sucking!

I almost jumped out of my own skin, the pointer leaping out of my hand, when Al clasped my neck and breathed in my ear, "They have a passion for practical learning, you see. All these fine young men with their firm young asses – waiting to be fulfilled by a man of experience. Your payment for teaching them."

I stared at the nude boys crouched down on the floor, at their humped buttocks sticking up into the air. Al helped me strip off my tee and jeans and briefs, led me by the hard, thickened cock over to the kneeling, gulping boys, slickening my dick with some substance as he did so. Compelling me to claim my just rewards.

I tried not to look at Stuart's shocked face and staring eyes, the twitching parts of his body that were still visible. His cock stuck out straight up into the air, vibrating as the boys sucked on him.

I focused my rapt attention on the pert, pale moons of the boy feeding on the vein in Stuart's left thigh, the one I'd first pointed out. Al released my slippery prick, and I gripped it, crouched down in behind the boy's mounded ass, plunged my shiny, bulbous cap in between his taut, round cheeks.

I squished against pucker first thrust. I pushed forward, popped ring, sunk into anus. The sight of my dark, gleaming meat gliding in between those two tombstone colored and textured buttocks was stunning; the feel of my mighty erection getting enveloped in squeezing tunnel sensational. I plugged in balls-deep, pressing sack against ass. Then I grasped the boy's narrow hips and pumped mine, churning my cock back and forth in his chute.

He hardly seemed to notice, so intent on sucking off Stuart, like all of the other boys. But he did bounce his bum back a bit, in reflex rhythm to my deep dicking, turning me onto fever pitch. I rippled his cheeks with my thighs, thumping up against him repeatedly, pistoning his tight, sucking anus.

"They're all willing and able – open for your pleasure," Al's voiced reminded me from nowhere.

I pulled out of that boy and jumped over to the other boy sucking on Stuart's right thigh, got in behind his ass. I stumbled over Stuart's ankle. But that didn't stop me. There was no stopping me now. I was in on the frenzy big-time, whole-hog. I speared my dong in between the new boy's butt cheeks and plunged deep into his chute.

I fucked his ass, banging back and forth. I reached down and around and played with his hard cock, tumbled his shaven balls between my fingers, making the boy groan with his mouth full. Then I dug my dark digits into the white flesh of his waist and hammered my nightstick into his anus, rocking his bent-over body and Stuart's towering cock.

The frenzy mounted, me fucking, the boys sucking. I reamed the two boys feeding on Stuart's stomach and right arm, then leapt in behind the boy sucking on the laid-out man's left arm, sawed that kid's butt tunnel with a fearsome intensity, gyrating his cheeks with my cocking. Until, finally, there was only one cool hole left to fill, one rosebud to burst, and I hit it and filled it – the boy feeding on Stuart's neck.

I hardly heard the boys' impassioned sucking and gulping anymore, my own blood pounding away in my head and my cock. I rammed ass with mahogany member, bloating manhole and stretching sphincter, searing chute with the entire donging length of my boiling hard-on.

The boy snarled, knocked forward with my ardor. He snapped his head around and glared at me with yellowed animal eyes, tonguing the red smear off his lips. Then he turned back and clamped his mouth onto Stuart's jugular again, as I pumped his ass in frantic rhythm to his urgent swallowing. Stuart wasn't moving at all on his own anymore, his cock a pale rigid stake flagging the air.

It was too much, I'd held it too long. I pile-drove the boy's ass and then flung my head back and howled. All of the boys howled back. I was buffeted by blast after blast of orgiastic joy, splashing the boy's bowels with my jetting jism, coming like a madman possessed by crazy ecstasy.

And it was only when I collapsed down to my knees at the boy's glorious ass, my cock popping out with a torrent of semen, that I noticed that all of the other boys had pulled back. Giving me a blurred look at the pin-cushioned, red-ribboned body of what had once been Stuart McFarlane, fellow traveler.

I fled at the break of day, when Al and his "boys" were sleeping. Two miles cross-country, I finally skidded to a panting stop at The Stagger Inn, a dilapidated hotel crumbling right next to a decrepit graveyard. I breathlessly explained my plight to the proprietor.

"A college boy, huh?" the dead-eyed man said tonelessly. He slathered his liver lips with a grey tongue, rubbed his soiled hands on his tattered pants. "Why, yes, we can always use a man with brains here."

JUST BEFORE DAWN
By Jay Starre

Residing on English Bay in Vancouver, Canada, Jay Starre has pumped out steamy gay fiction for dozens of anthologies and has written two gay erotic novels. Contact Jay Starre on Facebook.

Count Renaldo watched the wrestling matches from the sidelines, his clothing impeccable, his blue eyes glittering, his skin pale as fresh milk. He was a figure of mystery to the others in the medieval town of Ferrara but known to be in the favor of the ruling Duke of Este. No one questioned him, and there was a visible circle of respect left open for him in the straw-covered building that housed the late night wrestling matches.

The Count's eyes roamed over the gathering. All who met those bright orbs turned away with a little shiver of fear, although they could not have said why. Renaldo himself wasted no time on the audience, rather focusing his considerable powers of observation on the brawny young Italian men who stripped down to battle across the roped-off area below. A feral grin danced across his patrician features at every toss and snatch and tumble.

It was late in the evening when one particularly handsome lad slipped into the ring. Willowy slim, the young man raised hoots and catcalls from the crowd. But when he removed his clothing to stand in a pair of linen undershorts, the crowd cheered him. He was all muscle, with no fat marring his perfect form. And at his crotch, a noticeable bulge brought more catcalls, this time from the whores who circulated among the onlookers.

"Tonio Dellamarque, untested tonight, will meet his match in Josefe Nontono," the referee called out.

The Count's glowing eyes fixed on the wrestler as he stepped forward to the edge of the ring. Others moved aside, and Tonio was confronted with the tall, cape-adorned figure. Tonio blinked as the man seemed to flicker for a moment, a naked, ghostly figure replacing the elegantly gowned Count. But then the Count smiled, displaying sharp incisors in a white grin. Blue eyes held him in instant thrall. Tonio bowed, and suddenly knew he would do all he could to attain victory that night. Fate had touched him in that gaze, a fate he had yet to understand.

Renaldo, too, felt the kiss of fate brush his brow on that warm summer night among the crowd and the straw-strewn floor. The young Tonio was ravishingly beautiful. But there was more than beauty in his muscular form. There was innocence, and there was potency, an attractive combination that had the Count's deep hungers stirring.

Renaldo was all too aware of his hungers, lusts he managed to conceal and control with rigorous discipline. The bulge in Tonio's crotch and the tight curve of the young wrestler's ass called to those lusts. But stronger still, the flush of warm blood suffusing Tonio's body as he prepared for the clash of the contest inflamed Renaldo's desires. There was one that overwhelmed all others for his kind, one need, one hunger. It was strongest just before the dawn, irresistible and without mercy.

Tonio felt the Count's eyes on him as he grappled with his opponent, those icy blue orbs taking everything in. Strength infused his muscles as the crowd jeered and heckled. Their favorite would not be defeated by this scrawny interloper. But Tonio was a canny fighter. The two wrestler's bodies gleamed in the torchlight, muscles straining. Their buttocks tensed and jiggled with a sensual power as they pushed and shoved their way across the floor. The bulge in their drawers grew noticeably stiffer, as they both attained erections. There was a palpable aura of lust in the air as the crowd screamed its approval. Tonio stared into Josefe's eyes, willing the bigger man to submit to him, his own erection throbbing against his drawers. Josefe faltered, his eyes dropping to that stiff bulge.

Tonio tripped Josefe, who outweighed him by many pounds. As the Count grinned his approval, Tonio pinned the man in the straw. Their two bodies flopped and meshed as if lovers rather than combatants.

There was a momentary hush at the unexpected and sudden end to the match. Then the Count began to clap, a lone sound in the silence. Others hesitantly joined in then there was a rush of cheering as if no one dared any other response. Tonio rose and held up both arms, his naked torso gleaming with sweat. His face flushed with victory, and as his soft brown eyes met the Count's his entire body grew heated with an irresistible passion.

In the blink of an eye, the Count's hand was on his arm. "Come with me, young Tonio. I would reward you for your victory tonight."

The voice was melodious. The hand was slender but strong. Someone tossed Tonio his clothing as he was deftly extricated from the parting crowd. He held his boots, drawers and tunic over one arm, with the warm night embracing his sweating body as they went out into it. Renaldo moved quickly, hustling the wrestler through the winding alleys until they were suddenly alone. It had happened so swiftly, Tonio was still barefoot with his clothing draped over one arm.

He looked around. They were in a small plaza huddled up against the mountainside. It was quiet, just before dawn. The refreshing coolness of a splashing fountain wafted to where they stood against the wall.

"My reward?" Tonio asked in a quavering voice, surprised at his own boldness.

Count Renaldo stood close. His eyes bored into Tonio's while his hand retained its grip on the young man's arm. His breath was hot in the wrestler's face. He smiled, the sharp teeth again appearing. One moment of hesitation froze them both in a tableau of expectant lust.

Finally, the Count sighed, and his fierce smile grew softer. "I have a gift for you, but not tonight. It is too close to dawn. Just a kiss for now."

Again that melodious voice sent a shiver through Tonio's half-naked body. The Count wrapped his arms around Tonio, pulling him into the silken embrace of the black cape that draped Renaldo's lean body.

Lips came down. Tonio lifted his face and willingly opened his mouth. Awaiting that promised kiss, he shivered with desire. His cock was stiff against his drawers, pressing into the Count's waist. Another cock thrust back, equally stiff. Tonio mewled, his tongue out. A hand dropped behind him and slid into his sweat-drenched drawers. Slender fingers insinuated themselves into Tonio's asscrack. The fingers tapped at his asshole, and Tonio groaned.

Suddenly, the mouth descended, but not upon Tonio's waiting lips. Instead it clamped over his neck, biting and sucking. Tonio flopped in the strong arms that held him, suddenly weak with an all-consuming and capitulating desire. His cock grew stiffer, and stiffer as blood began to pump from him into the Count's mouth. Tonio was so weak he could not cry out. His asshole yawned open as fingers teased the rim and just inside the blooming sphincter. He spewed his release in a violent, twisting thrust against Renaldo's silk robe.

Then he was alone, staggering barefoot toward the fountain. He dropped to his knees and plunged his face into the cool water. He felt his neck, where a tender spot told him there really had been that kiss, that bite. He realized his linen drawers were down around his knees. His asshole pulsed with the remembered stroking. His cock dripped cum.

Count Renaldo was a blood-drinker! He had heard of them. They were called *vampiro*.

But, the whispers had claimed they sucked you dry and left you a dead husk in the night. Why was he still alive? Tonio staggered home, his body hot with the memory of silk and fingers and that mouth on his neck.

It took Tonio several days to recuperate. The medieval town buzzed around him with the news that the Pope's bastard son was on his way with an army to chastise the Duke. Ferrara was to become another jewel in the Pope's crown, another Papal State. But Tonio found himself uncaring. Lust throbbed in his crotch and between his ass cheeks. The fingers that had teased him, slender and delicate, had been full of intent. The Count had almost penetrated him, almost fucked his ass with those fingers. It had been so close. Tonio wanted that brief encounter to continue, more than anything. The rampaging hordes of a bastard Prince did not matter one bit to him.

Tonio was scheduled to wrestle again. With heart pounding, he entered the ring and searched the audience for the Count. This time the crowd was with him from the start, but lamentably the Count was not in attendance. Tonio tossed his opponent to the floor almost desperately. Where was Renaldo? Tonio fled with his winnings. He found himself at the fountain again. It was earlier than the last time by several hours. He would wait. He massaged his cock into a stiff bone as he remembered the night of the kiss, and the bite.

"Hello, my Tonio. Did you not have enough of me the last time?"

The voice came from behind. Tonio's hand was on his hard cock. He felt suddenly elated, straightening his back with a fierce determination as he turned to face the Count. Their eyes met, soft brown and ice-blue. The young wrestler said nothing. Instead he began to remove his clothing. Trembling with both passion and a giddy fear, the slender

71

Italian bit back a gasp when Renaldo lifted his black cape like the huge wings of a crow and tossed it aside.

He was naked beneath!

Tonio's hands froze at his waist where he was unbuttoning his drawers. The shimmering light of the moon reflected off the fountain's splashing water. The Count was no longer on the stone paving in front of Tonio. He now stood paces away, knee deep in the pool, bathed in the moon's ethereal glow.

How had he moved so quickly? Tonio abandoned the thought as his eyes took in the vision of Renaldo's tall beauty. Skin shone like ivory, hairless and as smooth as the silk cape he usually wore. Muscles broadened the Count's shoulders, power evident in the thick biceps and well-shaped chest. Renaldo had a perfectly flat belly, with long and lean thighs. His cock reared from his crotch like a battering ram afire with white light.

Tonio mewled deep in his throat as he tore off the remainder of his clothing, feeling his own cock stiffen even further while his asshole palpitated with a fierce hunger. He was speechless, although screams of lustful wonder bubbled up in his chest aching to escape.

"Bend over here, Tonio. I want your potent seed sack in my hands, and your lovely ass wide open."

The Count smiled gently as he spoke. His voice, that deep but soothing baritone, washed over Tonio and drew him forward. He turned and bent over, as asked, feeling his thighs quiver and his ass cheeks twitch as he spread his legs wide. A hand cupped his ball sack as it dangled down above the pool. He shivered as the Count's hand rolled his vulnerable sack and tugged at it. He felt a wet tongue sliding up into his open butt valley. He moaned and fell to his knees. His head on the tiles, his ass was parted and offered up for the taking.

Renaldo stood in the cool water of the fountain behind the wrestler. He massaged his hefty balls with one hand and stroked his own rampant erection with the other. He smiled, his sharp incisors showing for the first time that night. He checked himself for a moment, determined he would not drink, not yet. Instead he leaned over and buried his face between the delectable amber nether cheeks presented for him. Tonio's ass was firm as marble yet red-hot with life. The cheeks quivered as he swiped his tongue over them, tasting the salty sweat of a living man. He tickled up the crack until he found the pulsing asshole. He settled on it and sucked gently while twirling his tongue all over the tight rim.

Tonio felt the delicacy of the anal kiss as a sweet surprise. He wanted to be fucked; he wanted to be taken by this Count whom he knew to be a blood-drinker. He wanted it all, whatever it was. His body quaked as tongue began to slither into his guts. The tongue was so long! It opened him, lapping at his insides. Tonio spread his thighs and hung over the edge of the fountain, wide open for that snaking appendage. The hands on his balls massaged the sack and pulled him back into the anal lapping. He felt heat invade him along with the *vampiro* tongue.

He was getting fucked by a blood-drinker's hot tongue!

The gentle splashing of the fountain was a melody in time to the slurping of that tongue and lips on his asshole. He floated in the ass-kiss. His cock was stiff against his belly, leaking pre-cum. His body shook with desire. He felt aroused and denied at the same time. The tongue was driving him mad! He wanted cock. Suddenly, that was all he could think of as that tongue tickled and teased him to distraction.

"Please, fuck me, Count Renaldo! Fuck me up the ass with your hard cock! Please!"

Tonio's hissed plea stirred the crouching vampire. Renaldo knew what he was doing. His long afterlife had taught him many things, with sexual pleasures being his chief delight. He could play this young wrestler like an instrument. But there was something about Tonio that made him hesitate, as much as possible for any blood-drinker with the needs of his kind.

And his need was to fuck, and then drink. Especially when dawn neared when he must return to his slumber, fed.

To his own amazement, that fierce desire for satiation was not the only thing on his mind that night. Tonio's obligingly spread thighs, his willing moans, and his cry for Renaldo to fuck him, it was all so sweetly and poignantly yielding. The victorious wrestler all at once happy in a defeat – it was a truly unusual and utterly compelling circumstance.

Tonio felt the vampire's tongue slide from his asshole. He groaned as cock replaced it. How the Count had done that was a mystery. That fat slithering tongue, then less than an instant later a column of throbbing cock meat replacing it, riding up inside him, filling him with its heat.

There was a slippery essence coating the invading rod, some concoction the *vampiro* had coated his cock with earlier in preparation for the inevitable anal plunder. The herbal goo was not only slick as olive oil, it was imbued with a peppery herbal substance that grew immediately hotter. It was like an oiled red-hot poker had plunged up into his guts.

"Oh God, I'm fucked," Tonio moaned. His hands on the stonework of the fountain, his arms upraised and his head tossed back, he faced the glowing moon with a look of total bliss.

That fiery cock drove into him from behind. Firm hips slammed against his own taut asscheeks. The lewd sound of wet hole and sliding cock rose louder than the splashing fountain. He was stuffed! He hovered on the edge of the pool, the vampire in the water behind him, the earth in front of him, half in one world, half in the other. Profane, hellish cock ravaged his asshole, pumping deep in a steady rhythm that sent waves of rapture through his quivering young body.

Renaldo touched every spot on Tonio's body he knew would elicit a response. The unearthly aristocrat fucked the wrestler's asshole with his cock while manhandling his dangling ball sack with rough tugs. Another hand reached between the kneeling wrestler's thighs to stroke his armpits and tickle his nipples. He fingered his navel and teased the piss slit of his leaking cock. He stuck fingers in Tonio's drooling mouth. He had the youth writhing and whimpering with those exciting tactile pleasures.

Tonio became only flesh. He thought of nothing. His body was more alive than it ever had been, with a *vampiro's* slick cock in his ass, pumping and pumping. He rocked back over that fleshy piston, eating it with his asshole, wrapping it lovingly with his anal lips, greedily suckling on it with his anal mouth. He fucked himself as the Count fucked him. The slim wrestler's abdication was so complete, Renaldo was caught up in it as never before in his long years of night.

It was just before the dawn when Renaldo halted his steady fucking. He turned the wrestler around so that he lay on his back at the edge of the fountain where the Count stood knee-deep in cool water.

"Make be cum. Take my seed," Tonio begged him as he gazed up at the burning blue eyes of his conqueror.

"I must go," Renaldo replied quietly.

"No, please. I am begging you!"

Tonio's pleas held him like a chain, a chain of brief love in the night. This was a dilemma. Love was a hunger Renaldo never allowed himself to satisfy, or even taste. It was too ephemeral, an emotion tethered by neither the day or the night and quite impossible to discipline.

An undisciplined vampire was at best nothing but a beast.

Tonio saw it, that flicker of love in the blood-drinker, that glimpse of heaven in the profane. The wrestler cried out again for the Count to stay, to fuck him longer, to fuck him forever.

The Count bent and sucked in Tonio's stiff cock. The youth spread his thighs apart and moaned with lust, shoving his cock deep into the vampire's mouth, pumping and pumping. Renaldo sucked voraciously, bringing the handsome young wrestler to the brink as he flopped about on the wet tiles in the throes of his rapture.

"Make me come, please Count! Please, take my seed. Take it all!" Tonio cried out as his orgasm approached.

Renaldo pulled his mouth from the throbbing cock and wrapped his aristocratic fingers around it. He pumped it as Tonio groaned and writhed. The pale thighs had fallen far apart, and down between them, an artery pulsed with blood. The blood-thirsty Count dropped lower and suddenly clamped his mouth over the tender inner thigh and sucked on the flesh. Tonio cried out, the hand on his wet cock pumping, the mouth on his thigh licking and sucking.

Tonio's orgasm hit him like a sweet hammer-blow. He squirted jizm in a flying arc, his body flopping wildly. Just then, the Count bit, his sharp teeth digging into Tonio's fleshy thigh, his mouth sucking the spurt of warm blood hungrily.

Tonio felt the pain as a sharp counterpoint to the ecstasy of his orgasm. His cum was draining out of him, his blood flowing into the vampire's gullet. He went limp with shaking exhaustion, giving up all he had, seed spurting, blood gushing.

Renaldo rose from the unconscious wrestler, his mouth red with his bloody meal. He sighed, just able to resist bending down for the final drink. Tonio would awake by dawn, tired and sore and satiated. Would he remember the Count? Renaldo wasn't sure. The naked body looked so composed, the dick still leaking, the balls full and fat. The thighs were open and the deep crack offered him a glimpse of the sweet asshole he had fucked for the past few hours.

He rose from the pool and swept up his cloak. Wrapping it around his naked body, he rose in the air and disappeared.

Tonio awoke with a groggy headache. He was naked, cum-stained and aching. His asshole throbbed. He had been fucked. He felt his sore and slippery anal lips with a pair of fingers and his cock stirred. He was far from satiated. Then he remembered. The Count! A fierce hunger coursed through him. He stumbled to his feet and dressed, not wanting to be discovered in such a state.

When he went out into the bright morning sunlight, he smiled. It was not over. Count Renaldo would want him again. He knew it with an absolute certainty.

Over the following several months events prevented the pair from meeting. The city was under siege as the Bastard Prince attempted to subjugate it for his father the Pope. The two men performed their duty against the enemy with admirable bravery, but their natures required them to do so at opposite times.

At night, a winged vampire descended on the enemy camp to drink the blood of its frightened soldiers. The Duke himself, not a vampire but a friend nonetheless to one, sanctioned this unholy warfare. The wrestler took up arms and fought by the bright light of day, awash in blood as much as the night creature he had fallen in love with.

Later that summer the Bastard Prince abandoned Ferrara for the time being, although he was certain to return such was his dark greed. For most, those who had not died or suffered grievous wounds in the battle, life continued on much as it had before.

For others, nothing was the same.

A cool breeze told of the approaching autumn as the late night wrestling match welcomed back their hero, the undefeated Tonio. The crowd parted as Tonio entered.

Only this time, he strode on the arm of the tall and regal Count Renaldo. When he entered the ring and stripped to his drawers, his half-naked body emanated an unearthly glow. The crowd stepped back in a hushed silence.

Tonio smiled at his Count on the sidelines. Sharp incisors glittered in both their mouths. Love, whether it be labeled divine or blasphemous, had won out.

SATYR DAWN
By Jay Starre

Zach considered himself a man's man. Tall, broad and dark-haired with a matching black beard, he definitely looked the part. A logger by profession, he lived in northwestern Washington state and spent his free time either in the gym sweating it out with other grunting power-lifting fiends or in the bar drinking his buddies under the table. No one cared question his All-American male image.

Because of his job, he spent most of his time in the forest. Even so, his favorite recreational pastimes also revolved around the woods. He was an avid hiker and camper and traveled throughout the western states visiting national parks and wilderness areas.

On top of that, when hunting season came around, he was off every weekend with his high powered hunting rifle and hi-tech hunting boots tramping through the mountains in search of prey.

It was his most recent hunting trip that would change his self-image, and his life, forever. It was a misty October dawn when the burly logger found himself waking in his tent to the sounds of voices outside.

It was barely light. As he rose to a sitting position, he could just make out his hunting partner in the sleeping bag beside him. Chris was sound asleep. Zach's cock stirred into a throbbing boner as he stared down at his hunting friend. The dude was blond, blue-eyed, cute as hell and had the most easy-going nature of anyone he knew. He was a jogger rather than a bodybuilder type and had the slim and athletic body to show for it. Chris was the manager of one of the town's banks and the pair had little in common other than their dedication to hunting season.

Zach kept his gay inclinations to himself, while Chris was comfortably out even in the redneck environment of their small town locale. The two had been hunting together for the past three years, yet the blond jogger had never once hit on his burly companion. Zach thought that was odd, considering his own undeniable male allure. He had assumed a gay dude would be drooling all over him, eager to suck his fat cock or take a ride on it with his sweet round ass.

He heard those voices outside again. Stirring from his gawk at his buddy, he got up to crawl over to the tent's entrance and peer through the flap. The mountain mist was thick, and he was at first unable to see beyond the wall of woods that surrounded their clearing to pinpoint the source of the floating voices.

Then, a pair of men appeared out of the swirling mist. Naked men.

He gasped, all at once aware of his own nudity. He slept without anything on, a habit of his he maintained even when out camping. Crouched on all fours and peering through the tent flap, he was keenly conscious of his stiff cock swaying between his powerful thighs, as well as his dangling balls and his parted ass-crack.

Just within the woods, the two men faced each other as they chattered away in some strange language Zach couldn't quite recognize. Waving their arms gaily, they laughed boisterously between animated statements. Who in the hell would be prancing around nude in the woods at dawn?

Zach couldn't help but notice that both were incredible specimens of manhood. The one on the left was all slender muscle while the other was beefy and built. The slim one was blond and the other was dark-haired with a short black beard. His eyes fell naturally to their crotches, and his eyes grew large as he spotted their rearing hard-ons.

Totally dumbfounded, while also totally turned on, he felt suddenly hot all over. He was nearly overcome with a compulsion to rise and join the pair, naked and sporting a boner in the forest dawn.

The bearded one turned his way. Their eyes met. Zach let out a startled gasp as he recognized the husky brute. Dark eyes under heavy brows, a broad nose and wide, generous mouth surrounded by a silken black beard - it was like looking in a mirror! He was staring at himself!

The other stranger turned his way as well. What the hell? Bright blue eyes and finely sculpted features – the dude looked exactly like Chris!

He let out a choked bark of laughter. He was dreaming. That was it! He was fucking dreaming.

His hard cock jerked and even spurted out a dribble of pre-cum, an all-too-real reminder that he felt totally awake. The naked pair stared directly at him, grinning mischievously, then raised their arms and waved him toward them.

They wanted him to join them! He couldn't look away, and he couldn't muster up the will to speak either. He must be asleep still! He had to be fucking dreaming!

# # # # #

My name is Zachariah. It was Zeus's forest my friends and I lived in during that mythical era. The Olympian wood was deep and ancient, inhabited mostly by those of my ilk. Wood Sprites we were called, and with us dwelled the flute-loving Satyrs. Males all, we spent our days and nights romping under the trees in naked delight.

On certain special mornings something unusual and magical would occur. We called it the Satyr Dawn.

It was just after sunrise when I felt the first stirring that morning. I rose from my bed of pine needles and oak leaves and sniffed the dewy air. Something pungent wafted into my nose. I stood full up and flared my nostrils. Yes, there was a musky odor in the air blowing in with the mist.

I felt a tingling quiver along my spine. Straightening up, I inhaled deeply. The quiver slipped lower, down into the crevice of my butt cheeks. I stuck my hand up into my naked crack between my ample butt cheeks. Heat emanated from the deep crevice, and I ran my fingers over my asshole to feel the wrinkled slot. It was particularly sensitive and very swollen. I shuddered, beginning to realize what was ahead.

My cock was hard, too, aching and leaping in front of me. I stroked it lightly with my other hand. I sniffed the air again and began to run my hands all over my powerfully muscled body. The solid flesh was hotter than usual, and trembling. Yes, something was happening.

It was then I spotted the trotting Satyr in the distance. I stared at the creature with a sudden longing as he flitted past the boles of ancient oaks. This was unusual. Satyrs and Sprites, although we share the woods, rarely interact. I moved forward and peered through the trees to get a look at him. His hairy thighs were powerful and confident. His hairy buttocks pumped and swayed insistently. He turned and peered back into the trees for a moment. The ink-black pool of his eyes gazed through the woods directly at me. Then I saw his cock, thrusting up from his furry crotch. It was enormous and oozing juice from the purple head. It jerked and pulsed – then the Satyr laughed out loud.

I realized he was heading for the Meadow of Satiation. With absolute certainty, I now realized what that morning heralded. Satyr Dawn!

My own cock felt like a granite pillar, exactly as my asshole quivered and gaped open. I gasped as an undeniable urge moved me to spread my thighs and open my crack. I felt my asshole abruptly grow sweaty and moist. I reached behind again to rub my searching fingers into my hairless crack. I felt the swollen lips of my distended slot. I shivered and moaned out loud. The hole was so slick, and hot! It convulsed under my touch as I found myself crouching down with a whimper. I rubbed my fingers around the edges of the hot opening and cried out. I recalled that huge phallus protruding from the Satyr's hirsute crotch. I rubbed the lips of my asshole and drooled just thinking of the monster staff.

Then I felt the call, and heard it. A Satyr's high-pitched fluting, a single note gone wild and savage. The strident note resounded through the misty morning. Another joined it, and another.

As a cacophony of shrill notes filled the air, I bent over and scrambled for the pot of herbal ointment all Sprites keep in their forest dwellings. An all-purpose cream, it served well to moisten dry hands and feet and ease the ache of sore muscles. It also served marvelously as a gooey lubricant for any kind of anal play a horny Sprite chose to engage in!

I scooped out a generous amount and immediately shoved two liberally coated fingers up my pulsing hole. I gasped and whined as the same time. Unable now to resist that warbling fluting, I rose up and ran forward, my feet flying through the soft forest turf. I was going to join the Satyrs!

I ran on shaking legs, a rising heat of adrenalin and testosterone flooding my entire body. I felt it in my tight nipples and tensed buttocks. I felt it in my cock, and especially in the heat of my flushed butt-hole. I was on fire from head to toe. The image of that passing Satyr and his waving fuck-stick had me running forward with all the swiftness I could muster. That screeching flute music beckoned me forward inexorably toward my fate.

All at once, I was there. The woods opened just as the sun broke free of the mountains. Bright rays of light dispelled the last of the morning mist and illuminated the scene. I halted in my tracks and gasped.

Satyrs danced in a circle in the middle of the dewy meadow. Blowing their flutes with raucous glee, they cavorted with pricks out-thrust. My head swam with heightened lust. Pricks! Hard and drooling and prepared for action.

I spotted the first of my fellow Sprites only a dozen paces away. Already under the spell of the Satyr Dawn, he was presenting himself. Obviously, he was heavily influenced by the Rut. I groaned and bit my lip as I recognized him. It was my dearest friend and sometime lover, Cristoforo.

The blond Sprite faced away from the dancing Satyrs, half bent over with his hands on his knees and his feet planted wide apart. With mouth open, his tongue was out licking at his lush lips. His head was cocked, his nostrils flared and smelling at the air. I shuddered as I looked down at his wide-spread buttocks.

The crack was parted in that position. He was presenting his ass! I shuddered and moaned as my eyes zeroed in on that open butt crevice. There it was. His swollen asshole flushed bright pink. He wiggled his delectable butt cheeks and arched his back, his quivering asshole gaping lewdly. A translucent pink coating of ointment glistened on his round cheeks and along the smooth crack. The hole itself shimmered with herbal cream. Each Sprite created his own ointment, color, smell and taste unique to each of us. Mine was a honey-gold in color and smelled like rich, woody walnuts. I knew from experience the smell and taste of my good friend's ointment, ripe pomegranate!

I moaned again as I felt my own asshole spasm and grow moist in response to his undeniable sexual signals. I lusted for my fellow Sprite, my cock stiff and oozing in front of me. But the sensations in my asshole dominated my emotions and outweighed every other consideration.

I was succumbing to the power of the Rut myself!

I stumbled into the clearing. The soft meadow grasses and small flowers beneath my toes were like a sensual carpet. All my senses were heightened as that wild music filled my head. The perfumed smell of crushed hyacinth beneath trampling feet mingled with the sharp odor of fir and pine needles and the stench of oak leaf and mushroom litter from the forest floor brought in on bare feet.

I saw others flooding into the meadow, Sprites and Satyrs intermingling. It was not immediately apparent who was who as we were much like human men physically, both Sprites and Satyrs – except for certain outlandish features the Satyrs possessed that Sprites and men did not.

For one thing, the Satyrs all had hairless upper bodies. Their chests glistened with smooth flesh, as well as their arms, shoulders and backs. But just below their navels, they sprouted hair in practically all the shades of blond, brown, black and red, as well as striped and checkered. The stark difference between upper and lower bodies lent them a distinctively bestial appearance where it counted – in their crotches and asses. Their pricks jutted out from their furry thighs like sleek purple fuck poles.

They also possessed certain exaggerated features. Their ears were large and pointed. Their noses were long and sharp, hovering above bulbous lips that were always glistening with moist spittle. Their hands and feet were oversized to an extreme. Long fingers boasted hairy knuckles. Their feet were stupendous, with splayed toes that were gigantic, especially the big toe, which was magnificently enormous.

We Sprites were hairy or hairless in a random fashion. We were also blessed with rounded asses that were plump and fetching. They jutted out behind us with sexually alluring immodesty. But otherwise, the features of both Sprites and Satyrs were alike and unlike indiscriminately, some tall, some short, some slim, some stocky, some deliciously plump and some lean as taut rope.

On this day, Satyr Dawn, we separated into two clearly distinct groups. The Satyrs proudly thrust their pricks out in front of them. We Sprites, too, sported stiff pricks. But it was our assholes that grew most heated with an overpowering, delirious hunger.

I found myself trembling all over at the sights, sounds and smells. I couldn't stop myself. I halted in a prominently visible position and presented myself.

Bending over, I clasped my knees with shaking hands. My feet went wide apart. The morning sunlight heated up my parted crack as it shined directly on the center of my lust, my pulsing, swollen asshole. I heard by own groans. I found myself wriggling my buttocks lasciviously and gazing around me in a frenzy of needy excitement. Where was a Satyr to satisfy me?

The wild music abruptly ceased. For one hair-raising moment, the stillness was absolute. It was as if we all held our breath simultaneously. Then, a sudden burst of gasping and moaning permeated the dawn air.

Nearby, my friend Cristoforo was first to meet his fate. A blond Satyr, very much like Cristoforo in facial features and build but with the smooth upper body and hairy lower body of his kind, moved forward on prancing feet to reach him. The assault of the Rut commenced.

The Satyr grinned lewdly as his hands came out to stroke the Sprite's bent-over form. Greedy fingers ran over his back then down into his parted crack. The fingers flickered over the distended anal lips, already wet with sweat and our particular herbal juices. The monstrous Satyr fingers stroked that orifice, teasing it open as the Sprite bent further over and cried out in a whimpering plea.

The bestial creature plunged a pair of fingers deep into the whimpering Sprite's gaping, well-lubricated slot.

I gasped, feeling my own asshole flush with moist heat. I shivered as Cristoforo moaned and wiggled around those penetrating fingers, his entire body vibrating and squirming.

Then it was my turn.

I was so intent on observing my friend's brutal seduction, I did not see my own assailant arrive from behind. "Ah, Zachariah! What a pleasant sight," a Satyr's merry voice boomed over my shoulder.

I shuddered. It was Xerses. I had run into him in the woods a number of times. He was tall for a Satyr, auburn-haired and sweet-lipped. I had also seen his cock, which was prodigious indeed.

"What lush raven locks you have, my sweet," he crooned behind me as his hands came out to stroke my hair. "What a broad back and sturdy shoulders you have," he chuckled as his hands moved down my body.

I shuddered at his touch, my asshole convulsing in eager spasms and my knees growing weak. I watched Cristoforo writhe under the assault of his Satyr, his asshole stuffed with a number of fingers as he cried out his pleasure, just as my own Satyr's fingers descended along my shuddering spine to my buttocks.

"Yes! Rounded to perfection. Swelling with power. Taut yet pliant. Cheeks of perfection."

Xerses waxed poetic as his massive hands slowly caressed my naked buttocks. Not only were Satyrs renowned for their talent with the flute, but also they were known for the garrulous tendencies, able to rattle off exquisite poetry at any time of day or night and at a moment's notice.

I trembled violently and wriggled backwards against the Satyr's roaming fingers. Anticipating their descent into my deep ass crack, I moaned aloud and arched my back, thrusting up my ass. Xerses did not disappoint me. His fingers trailed between my ass cheeks slowly but deliberately. I groaned. They found my hole!

He teased the lips, rubbing the outer rim as I continued to tremble and gasp. He laughed and crooned coarsely as he dipped a fingertip into the slippery center while I wriggled with agitation and thrust my buttocks back to meet the rigid digit.

"Ah yes, my studly Sprite. You are ready for a good fucking, aren't you? Feel this," and he immediately drove a finger deep into my quivering quim.

I shouted out as I backed onto that probing finger. The stiff thing rode into my hot hole, rubbing my inner tunnel and banging against my prostate. The gnarled knuckles massaged my innards as I bucked and squirmed over them, loving it but wanting more. More!

"Give me your cock, Xerses. Please!" I cried out.

The bestial creature chortled with glee. His finger slid from my steaming slot, but he was then pulling the lips apart with more fingers. I groaned and wiggled my buttocks. His fingers spread me open lewdly and teased the exposed inner flesh. I gasped. He held my asshole open and laughed with nasty joy. I felt completely vulnerable, my asshole a gaping pit of desire, waiting impatiently for fulfillment.

I felt the head of his thick poker rub up against my gaping hole. I shivered and whined. The plump crown was slick with drooling pre-cum while my asshole dripped with my own special lubricant. He rubbed that fat knob all over my swollen ass lips, teasing and taunting me as I moaned out my need.

I could hardly recognize my own voice, usually so deep it was almost a growl, now a mewling whimper as I begged for cock. "Please, Xerses! Please fuck me!"

It thrust into me. I groaned and spread my thighs far apart, willing my hole to open and swallow that invading meat. Xerses laughed and laughed as his cock drove up into me, spreading my lips apart and riding deep into my guts. I felt stuffed. And fulfilled.

He began to fuck me in earnest.

That huge prick reamed my guts. Pleasure emanated from my asshole outward to envelop my entire body. Xerses caressed my writhing body all over with his immense hands as he pounding his cock in and out. I moaned and pleaded — for more, for deeper, for faster.

Regardless of the intense spell of the wild fuck, I still noted what went on around me. The meadow had become a sexual paradise of fucking men. Sprites and Satyrs were similarly engaged in unrestrained encounters all about me.

Cristoforo squirmed over most of a brutal hand stuffed up his dripping asshole and apparently was loving it. Another Sprite nearby was in the same position, only bent further over. A Satyr with flaming red hair was on his knees behind the Sprite. As I watched with fascination, the Satyr's big tongue came out and swabbed at the Sprite's swollen anal lips. That fat tongue tickled and teased the lathered slot obscenely. The Sprite shoved his butt back over that tongue and grinned with crazed passion. He wiggled his ass all over that tongue as the Satyr ate his ass with smacking triumph.

Another hapless Sprite lay face down in the trampled grass and crushed hyacinth. Above him a magnificently muscular Satyr pinned him down with one monstrous foot. He chortled with savage delight as he plunged the other foot deep between his plump ass cheeks and rooted around for his primed hole.

I gawked with shuddering empathy as the Satyr's enormous big toe found the ointment-leaking Sprite's ass slot and burrowed inward. The bestial creature guffawed wildly as he wriggled that big toe in circles deep within the poor Sprite's quivering hole.

Another nearby Sprite squatted over a prone Satyr with his plump ass rubbing back and forth over the grinning creature's face. His distended asshole met the bulbous, slippery lips of the Satyr's beard-rimmed mouth. An enormous tongue pushed upward to impale the gasping Sprite. The red-headed Sprite was lusciously round, and his body jiggled and heaved as he sat down over that greedy mouth and probing tongue. A second Satyr stepped up to take advantage of him. By coincidence or design, both Satyrs assaulting the Sprite were red-heads, too. The second one grasped his thick red locks and pulled his face over his rearing pink erection. While one red-headed Satyr ate out his nether hole, the other plunged a prick deep into his throat. He was gutted from either end.

The rigid cock in my ass thrust deep into my guts all the while. Deeper, and yet deeper as the Satyr's meat miraculously expanded with his increasing lust. That was another of their particular physical eccentricities. Their pricks grew to a tremendous size when aroused, but were also capable of growing ever larger as they rubbed or stroked them. So, as he pumped in and out of my hole, the very act of rubbing against my steamy anal walls and slippery sphincter served to increase the length and girth of his monster tool.

His hands on my body had grown more insistent. He plucked at and pinched my nipples, sending shock waves of electric sensation coursing through my violated form. He ran his knuckles savagely up and down my torso, then around onto my back and along my spine. He slid the gross paws around my heaving belly, then into my crotch. He gripped my stiff cock and cupped my dangling seed sack and squeezed both with rough greed.

I jerked from head to toe as his enormous cock slammed into my aching ass.

"Unload for me, sweet Zachariah. Release your semen while I fuck your hot asshole to mush!"

The words were whispered in my ear as a hot tongue snaked out and swabbed at it. I shivered and squirmed as his hairy paw flailed my cock. Yet the center of my passion remained in my sensitive asshole and the savage pounding it received. The steady ache grew more and more exhilarating.

Exhilarating, too, was the riotous scene unfolding around me. Other Sprites were bent over with cocks slamming into their juicy asses. Just as Xerses rammed deep into me, I turned my eyes toward Cristoforo beside me. His Satyr's purple pole thrust up into his dripping butt orifice beside the trio of fingers already planted within. The glistening tube parted the moist anal lips, sliding and slurping as it shoved deep and then pulled out. The buried fingers twisted savagely before the cock slid in beside them once again. Cristoforo's glazed blue eyes met mine. We shared a moment of true

90

ecstasy as both our balls roiled, our assholes burned and we achieved orgasm.

Eyes locked together, semen spurted in a rocketing spray from both our cocks. Our assholes snapped and convulsed in an orgasm of their own. The milking muscles sucked a load from both our savage Satyrs.

"Yes, sweet Zachariah! Drain my cock with your hot hole! Spray the grasses with your redolent man juice. We are coming!"

I fell to the grass on my belly, wallowing in my own jism. The Satyr laughed with rabid glee as he covered me with his half-hairy, half-smooth body. He began to fuck me all over again.

I succumbed to it with moaning pleasure. It was Satyr Dawn.

# # # # #

Zach returned to the present in a rush of heady lust. He was still on his hands and knees peering out of the tent flap at the misty dawn. Only now, he felt the slim body of his hunting partner perched over his own powerful frame. The blond breathed in his ear, grunting as he rammed his lengthy pink cock in and out of Zach's well-lubed and aching asshole.

The pair of Sprites were turning away, arms across each other's shoulders. They offered him a final jaunty wave and smirking grin as they strode off. Both their naked asses were flushed and slick with Sprite oil. He knew with certainty their slippery holes buried between those firm ass-cheeks had only recently been well-fucked by lusty Satyrs.

Chris's soft voice whispered in his ear, bringing him back to the present and the aching pleasure of cock sliding in and out of his own hole, here and now.

"What the hell has gotten into you this morning, Zach? You sure were asking for it, waving your naked butt and moaning with your eyes closed and a big boner between your legs. I couldn't help greasing you up with a good coating of hand cream and sliding my cock into your hole. You seemed to be loving it, so I kept going. Now that you're awake, are you OK with it?"

The burly logger took a deep breath, then exhaled slowly. What the hell. No use in pretending anymore! Something had changed inside him, and he wasn't about to go back to who he had been before.

"Fuck the hell out of me, Chris! You been wanting to for years, and I've been wanting you to. Hell Yeah! Fuck ... my ... big ... logger butt!"

Chris didn't argue. Especially since he'd just had the wildest dream of his life, some crazy fantasy about fucking in the woods with a bunch of naked Satyrs and Sprites! Fucking Zach's beefy butt was a dream come true, and he wasn't about to let the opportunity pass him by.

Neither was Zach. The burly logger arched his back, slammed his hefty ass backwards, and swallowed up all the cock he could get.

Life was good!

THE GROUP
By Mark Apoapsis

Mark Apoapsis currently lives alone, having eaten his roommates. He has no website at the moment but may be reached at mapoapsis@excite.com.

"It would have been easy enough for someone to steal all my clothes while I was in the lake," I finished sheepishly, "considering how drunk I must have been."

"You're just lucky you didn't drown," said a guy I didn't know yet, seated on the far side of our small circle of folding chairs.

"Yeah, believe me, I realize that."

"How do you know you didn't just forget where you put them?" asked a guy I'd met a couple of weeks before. His name slipped my mind, but I definitely remembered his story. He was a veteran and probably a recent one since he looked no older than I, maybe younger. He had skipped the previous week's meeting, so he'd only heard my original story of why I was here; this was the first time he was hearing the extended version of how I was dealing with it.

"I don't. I mean, like I said, I don't remember stripping. Or getting into the water. Or getting out again. Or even leaving the bar. So I guess I could have left them anywhere between the bar and the lake. Or maybe I stripped while I was swimming, and my clothes are all at the bottom of the lake. I don't remember anything until I woke up on the edge of the water."

"That's what happens when you try to drown your sorrows in drink," said the first guy.

"Thomas," Matt told him gently, "I know A.A. has really helped you and a few of the other guys here, but remember,

93

this isn't A.A. This is a safe place for men to talk about their grief. We don't judge each other in this group. Each of us is dealing with the loss of a buddy in his own way, and what's self-destructive behavior for one man may be a useful coping mechanism for another."

A fourth guy, speaking for the first time since I'd started, said supportively, "As long as you weren't driving, Jake, I've got no problem with it." His name I remembered: Andy. The poor guy had lost both his gay lover and his best friend to a drunk driver. Recently enough that his own arm was still in a cast.

"The bar I go to is less than a mile from my house, and I always leave the car at home," I assured Andy, just as I had my second week. "Although I don't think I had all that many. I guess I just can't hold my liquor as well as I thought I could."

"Or you lost count," Thomas said.

"Could be."

"How did you get home?" someone asked curiously. The one whose brother had committed suicide, if I remembered correctly.

"What could I do? I started walking, even though it was broad daylight by then. Someone must have called the police. The cop was really nice, though; he let me off with a warning and even gave me a ride home. And a blanket. It was bad enough having to go knock on the super's door wearing only a blanket; I'm glad I at least had that!"

"That's one of the times when having a roommate would really have helped," another guy said quietly. He looked vaguely familiar from somewhere. Not from this group, I was sure. I supposed he was close enough to my age that we might have gone to college together, but if so, he couldn't have been someone I'd really known; college wasn't so many years ago that the memories would have gotten this fuzzy. Maybe high school. No, I decided, I'd never have forgotten those eyes, a

94

striking shade of blue. They'd be hard to forget, even on another male. No, I was probably half-remembering someone who resembled him except for eye color.

Everyone had been amused by my story – the ending, anyway – and obviously trying hard not to laugh out loud, some succeeding better than others. And the thought of my having had to explain my nudity to a roommate, who would have felt free to razz me about it, instead of to a super who was just doing his job and had to be polite, should if anything have made it even funnier. But, something wistful in the way the guy said the word "roommate" sobered the room up. The other guys stopped snickering and looked at him curiously. Maybe it was just because it was practically the first comment he'd made all night. This was his first meeting, I'd decided. I hadn't seen anyone greet him as we were gathering. except Matt, who'd shaken his hand and spoken to him for a few minutes, gesturing vaguely around the room. Everyone else here seemed to be regulars, even Thomas and a few others I was meeting for the first time because they'd missed a couple of weeks.

The new guy had seemed riveted by my story in particular. Not just the embarrassing part at the end; the tragic and brutal beginning had caught his attention right away, even after an evening of hearing one story after another almost as horrible as mine.

I told him, "Yeah, I've always been enough of a loner to prefer having my own place, but you've got a point. Anyway ... The super must be a heavy sleeper because I had to knock pretty loud, and by the time my pounding woke him up, the guys in the apartment next to his were poking their heads out and laughing at me. I'm pretty sure I woke them up. I mean, it was early, and they're always out partying late – or in partying late; their apartment is directly below mine, so ... Anyway, they looked like they just got out of bed." Judging by their bare shoulders, I meant. Although for all I knew, they went shirtless at home all day. That would be in keeping with my slovenly impression of them. They were several years younger than I, about the right age to be frat boys who'd just graduated – or been kicked out of – college.

#

"Any updates from this week?" Matt asked. "How have you been doing?"

"Still grieving, but it gets a little better every day. Oh, did you mean the drinking?"

"Not really, but if you'd like to share that ..."

"I've kept drinking, not too excessively. You know, mostly on Friday and Saturday nights, so it hasn't interfered with work or anything."

"And no more blackouts?"

"No, that was the only one in the six weeks since ... it happened."

Andy said lightly, "Be sure to tell us if you ever strip naked and dance on the bar. Preferably in advance."

"You'd like that, wouldn't you?" I was getting comfortable enough with Andy, after three weeks, to banter with him, but I felt myself blushing.

He grinned at me. "Damn straight!" After a pause, he said, "Anyway, if you're done? Should I go next? If no one else was about to ...? OK." He took a deep breath and retold his story – which didn't get any less heartrending on the third hearing – of watching his best friend and his male lover both bleed to death as he himself lay pinned in the wreckage of his car, unable to help them. I noticed he told it with a different emphasis each time. The first time I'd heard the story, he'd mentioned the friend only briefly and unemotionally, as if the guy's death was so overshadowed by the greater tragedy of losing his lover as to seem insignificant. I'm pretty sure he hadn't used the phrase "best friend" until my second week. Tonight he was crying unabashedly as he talked about his friend's death and how much he missed him.

96

"As for recent progress, I've been doing a lot of thinking, and I realized something. Everyone I know, gay or straight, understands – or thinks they do – how I feel at losing Jim, my partner. We were together for ... well, it would have been two years next month. We might have gotten married if it were legal in this state. But Tyler was my best friend. I knew him since college. And I'm not sure people understand that in its own way, losing him was just as bad. Maybe even ... The truth is, I've been afraid to talk about Tyler, because it might sound like I miss him more than my own partner."

"Do you?" Matt asked.

"Is that horrible? Does that make me a bad person?"

"No, and that's exactly the point of this group. Men in our culture don't feel like it's okay to admit how much our male friends mean to us, even when we lose them. What I hear you saying is that people have made an exception for your feelings about your partner because you're gay, and they sort of translate it to their own opposite-sex relationships and overlook his gender. But they don't give you permission to express your feelings about your buddy. Exactly what people do to the rest of us."

"That's how I feel," one of the other men said. "This is the only place I feel I won't be considered weak, or, you know ... gay – no offense, Andy – for being devastated after my closest friend died."

Several others voiced the same sentiment, and Andy said, "And, the other thing I decided is I owe all you guys an apology. I realized I've been treating you guys as bad as the rest of the world does, acting like I thought your grief was less valid because you didn't lose the person closest to you. Like you don't know what it's like to lose a man you really love. I was trivializing your friendships and your grief. I think it's because I was afraid to admit how much my friend meant to me."

"That was a very natural defense mechanism, Andy," Matt said, "and I'm glad you figured it out on your own."

97

Andy continued, "I understand now we're all in the same boat." Looking at each of us in turn, he added, "Whether we lost a lover, a friend, a brother, a comrade in arms – did I miss anybody? We all lost someone close. Also, it was just plain stupid of me to claim that watching someone slowly bleed to death was somehow worse than seeing him instantly blown to bits by a land mine, or finding him hanging by the neck, or watching him dying in a hospital bed from a lingering illness. Although I have to say, seeing a buddy torn open and eaten alive has to combine the worse parts of 'gory' and 'not over quickly.'"

He had turned to look at me for the last part, of course. "Thanks, Andy," I said. I swallowed hard and remembered to add dutifully, "But really, there's no good way to watch a friend die."

"Anyway, I promise all of you that I'll try to be more supportive from now on." He looked at the blue-eyed newcomer. "I didn't catch your name ..."

"My name's Ethan."

"You're new, aren't you? Are you ready to tell us what brought you here?"

"Funny you should ask. Believe it or not – and I brought in the newspaper, so I can prove it – my story is a lot like Jake's. Uh, not the naked part at the end!"

That would have gotten a laugh under other circumstances, but everyone knew how my story began. Every man in the room was leaning forward with various mixtures of sympathy and morbid curiosity.

"Only in my case," Ethan continued, "it wasn't out in the woods. We were at home. It was a very warm evening – remember how nice it was the weekend before last? – and we had our door open, with the screen door shut and locked. It smashed right through the screen and attacked us. Me and my roommate. I made it. He didn't. You really want the gory details?"

"A lot of guys find it helps to talk about the traumatic event," Matt said tentatively.

He took a deep breath, looking down at his hands, which were clenched together in his lap. "I rushed into the living room when I heard the screams. Brandon was lying there, still alive at that point, with his shirt ripped open and red gashes across his chest, and this animal was pinning him down, and slowly and deliberately ..."

I always helped put away the folding chairs, along with several of the other young and physically fit men in the group – fit and able-bodied, that is; I didn't blame Andy for not helping as long as his arm was in a cast. Ethan certainly qualified on all three counts, and he pitched in without being asked. I liked him for that. Afterward, right after Matt locked the door behind us, Ethan and I were almost the last ones left. I offered him my hand and said, "Ethan, right? I'm Jake."

He clasped my hand warmly. "I remember. And I definitely remember your story! I didn't expect to meet anyone here who'd had an experience so close to mine."

"And I didn't think it was possible for someone to have a worse experience than me. You know that what I said before was polite bullshit, right? When I told Andy that any way of watching a buddy die is equally bad? That's the party line, but I don't care what anyone says. I try to be supportive because I know these guys are hurting in their own way, but you and me? We have to be even more ... scarred than any of them."

"I know, right? I didn't think I'd find anyone who really understood."

"I mean, dude! At least mine was in the dark, and I was lying on the ground, distracted by physical pain, because it attacked me first. You were on your feet, not even injured yet, in a brightly lit room." He hadn't been kidding about giving us the gory details. He'd described seeing his roommate's

99

internal organs exposed, heart still beating as it pumped blood all over their floor. As he remembered it, it was only when the animal ripped into his friend's lungs that the screams cut off. And it had just gotten messier from there.

I wasn't crass enough to repeat any of those horrible details now, of course, but it gave us both pause, as his memory no doubt replayed the scene against his will, and my overactive imagination forced me to picture it as vividly as if I were watching an old-time horror movie whose director had forgotten to turn the camera away from the most graphic details and focus discreetly on the dark blood soaking into the light-colored carpet. I could picture his poor roommate's dark shirt ripped open to reveal the pale, nearly hairless chest underneath, hear his screams, even smell his fear, then his blood.

Finally, I continued, "And it seems so unfair. At least my buddy and I knew, in a vague kind of way, that there's a tiny risk of an animal attack when you camp in the woods. But for a wolf to enter your house in the middle of town! You did say a wolf?"

"It looked like a wolf, or a huge dog or something, but I'm no expert. And of course, I was scared out of my wits. You never said what yours was."

"That'd be because I don't know. I didn't get a good look at it. It could have been a bear, attracted by our food. Or a mountain lion; it certainly played with us like a cat plays with a mouse. But now that you mention it, the rangers said the next morning that when they followed the trail of broken branches to the riverbank, they found what looked like wolf prints in the mud. They tracked them as far as the point where they were obliterated by footprints from some camper apparently coming back from a swim further downstream."

"Do you find it helps, having this support group?"

"A little. Mostly I just feel this strange need to be surrounded by other guys since it happened."

"What's strange about that?"

"Just that I'm normally such a loner. Maybe danger sets off an instinctive need for the safety of the herd."

"'Band.' It's called a 'band' of man, like a 'flock' of birds or 'school' of fish."

"That does sound less lame than 'herd.' Yeah. This is the first time I've ever felt the need to be part of a band of brothers."

He grinned and clapped me on the shoulder. "Want to go grab a drink, bro? We can compare scars."

"Uh, we're still talking about psychological ones, right?"

He laughed. "Yeah. I mean, this group is great, but I really need a friend to help me through this."

"Me, too. Maybe we can both help each other through this."

"And hey, we can compare the physical scars, too, if you want. Don't get me wrong: It's not a come-on. I'm straight."

"Me, too."

"They're only on my upper chest, anyway." His grin faltered. "Same place it started digging into Brandon, before it worked its way down. I was sure when it knocked me down that I was in for the same slow death, but it was almost like it was playing with me. I think it could have torn me open with one swipe, but it took its time, ripping away my shirt, watching me squirm for a few minutes like it enjoyed having me at its mercy, and then scratching me just deeply enough to draw blood. What the hell kind of wolf does that?"

"The rangers told me that it was unusual behavior for almost any species."

"Why it let me live, when it killed Brandon, I'll never know."

I patted his chest, right about where the scars later turned out to be. "Matt is always telling us not to fall prey to survivor guilt. Tell you what, here's the plan: I'm never drinking and driving, not even under the legal limit. Not after hearing Andy's story. So, we drive to my place, walk to the bar and have a couple of stiff drinks, and then I've got plenty of beer at home. And if you were serious about ... well, mine are just on my shoulder, so why not. Then we call you a cab, or you're welcome to crash on my sofa."

#####

"Dude!" Ethan said, laughing at me as he finished buttoning his shirt. "For a guy who skinny-dips, you were awfully shy about taking your shirt off."

"I was drunk then!" I protested, tucking my shirt in.

"You're drunk now."

"Not very. Not blacking-out drunk. Although I didn't think I was then, either. Anyway, I was skinny-dipping alone. As far as I know."

"I can't believe those guys downstairs! Did they really stand there laughing at you, instead of inviting you in and lending you some clothes?"

"That didn't even occur to me," I said, shuddering at the thought of throwing myself on the mercy of the frat boys by entering their apartment naked and defenseless. "I was pretty desperate for a few minutes. Maybe if they'd handed some clothes out to me ..."

"I mean, I haven't seen them so I don't know if they're your size, but some sweat pants at the very least."

I still wore the same pants size as I had when I was in college, so maybe. "I've never looked at them that close, but guess they're both medium build, maybe on the muscular side, like me. And you."

"Well, I'd give you the shirt off my back anytime you need it, bro. He looked down at my waistline critically. "I think you could even get into my pants. I mean ...! I mean they'd fit."

"Yeah, I know what you mean," I said, laughing with him.

"Well, this has been fun. See you next week?"

"Wow, I didn't realize how late it was getting. Even Nick and Chip seem to have settled down. That's the guys we've been talking about – and hearing through the floor all night." I knew their names from the mailbox right below mine. And from the occasional shouts of "Nick, get your ass out here and help me with this keg," or "This isn't funny, Chip! Come back here and untie me!" I'd never figured out which was which, and didn't care.

"Yeah. I have to work tomorrow. Listen, in case you want to get together before next week ..."

"Hey, take that jacket off. The plan was for you to crash here, remember?"

"That was before we found out I only lived two highway exits away."

"Do we know how long the drunk driver was on the highway before he smashed into Andy's car?"

"I'm probably under the legal limit."

"That's what I thought a week and a half ago, and next thing I knew I was waking up aching and dizzy with no clothes on."

"OK, OK! You win." He had his jacket off and was untucking his shirt. He began unbuttoning it from the bottom this time, exposing his flat, hairless belly.

"I'll get you a blanket. I've, uh, got an extra one."

# # # # #

We exchanged phone numbers after breakfast and wound up getting together again that weekend. After a couple of drinks, we spent the rest of the night watching an old movie, *Animal House*. It was Ethan's pick.

"I feel like I'm living upstairs from it," I said. "I want to kill those guys sometimes." From the muffled whoops and shouts, I couldn't tell yet whether Nick and Chip were watching a football game or staging one of their testosterone-soaked mock battles.

"Aw, they're just having a good time," Ethan said, sounding a little envious. I remembered he'd lost his own roommate all too recently and felt like kicking myself.

The next week, we met for pizza and beer before the meeting and went to see a movie afterward. Then we spent the next Saturday playing cards and watching a ballgame. Sunday, we just tossed a ball around in the park near my place. That was surprisingly fun: even chasing after the missed catches was a blast. We started deliberately making each other chase after wild throws and bring them back.

It came as no surprise to the group that we were hanging out together. A few other guys had buddied up for the same reason: Not only did we have a tragic experience in common, but also we now both had a gap to fill in our lives. I'd lost my closest friend – there were people I saw a lot more often, but I didn't consider any of them more than casual friends. And Ethan had lost a friend who had been part of his daily life. Right after the attack, he'd moved away from the scene of the bloodbath and into a one-bedroom apartment. He could barely afford it, and he found he didn't like living alone. He was spending almost half his nights on my sofa anyway, and even in uncomfortably close quarters, we were getting along very well as quasi-roommates. We were already talking seriously about looking to rent a two-bedroom place together, somewhere with quieter neighbors and no one who knew about my ignominious early-morning return, about four weeks ago now, clutching the nice young cop's blanket around me with one hand and banging on the super's door with the other.

#####

Yeah," Ethan told me the following Friday at a restaurant, after we'd been friends for a couple of weeks, "I haven't felt like trying to get laid either. Too depressed.

Brandon and I used to spend most Friday nights trying to pick up girls, but I figured it would take a while." He stared down at what was left of the plate of spaghetti he'd ordered after picking clean a full order of ribs. He'd eaten all but a couple of the meatballs but had mostly played with the pasta rather than eating it; some strands were threatening to spill over the edge of the plate and already dripping red onto the table. "But I'm feeling kind of horny tonight for some reason." He picked up his fork again and began toying with the remaining two meatballs.

"You, too? Must be something in the air." I speared one of his meatballs without asking his permission, and popped it into my mouth.

He gave me a wry grin and devoured the remaining meatball while he could. We chewed together, and then he asked, "Is this the first time you've felt like picking up a woman since your attack?"

"Uh, well, once before, a couple of weeks ago." I paused to cut another chunk off my steak, which was nice and thick and lean like I liked it, and still pink inside. I'd never known how much taste I'd been missing, eating well-done steaks all my life. I chewed on it appreciatively.

"How did it go?"

I considered making up a story I could boast about but decided I had nothing to hide from Ethan. Sheepishly, I said, "I seem to have decided to cool off the desire by jumping into a cold lake."

"Oh." He grinned and punched me in the shoulder. "Tell me that story again. I never get tired of hearing that."

"Dude, going through that once a week is enough. Anyway, you know it by heart by now."

He slid around the horseshoe-shaped booth and playfully poked me in the ribs, saying, "C'mon!" When that got a reaction, he started tickling me. "Tell me again, or I'll go talk to your neighbors – Chip and Nick, was it? – and hear it from their perspective. That should be good!"

I trapped his head under one arm and tried to tickle his ribs in retaliation. I got disappointingly little reaction. Maybe if his damn shirt wasn't in my way. I said, "I've got a better idea. Let's finish our food and go to the bar and pick up some girls."

# # # # #

I'd always done this alone before, but it was more fun with a buddy along. We struck out a few times, but we finally hit on two girls sitting at the bar together who seemed vaguely interested in us. That is to say, when we offered to buy them drinks they didn't decline. We took the stools flanking theirs, implicitly each staking a claim to one of them. We hadn't exactly discussed it or thought through the logistics, but I guess the idea was that if Ethan got lucky he'd take his back to his place – in a taxi, if I had anything to say about it. He lived a little too far away to reasonably walk. I had the home-territory advantage; I figured I could take mine out for a stroll and subtly herd her toward my apartment.

Odds seemed to be looking fairly good for me, less so for my buddy, when I made the tactical error of going to the men's room. But what choice did I have? I'd had three beers by that point; it was that or pee in the corner. When I staggered back – was it really only three beers? I felt as if I didn't concentrate on staying upright, I'd wind up crawling the rest of the way – the girl who Ethan had been talking to was gone. I'd already forgotten both their names, to tell the truth, but I saw that Ethan had moved to the stool his girl had vacated and was now talking to my girl. Worse than that, he was leaning close and resting his hand on her wrist. She wasn't exactly pushing him away. Not that was she leading him on, unless you count taking his hand in hers when it started to wander somewhere more interesting. When I sat down, they barely glanced at me long enough to explain that the other girl had left, pleading exhaustion from a long day at the office. Then they went back to focusing on each other. It wasn't unusual to have an attractive woman ignore me, but it bothered me that even my buddy was acting as if I wasn't there. I sat there fuming for several minutes, then slid to my feet and put my hand on Ethan's shoulder. "Can I talk to you? Outside?"

They both looked annoyed at the way I'd interrupted their two-way conversation. For a second, Ethan actually looked angry; I'd never seen him mad at me before. I almost thought he would slug me, but he controlled it and said. "Sure, buddy, in a few minutes. We're ..."

"Now!" I said, squeezing his meaty deltoids hard and grabbing his collar with my other hand, physically yanking him off the stool. Out of the corner of my eye, I saw the girl jump to her feet in alarm and back away a few steps, but I was focused on Ethan, whom I was already half-dragging toward the back of the bar. I knew there was a back docr somewhere; I could smell the faint, not-unpleasant aroma of garbage from the dumpsters out there, even through the intervening aromas of men and women and a dozen kinds of drinks inside. I followed my nose to the door and shoved Ethan through it. I didn't mean to send him sprawling, but either I was stronger than I thought or he was as unsteady on his feet as I was. Next thing I knew he was on all fours. I rushed toward him, part of me wanting to help my friend to his feet and part of me wanting to pounce on him, flip him over, and pin him to the ground beneath my weight.

Before I got close enough to do either, he scrambled to his feet and staggered toward me, aiming a wild punch that I easily dodged. I grabbed him by his shirtfront, lifted him off the ground, and shoved his back against the brick wall. The friction against the rough bricks must have supported some of his weight because it was amazingly easy for me to hold him there with one hand, his feet dangling.

"What the hell, man?" he said.

"What the hell do you think you were doing in there?"

"Hey, just because you were sitting closer to her doesn't mean we'd agreed who got which girl. She seemed to like me ..."

I pulled him toward me, only to slam him against the wall again, knocking his breath out of him.

"OK, I'm sorry! I should have asked you. You can have her, bro. Let's just go back inside."

"She's probably gone by now. Anyway, you know what? I don't even care about the girl anymore." And it was true; all I was thinking about at that moment was how good it felt to have my friend and rival against the wall with his shirtfront twisted in my fist. I was especially conscious of how his shirt was hiked up, exposing his belly. I had him where I wanted him. I was enjoying this, I realized. This was actually the most fun I'd had all night.

I continued, "This is about you and me, and whether I can trust you." Because that sounded better than this is about who's top dog and making you submit to me.

"Hey, take it easy, man. Look, no one-night stand is worth pissing you off. We're bros, right? I'm sorry I, you know, treaded on your turf or whatever. It won't happen again."

"Good. Because I really didn't want to have to hurt you, man." The idea of making him bleed, let alone breaking his bones, didn't appeal to me now that he'd backed down. Now that I had him at my mercy. I set him down on his feet and made a show of smoothing down his rumpled shirt, half a pacifying gesture and half making a point: I could do whatever I wanted with his clothing and his person, and he would stand still for it. As I straightened his collar, my fingers could feel the chest hairs curling up at the base of his throat, and the racing pulse further up. He really needed a shave, even though I'd seen him shave that morning before work, having crashed at my place.

"Are we okay, then?" he asked anxiously.

"Sure, buddy. We're good." I squeezed his shoulders. He put his arms around me. I slid my hands down his back and we drew each other into a bone-crushing hug, half affection and half a contest of strength. I kept him slightly off-balance, as if I were about to throw him. Burying my nose in his shirt collar, I realized his scent had grown very familiar to me over the past couple of weeks without my realizing it, and that I kind of liked it. Still hugging him with one arm, I slid my other arm between us, so I could undo a button on his shirt. Pushing his shirt open a little, I buried my nose contentedly in his chest hair. I hadn't noticed how hairy his chest was, back when we'd first compared scars, or when I'd glimpsed him stepping out of my shower wearing only a towel the one or two times he'd been in too much of a hurry to stop at home on his way to work.

"Dude, what are you doing?" he said with a tolerant laugh, halfheartedly trying to push me away. "Stop messing with my shirt."

"Don't tell me what to do," I growled softly into his chest, rubbing my stubbled chin against his bare skin to punish him for daring to object.

"OK," he said, and I felt him holding his hands up placatingly.

He hadn't tucked his shirt back into his pants and I hadn't done it for him; it was still hanging loose. By feel, without taking my head away from his chest, I yanked his shirt up in front, exposing his belly again. I stroked the smooth bare flesh with my fingers, forcing a laugh from him. He tried to squirm away, but I dug my fingers deep under his belt and pulled him back toward me, relishing the feel of my knuckles digging into exposed skin, and still stroking his belly with my thumb. "I can do whatever I want to you now. I just kicked your ass. You're mine."

His only reply was a whimper, so soft I only heard it because his lips were less than an inch from my ear. His belly was smooth, completely hairless, above the navel, but he had a silky-feeling trail of hair starting just below his navel and continuing further down than my thumb could explore just at the moment.

I wiggled my fingers and found that the sensitive skin below his belt was even more ticklish; he started laughing again.

"OK, OK, whatever you say! I screwed up, you kicked my ass, and now you own me."

"Damn straight." I stepped back from him, not releasing my grip on his belt, and fingered his shirt with my free hand. "I ought to take you back home, stretch you out on the floor, rip your shirt wide open, and give you a pink-belly, at the very least."

"Let's do it, if that's what it'll take to make things right. I won't resist, I swear." Again he held up his empty hands in a placating gesture.

"Maybe later." I patted his belly possessively and pulled his shirt back down. "Come on, let's go back inside." I released the grip I still had on his belt then steadied him with a hand on his chest when he stumbled.

"Sure! I'll buy you a drink." He added in an undertone, as if to himself, "Because you're obviously not drunk at all yet."

"I heard that. You're not exactly steady on your feet yourself." I mussed his hair affectionately.

"You're right. I must be drunk because I let you do all that to me, and I don't even mind. The drinks here must have been stronger than I thought." Grinning at me, he said, "But then, so are you." He gave me a playful push, not hard enough to make me stumble, which wouldn't have taken much.

Sliding my hand inside the back of his loosened collar, I steered him toward the street with my fingers clamped around his bare neck, half vise grip, half massage. "Come on, let's go back through the front door, like civilized men."

He threw his arm around my shoulders and we stumbled out of the alley, needing all four of our legs working together to keep the two of us erect.

# # # # #

"And that's the last thing I remember clearly," I admitted. "Until, well ... the next morning."

"Wow," said the guy whose brother had killed himself. Everyone else just stared at me.

"Alcohol can really change a man," Thomas finally said.

"You apologized to Ethan, I take it," the veteran said.

"It wasn't as bad as he made it sound," Ethan said quickly. He was sitting beside me, his folding chair pulled so close to mine that our knees almost touched. "Turns out, being roughed up in a dark alley by a close friend isn't anything like it would be with a stranger. I knew Jake wouldn't seriously hurt me. When he had me up against that wall, it almost felt ... I don't know." He grinned at me shyly.

Matt looked at him expectantly. When nothing more was forthcoming, he turned to me. "Jake, you seem embarrassed when you mentioned the next morning."

Looking searchingly at Ethan, I asked quietly, "Are you sure you're okay with telling them, man?"

"I trust these guys. I think we can tell them anything." But he looked away, embarrassed. We had trouble meeting each other's eyes these last few days when we talked about Saturday morning.

Matt said, "Anything you tell us never leaves this room. You know that. Everyone here understands that." He turned to our newest member, seated almost as close on my other side. "Nick, you understand that ground rule, right?"

Nick, still looking pale and grave after telling his own story for the first time, nodded earnestly.

I said, "You almost saw this last part for yourself, Nick, just like you and ... like when you caught me coming home after the first time I blacked out. You were right there outside the apartment house, and under normal circumstances you'd have seen us sneaking around the back. So would the entire crowd of people around you. Maybe some of them did, but I think ..."

"They were too busy gawking at me, and the paramedics bandaging my scratches," Nick said numbly. "And at ... at ..."

I squeezed his shoulder sympathetically. I felt incredibly sorry for the poor guy. My own grief had only just started to fade to a dull ache after two months, and even Ethan's had, what was it now, four weeks? But Nick still had fresh raw memories of watching his roommate being stuffed into a body bag – over the course of maybe half an hour. I just hoped, for Nick's sake and for the sake of all us neighbors who might stumble across something, that they got it all. Or at least, all the bits of Chip that hadn't wound up in the stomachs of the two wild animals that had torn him to pieces right before his roommate's eyes. I'd found that now I actually missed their cheerful rowdiness. The apartment downstairs was heartbreakingly silent with Nick living there all alone.

No wonder the poor kid had been following me around like a lost puppy ever since. He'd never been anything to me before except a noisy neighbor, but tragedy has a way of bringing people closer together. Now we were spending all our free time together, along with Ethan, who'd been dropping by every day. We had a common bond, our little ... band, was it?

Already Nick had been there when I needed him: He'd been really helpful this week, driving me and Ethan to work and to the DMV. And physically, he was just the kind of guy I instinctively wanted beside me in case things ever got tough. His meaty shoulder felt pleasingly solid under his T-shirt sleeve as I squeezed it. He was sturdily built, almost the equal of his late roommate: I'd seen him with his shirt off and pants down by now, when he and Ethan and I had compared scars, Nick's being on his chest and upper thigh. As for Chip, I'd never consciously taken a good look at the guy, could have barely told the two roommates apart, but I must have subliminally sized them up at some point. Maybe I'd once glimpsed them wearing tighter T-shirts than the one I was now squeezing Nick's shoulder through. Or maybe it was the morning I'd seen them peering out their half-opened door, Nick's hand resting casually on his roommate's bare shoulder as he leaned out for a better look at their blanket-clad neighbor pounding on the super's door. Or maybe I'd been subconsciously keeping score of who kept coming out on top of their endless wrestling matches, based on the muffled taunts I'd frequently heard through my floor. For all that Nick was a big strapping guy, I'd definitely formed the impression, somewhere, sometime, that Chip had been the brawnier of the two. I vaguely remembered Chip as being solid and beefy, with a thick layer of chest muscle under only the most minimal layer of fat.

"I'll never know how we managed to sneak around back without anyone in that crowd of people seeing us," Ethan said.

Matt said, "They've done studies that show that if people are distracted enough, a guy can literally walk by in a gorilla suit and they won't see him."

"Well, we weren't wearing gorilla suits," Ethan mumbled, staring at his shoes, a very scuffed old pair. "Or ..."

I took a deep breath. "We – look, I swear we're not gay or anything."

"We were just drunk," Ethan added quickly. "We're not gay. I mean, I know for sure I'm not ..."

"I'm not either. Really!"

Matt said, "You know it's perfectly okay if ..."

"But we're not," both of us said in unison.

"It's not like we even remember ... doing anything," I said.

113

"But we probably ... I mean, we woke up right next to each other ..."

"Sort of cuddled up," I added reluctantly.

"Hey! It was freezing out there!"

That was an exaggeration, but certainly the morning air had felt uncomfortably chilly against a man's skin, so it was natural that another man's skin would feel pleasurably warm against it. The truth was I could have stayed like that all day. And I still hadn't admitted to Ethan that I'd woken up with this oddly satiated feeling, as if during the night I'd fulfilled needs, satisfied hungers, that I hadn't known I had. So I sure wasn't going to admit it to these guys. Instead, I stuck to the bare facts: "We somehow wound up under a bush."

"In the park," Ethan explained. "That's where we woke up the next morning."

"Sore all over," I added. "Both of us." I didn't mention that there'd been some kind of unfamiliar taste in my mouth; I had a feeling these guys would consider that a little too much information.

"And we were ... well ..."

"We eventually found Ethan's shirt a hundred yards away."

"Yeah, it looked like it had been ripped right off me."

"I don't remember doing that, I swear! But, well, it might have been me." Because I did remember fantasizing about it before I blacked out. During that brief moment when I'd had Ethan on all fours after I'd sent him sprawling into the alley, when part of me had wanted to flip him onto his back and pin him there, I'd actually visualized ripping his shirt wide open. At the time it felt as if that would give him the proper perspective while we had a nice long quiet talk about just who was boss. I didn't feel that way about him anymore, of course; now I just wanted him by my side, not groveling at my feet. But that night, I actually had threatened him more than half-seriously with a pink-belly. As a substitute for a full-on thrashing, it had held a surprising appeal for me at the time. I never did go through with it, as far as I remembered. But then, neither of us even remembered ever reentering the bar.

Even before that, at dinner when I'd tried to tickle him in the booth, I'd felt frustrated at the layers of clothing and skin and flesh and fat and muscle between my fingers and his ribs. If we hadn't been in a restaurant I'd have been tempted to strip away the outermost layer. It was like I'd been a different person that night. But I still remember how it had felt. The desire alone, the anticipation, had felt good, incredibly good

"We never did find the rest of our clothes," Ethan said. "Not that we exactly felt free to search very far. We mostly stopped looking when we found Jake's keys in the grass. Thank God his apartment is close to the park."

"Not as close as we'd have liked," I said ruefully.

"Other than those two garbage men, I don't think anyone saw us. There weren't too many people on the streets at that hour."

"Until we got near the apartment."

"And then it was a zoo."

"So," Andy said slowly, "when you woke up together under that bush, you were ..."

"Yeah," I admitted. "We have no memory of how we got that way."

"But we know full well what we must have been doing, so you can wipe that smirk off your face, Andy!" Ethan took a deep breath. "And I have to admit, sore as I was, I woke up feeling, I don't know ... Satisfied somehow. Not that I feel like ever doing it again! It was a one-time thing, I'm sure!"

It hadn't occurred to me that Ethan had felt the same way. About the physical part, I mean. Interesting. So, what now? Probably nothing. We'd continue hanging out together, of course, but we'd stay completely sober, and it would never happen again.

"How you got what way?" Thomas prompted as we both fell silent, lost in thought.

I returned my gaze to my brand-new pair of shoes, which I'd been examining throughout most of my story, even though they were identical to my previous pair, the pair that had lasted all of a month. "We were both, you know ..."

"Stark naked."

FROM HERE TO ETERNITY (OR PRETTY DAMNED CLOSE)
By Michael Roberts

Michael Roberts has published his sexual flights of fancy in eleven anthologies. He has written for www.cruisingforsex.com and several leading adult gay magazines.

"Aren't we getting a bit long in the tooth to be doing this?" I said.

"You used that line before," he said. "I was only moderately amused then, and I'm even less so now. Lie down and open up."

I did, and he fucked me.

One of the problems with being fucked by the same man for four-hundred-three years is that pretty much everything is predictable. We've tried a lot of things to make our sex life interesting: a bit of B&D, S&M, SWF (Suck While Fucking), FWS (Fuck While Sucking), FWHUDFAT (Fuck While Hanging Upside Down From a Tree). But it seems that the best way of doing things and each other is tried and true: me on my back with my legs over his shoulders staring up at him (with only slightly exaggerated adoration) as he stabs in and out and in and out, etc.

Over the years, his cock has grown longer and thicker. Maybe it is gravity; I know that women's breasts sag lower and lower as time goes by, and as a lot of time goes by, maybe that happens to vampire's dicks, too – in a different way, of course. Consequently, he keeps finding spots inside me that he hasn't reached before and filling me up, in several ways, more and more and, incredibly, more.

With me, my asshole is getting smaller and tighter, although perhaps it just seems that way because he is enlarging so consistently – or perhaps he appears to be enlarging consistently because I am shrinking in certain parts of my anatomy. But no, it is obvious that his schlong is progressively lengthier and bulkier. My dick increases only moderately – but then, he is one-hundred years older than I (give or take a decade), so further enhancements may yet be mine.

The good thing about being fucked by the same man for three-hundred-four years – or is it four-hundred-three years? After so much time, my memory isn't what it used to be – is that he knows how to excite me, just as I know how to excite him. We are familiar with each other's pressure points, each other's preferences, the touches that bring us to and past the point of explosion.

He is so good at what he does that usually I come without stroking myself, and if he shoots his spunk (is that the right word? It's so difficult to keep up with the vernacular) down my throat, I feel such a headiness (is that a pun? My partner in vampirehood, Jason [his name is not really Jason, but the contemporary variation at least approaches what his real name is] tells me I am just too clever for my own good) that I am quite inebriated with the elixir of his fantastic fluids, and sometimes, due to my expert anal fluctuations, with an ear-splitting bellow, he explodes into me after just four or five days of fucking, rather than the usual seven or eight (when you are going to be alive forever, several days do not seem that protracted a time).

Then, of course, since we are vampires, he will lean over in the diminishing throes of his orgasm and fasten his teeth into my throat and suck away. And sometimes, if he is feeling benevolent, he will tilt his neck and allow me to latch on to him and suck away.

So yes, we understand each other well, and yes, the sex between us is generally good, occasionally more than that, every so often much more than that. Still, at this particular coupling, I said:

"Maybe we need some new blood and sperm."

Jason stopped in mid-stroke and stared down at me.

"You think so, Roberto [not my real name, either, just an approximation]?"

"I think so."

Then, after a pause, he said, "The produce man."

I tried not to flinch guiltily, but I might not have succeeded, because his eyes narrowed, and to cover my possible *faux pas*, I said, in what I hoped was a normal tone of voice, "The produce man?"

"Yes, the produce man," he said, with what I thought was a suspicious expression as he squinted at me.

The reason I was so startled he had mentioned this particular target was that I had cruised – again, I am not sure of the correct terminology – the produce man myself more than once at the food store at which Jason and I shopped.

The first time, I was looking through the potatoes and noticed him at the cucumber display. The way he was standing revealed a rather sizeable bulge down his left leg. I walked over to him and looked at what he was sorting and then downward and said, "A very nice cucumber."

He turned and glanced at me, then tilted his head so that he was gazing behind me and said, "Nice cantaloupes."

"Thank you," I said graciously.

"Are you looking for something special?" he asked.

"I was hoping for some fresh juices," I answered coyly.

It had been only a few hours since Jason and I had finally finished fucking, so Jason's sap had revivified me (insofar as a vampire can be revivified); thus I knew that I was reasonably attractive to a handsome young man in his thirties – although, of course, the evidence of generous endowment had a great deal to do with my finding him fetching and therefore attempting to fetch him – I can be a bit of a slut.

After a few moments of silence, he said, "I have those in the storeroom. Follow me."

I did.

Watching his retreating butt in his jeans was arousing, and I did not walk as agilely as I usually did. Perchance my masculine appendage was more substantial than I thought. It was indeed, at that particular moment, bloated.

As I trailed after him, I wondered if perhaps Jason was correct, that I was too clever for my own good and should not be lingering with produce persons, but I was able, as usual, to resist my wiser inhibitions and continued walking. He pushed open a swinging door, held it for me, and I tagged along as he turned down an aisle loaded with fruits and vegetables.

"We'll be safe here," he said. "It's closing time, and all of the stockers are gone except me, and they know I'm working overtime."

He yanked off his apron, yanked down his zipper, and yanked out a specimen of manhood that was even grander than had been implied by the protuberance in his pants.

I knelt before him and began orally exploring his fleshly extension. It had quite a nice taste to it. I had not fellated anyone but Jason for quite a while (which, to be sure, is in vampire time a most relative term), but the flavor of the young man in front of me precipitated a flow of reminiscences and also a flow in my dick.

He said, "Hmmm," which indicated to me that I was doing something right, so I continued doing it, exploring a thick shaft, a nicely rounded head, and substantial balls with my well-practiced tongue.

Then he raised me by my armpits and said, "I want to fuck you," and he turned me around, slid down my trousers and underwear, and bent me over so that my head was between some cabbages and some Vidalia onions, and he did just that.

There was a momentary pause during which I heard the ripping of a condom package (presumably) and a tube of lube, which was interesting – I mean, what produce clerk has a condom handy unless he makes a practice of noodling in the crops – and the snap as the condom was applied – I guess – after several hundred years, I still have not got accustomed to condoms – and then he got down to harvesting me.

His prick was not Jason's prick, but that was what I wanted at the moment, a prick that was not Jason's.

There was a freshness to his fucking, a vigor, a novelty, a newness – a force.

At that juncture – I used the word advisedly – it did not matter if my asshole had constricted. My asshole and his prick were a cunning fit.

"Fuck me," I whispered to the arugula, and that was a sign of how much I needed something delightfully diverting such as the produce man's tool; it had been a long time – a long, long time – since I had said something like that to Jason. "Fuck me, fuck me, fuck me."

Well, that inspired him to new heights – or new depths – of plunging into me, so that soon my face was right up against the leaves of the cabbage, and with the fortitude of the young – which to me was everyone except Jason – he pounded and packed his prick into my ass and – I would not have considered it possible – he found places and points and locations in me that even Jason, in all of his prodigiousness and skill and knowledge of the terrain, had not been able to access.

He ferociously grabbed my hips and let out a cry that would have been heard at the cash registers, if anyone were at the cash registers, and aimed a final thrust and came in the willing recesses of my ass.

"Oh, Arlen," I sighed, for I had established his name by the tag he wore on the apron that now rested on a pallet. I didn't come, of course – it always took four or five days for me to reach climax – but I made sure that he thought I did, for I wished to thank him, at least tacitly, for the spectacular sensations he had just supplied me. Who would have thought that after hundreds of years, I could have such an inspired, inspiring, perspiring experience?

He collapsed over my back, and we rested that way until he had recovered, and he rose and popped moistly out of my rear access, and he said, "Wow," and I said, "Wow."

With something of a flourish, he divested himself of his condom and threw it on some spinach, which meant that whoever purchased that particular batch would get something extra, then wiped himself off with his apron, smearing his fresh juices and the juices of a number of fruits and vegetables over himself. We pulled our clothing and ourselves together, and I said, "That was – that was ..." Rarely was I at a loss for words, but I was then.

"I'd better get out to the produce," he said. "You never know when the boss'll show up."

"Yes," I said. "That was ..."

Even if I had thought of something to add, he had gone through the swinging doors, and when I emerged from the storeroom, he was covering the displays for the night. Without looking at me, he gestured toward the back door of the store, and I slipped into the alley and thence home and tried guiltily to convince myself that Jason did not regard me suspiciously – although Jason frequently regarded me suspiciously, since I could be a bit of a slut. Of course, how many times would I need to stray during a few hundred years to make me not merely a sort of explorer but a slut?

A couple of weeks later, as I was passing the produce presentation and avoiding only by a split second walking into the peaches and pears as I perused Arlen's ass, he said, without turning around, "I'm working late again Thursday."

Thus Thursday night, I was there at closing time, and again he went into the storeroom, and again I followed him, and again I blew his succulent shoot, and again he raised me and turned me around and fucked me with his particular youthful fervor, and the experience was pretty much as it was before – quite agreeably so – except that he did find a new and novel use for a rutabaga.

I hadn't bitten him the first time, not wanting to put forth the effort if our experiences were not repeated, and they were, so I moved toward him as if I were going to kiss him, whispering, "Arlen, Arlen," to deceive him into thinking that I was just declaring my gratitude for the inspired screwing he had given me, and then lowered my lips and fastened onto his neck and perforated it and drew in the intoxicating, the aphrodisiacal taste of blood, and he was mine.

When Jason said, "The produce man," I was sure that he knew of my perfidy, and I said, "Yes, the produce man."

"Wednesday night, we'll see the produce man," he said, and I said, "Yes, Wednesday night."

I brought Arlen back to our house and waited apprehensively for Jason, and in a half hour, he got home and brought into the living room a young man, and I looked at the young man, who seemed familiar, and Arlen looked at the young man and said, "Tony!" and Tony said, "Arlen!" and I then recognized Tony.

Arlen was the produce man at the Jewel supermarket, and Tony was the produce man at Safeway. And Tony had two teeth marks on his neck, and I looked at Jason, and he looked at me sardonically, with his eyebrows raised as far as they could go without merging with his hairline, and I understood that Jason had been dallying with Tony while I

123

had been dallying with Arlen – what was sauce for the vampire was sauce for the vampire.

What I had thought would be a threesome turned out to be a foursome, and this foursome would (at least might) be together – really together – for a very long time – hundreds of years, thousands, who knew? An eternity, or pretty damned close. We could all imagine the future – the long and winding future – and so we looked at one another and laughed a trifle hysterically, and then, we did what we were ordained to do.

We fucked.

LOVE BITES
By Michael Turner

*Michael Turner lives in South Wales, UK, with his
partner and a mad Springer Spaniel. He divides his time
between writing, painting and walking the dog. E-mail
galadann100@gmail.com*

Port Camelot was nestled in a cove. It's landward side
guarded by a steep ravine with one twisty, winding road
allowing access. The views from the top of the cliff out over
the azure Atlantic topped with white rollers was breathtaking
and one of the primary reasons the Port was a Mecca for
tourists.

The town was one of those sedate, tranquil places, which
attracted artists, writers and those seeking solitude and quiet
contemplation. It had three large golden, sandy beaches,
which surrounded the prominontry and attracted more than
its fair share of surfers all year round.

Along with the surfers, the quiet town normally attracted
the attentions of the armed forces. Port Camelot was the
second closest town to Samuel's Air Force Base and Peard
Army Base. Both were located on the moors above the town
but at the opposite ends.

Samuelmouth, four miles away housed the Naval
presence in the area and whilst the largest town and the
playground of the armed personnel, those in the know headed
for Port Camelot for a night out. Not only were the pubs
cheaper, but also the locals friendlier and the town less
crowded despite the surfers and artisans; there was also a
smaller chance of running into military police or Shore
Patrols.

Port Camelot was quiet. Too quiet for this time of year and this time of night.

I glanced at my watch. It was barely ten o'clock at the height of a summer. The sky was still light, the clouds illuminated softly in the muted light. I sighed. As I stared out across the tiny harbor, the waves gently lapped at the retaining wall upon which I sat.

I'd lived in Port Camelot on and off for more than two-hundred-fifty years of my two-thousand-one-hundred-thirty-five-year existence. I'd lived in a large house on top of one of the cliffs passing the property to myself posing as a faceless stranger every generation or so and disappearing, usually in unusual circumstances to make it look more real to the mortals of the town. So far, I'd been stabbed, drowned, shot during the war, killed in a car crash and just plain disappeared. So much so that over the years the rumor of bad luck and a curse had grown up around the house. Now none of the locals would buy the property even if I had been selling it for one pound.

Every successive time I morphed into a new persona, I had to hear the stories and seeing that I could only return every other generation or so they always intrigued me. The amount of embellishment seventy years can add to a story is amazing.

None of the stories come anywhere near the truth though. If the locals found out an honest to goodness (I'm not so sure about the goodness part, but I am wherever possible, honest) vampire owned the house I'm sure they would freak – although in this modern culture, I'd probably be described as neat or cool. I shuddered. Not exactly the best description a vampire could ask for but it was better than being burned or staked.

The tinkling sound of a glass bottle hitting a wall drew me from my reverie. Looking over my shoulder, I glanced into the shadows of Jerusalem Lane. The street light was out, a gross oversight by the local council given the number of killings to have occurred in this part of the world recently. To be fair to the council, the light had been working up until an hour ago when I'd smashed the bulb.

Many of the quaint pubs in town faced onto Jerusalem Lane, and it was my favorite hunting ground, so I regularly smashed the light. Usually the council wasn't so fastidious about replacing the bulb – after all, the light only ever seemed to last a week before it needed replacing again.

Attempts to replace the light over the years by the council had also ended in failure; not surprising given my nocturnal activities and my assurances that it never worked. Eventually, they gave up, and a legend of its own grew up around the light. I encouraged the legend even making sure the light remained off during the periods I was away from Port Camelot.

I always ensured whomever used the street was safe though. The last thing I ever needed was the authorities applying too much investigation. Like now.

I'd been gone from the Port for the last sixty-six years, and I'd just inherited the house on the cliff from ... well, me so I'd moved back a month ago only to find a small coven of my colleagues had moved into a cave further down the coast and had been terrorizing the area for the past five years.

The authorities were at a loss what to do. Bodies kept appearing at regular intervals as my colleagues feasted indiscriminately, unable to control themselves.

I only ever bite to feed not to kill. I guess you could say I was kind of a good vampire. I ensured my ... donors were as healthy when I finished as when I started – minus a pint or two of blood of course. They would wake up with a slight headache and a loss of memory of the last few hours – always blameable on having drunk too much. Alcohol doesn't affect a vampire, so drinking intoxicated blood was never a problem.

My colleagues weren't that considerate. People had been going missing for the last five years and, until a month ago, never being seen or heard of again apart from the occasional body.

That was until an anonymous tip off to the police had led them to a cave in the cliffside then miles away from the Port where they found a huge pile of bones which DNA testing later identified as the numerous missing persons lost over the years.

The five vampires they never found. After I killed them, I disposed of the bodies in the appropriate manner, so the mortal authorities would never know what really happened. The supernatural authorities, the Vampire Council, approved of my clean up and left me alone.

Devil worshipers got the blame for the murders, and whilst I was mortified that another branch of the underground took the blame, it was preferable to my kind being discovered.

The clinking of glass came from the alley again. This time when I looked, I saw a shadow moving in the darkness of the lane. The man staggered slightly and I smiled. He was drunk.

My eyes darted around. There was no one else about. Not surprising really. Ever since the discovery of the cave and its gruesome contents most people in and around Port Camelot were behind locked doors by the time darkness really took hold.

The man staggered down the middle of the lane singing softly to himself, quietly giggling every few seconds. I couldn't help but grin. His shock of soft-looking blond hair glowed in the starlight, the darkness no impediment to my vampiric vision, making him look cute and lost; like a little boy.

My cock twitched. The lad was handsome. His face was thin with good bone structure, high cheekbones and a manly square jaw that was covered with fine blond stubble. Tall and slim, his body moved lithely down the lane despite the apparent amount of alcohol he had imbibed.

He was wearing a plain white shirt, open to the navel revealing a broad, smooth chest and a flat stomach. Where the shirt disappeared into his jeans was a wide leather belt, cinched tightly, revealing a narrow waist. The man's groin was full, the denim molding itself to his bulge.

I licked my lips. The sight of his full groin coupled with the sweet smell of his blood and a slight salty tang I knew from experience meant he was a sailor, had my pulse pounding with desire. It was all I could do to restrain myself from flying over the road, grabbing him and fucking him there and then. Undead I may be but I am not and have never been a monk.

Instead, taking a deep breath, tinged with salt and blood and man-milk I stood up and casually walked across the street. "You okay, mate?" I asked solicitously as I came to stop in front of him, my hand resting on his shoulder in a friendly manner.

The lad looked up at me. He couldn't have been any more than twenty, probably on his first leave from the naval base. He grinned at me. "'m fine," he slurred, the smell of beer assaulting my nasal passages, his light blue eyes twinkling at me.

Taking a step forward, he misjudged his timing and tripped, landing against me. I took advantage of the opportunity to slip my arm around his waist and pull him tight against me.

All his muscles were hard, as I knew they would be, being military, but it was still a pleasure discovering so. There's nothing like a strong young man to turn me on even after two-thousand-odd years.

"I've got you," I said, holding him tight.

He grinned up at me again. "Thanks." He hiccoughed. "Oops." He started chuckling.

"What's your name?" I asked.

"Gareth."

129

"A nice name."

"Sank you."

I grinned as he slumped against me again, my arm tightening around his waist. "Come on," I said, friendly. "I know a quiet place you can lie down and sleep that off."

Gareth looked up at me, smiling. "You're very kind," he said, raising his hand to stroke my cheek. "Handsome, too."

I grinned back at him. "Not as good looking as you though," I countered.

Gareth ducked his head but not before I saw him blush redder than a London bus.

"Come on," I hoisted him closer to my side, careful not to allow my superhuman strength to show. I could have easily carried him in my one arm, but even Gareth wasn't drunk enough to have missed that ... and if anyone else was out in town I wouldn't want them seeing it and asking questions.

Slipping Gareth's arm around my shoulder we started down the wharf. The sea lapped quietly against the harbor wall to our right in a melodic tune as we headed for Mason's Pier, which jutted out into the sea running parallel to the wharf and forming part of the harbor wall.

Huge stone archways supported the pier, their thick walls forming the defense against the Atlantic; the space beneath these archways formed manmade caves. The one we were heading for always stayed dry and had become one of my favorite places.

"I got somefink to ask you," slurred Gareth merrily.

"Yes?"

"You know I'm a sailor, right?"

I nodded, not that Gareth could see me in the dark and his inebriation. "I know."

"Really?" queried Gareth, pleased. "How?"

"I've lived in Port Camelot long enough to tell," I replied. "You have that manly sailor look about you."

Gareth beamed proudly and tried to stand taller, chuckling when he fell over his own feet. "Oops," he giggled.

I laughed along with him. The kid really was cute.

We staggered in each other's arms down the slip and onto the sand. Our going slowed and I lifted Gareth so his feet barely touched the golden grains as I kept up my pretense.

"You wanted to ask me something," I prompted seeing as Gareth had completely forgotten.

"Oh yeah," he weaved on the sand," Umm ... are you gay?"

"What makes you ask that?" I enquired, wishing I had the power of thought reading like my maker.

"Don' know." He paused then continued in a rush. "I'm just hoping you are."

"Really? Why?"

He nodded and waved a finger admonishingly in my direction. "I'm hoping you're gonna ... gonna take advantage of me."

"You want me to take advantage of you?" I asked seeking clarification.

"Hell, yes!" shouted Gareth, his voice echoing from the wharf wall.

"Sssh," I said quickly, quieting him. "You'll get us in trouble."

"Oops," he giggled again, placing a finger against his lips and shushing me loudly.

I couldn't help but grin back at him, he was so cute.

"Will you?" he whispered loudly.

"Will I what?"

"Fuck me!" he seemed exasperated at my denseness. I knew exactly what he wanted I just wanted him to say it; to be absolutely clear. I grinned at him. "Depends," I replied.

"On wha'?"

"Whether you can take eight solid thick inches."

Gareth's beautiful blue eyes glazed over, and he moaned appreciatively, unconsciously licking his lips. "Yeah," he vigorously nodded. "I can take it."

"Then I'll willingly fuck you," I whispered into his ear, "after I've sucked you off."

Gareth moaned again. I glanced down at his groin, which seemed fuller than earlier.

At that moment, the manmade cave loomed before us. The sand was dry and soft beneath our feet. "Here we are," I grinned as I gently lowered Gareth to the ground.

"Hmm," he sighed in contentment as he pulled me down on top of him, his arms locking around my waist. "Don' go," he muttered. "Stay wiv me." His legs wrapped around my waist, trapping me.

I grinned into his handsome face. "Looks like I'm trapped," I laughed quietly, thrusting my groin against his. "I couldn't get away even if I wanted to." I played to his desires knowing I could break his leg with my little finger if I really wanted to.

Gareth chuckled, wrapping his fingers into my shoulder-length black hair. "Mine," he teased, pulling my head down.

"Yours," I echoed as my lips gently met his. They were hot and plump and soft and tender and very kissable.

Gareth gave way under my insistent probing, opening his mouth, allowing my tongue access, which I quickly claimed.

He tasted of stale beer and garlic which, unlike Hollywood's insulting portrayal of my kind, I actually liked.

Gareth kissed me back hard, his tongue dueling with mine, his mouth sucking at me. It was as if he hadn't kissed a man in quite a while, and knowing our armed forces, that was probably the case.

I pulled back. "Calm down," I said soothingly. "I'm not going anywhere."

Gareth's response was to grab my head and mash our mouths together so hard he split my lip, our teeth clashing. I pushed him away, gently, knowing my own strength, wiping at my bloodied lip, which healed itself almost instantly.

Gareth had seen the blood, his eyes wide. "Oh God, I'm sorry," he whimpered. "I didn't mean to hurt you. It's just ..."

"Ssshh," I soothed him, pulling his into my arms, nuzzling his neck. "It's okay," I murmured inhaling deeply, the smell of his blood intoxicating as it throbbed through his vein millimeters from my mouth. I felt the tingle in my gums that announced my fangs were about to descend and pulled back, fighting my desire to sink my teeth into him.

The wound had already healed. I only hoped Gareth wouldn't notice and freak out on me. I knew I had the power to mind-control him but I hated doing that. I preferred to take a man knowing he was there because he wanted to be and not because I'd forced him. Yup, you've guessed it. A vampire with a conscience. I wasn't certain there had been another one of us since Louis in *An Interview with a Vampire* and that was hardly nonfiction.

Gareth whimpered and clung to me. "S'rry," he muttered. "Been so long since I've had a man."

I leaned back and grinned at him, trying to allay his fear that he'd hurt or annoyed me. "I'm gonna make this special for you," I whispered, pushing my hand inside his open shirt, my fingers walking along his hard pectoral muscle until I found his nipple.

Taking it between my forefinger and thumb, I pinched the nub of flesh pleased with the way Gareth hissed and arched his back, pushing himself closer to me.

"Like that, huh?" I teased, squeezing again, rewarded with another hiss.

"Yeah. Love my tits being played with," Gareth moaned as I squeezed again.

With my other hand, I ran over his thigh feeling his thick muscle hard and firm beneath my grasp. I did love the armed forces. They were always muscular and horny – a perfect combination in a man and when combined with their blood which always had more than its fair share of adrenaline, totally enrapturing.

Gareth groaned again as I continued to play with his nipple. My hand stole across his thigh and between his legs, coming to rest on his genitalia. Gareth sighed into my mouth as my hand squeezed his crotch. His balls were large, full of unshed spunk I guessed, and his cock was hard, confined in his denim.

I ran my hand along his denim-clad erection enjoying its hardness and length. Gareth certainly had nothing to be ashamed about in that department. I couldn't wait to get him undressed.

My longing must have communicated itself. Gareth broke our kiss, his blue eyes earnestly staring at me. I recognized the pleading in his gaze and in one swift movement, tore his shirt open wider.

Leaning forward, I captured his left nipple in my mouth, sucking hard. Gareth's groan was protracted, pure and heartfelt. I grinned around his firm nub of flesh ignoring the almost overwhelming desire to sink my teeth into his chest and feed. The pounding of his heart so close made it almost painful. I was so close I could practically taste the sailor-boy blood.

I fought off my desire to feed, the denial making the longing more pronounced but knowing that when I did, the taste would be all the sweeter. Instead, I focused my attention on my other desire. My blood pounded through my cock, my eight inches of vampire manliness throbbing painfully. The delicious ache radiated from my groin, my stomach fluttering.

Gareth groaned again, and his hand came to rest on the back of my head, his fingers tangling in my collar-length black hair, gripping hard. "Oh, yeah, suck me," he moaned.

I glanced up at his handsome face. His head was thrown back, resting on a rock, his eyes closed, a look of sheer ecstasy spread over his features. I grinned around his nipple again. He was adorable, looking like a fallen angel.

I snorted at my own sentimentality. In reality, Gareth looked nothing like any of the fallen angels I'd ever known ... and there had been a few.

I hurriedly banished the specter of ice-blue eyes that rose in my mind, banishing the image before it had time to register and sour my mood. Instead, I concentrated on the fabulous piece of manhood laying supine beneath me.

Gareth, like all humans, was super-responsive once you'd broken through the wall of reserve and guilt they now carried. Silently, I cursed the Victorians and their prudish ways and attitude to sex, lamenting the passing of the promiscuous Georgian era.

Squeezing Gareth's rock hard manhood and eliciting another moan from him, I let go of his nipple. Slowly, I rained gentle feather kisses across his pectorals enjoying the tickle on my chin of his forest of blond hair buried between his muscles, to his other nipple.

I teased the nub of flesh, flicking my tongue over it and running the tip around his areole until it was standing as tall and proud as a Masai Mara warrior. Another pair of eyes rose in my mind, and they followed the blue eyes of my earlier image into banished oblivion.

Sitting back on my haunches I smiled at Gareth as he opened his eyes and looked at me. "Why 'u stop?" he slurred more in confusion that annoyance.

"It's called teasing," I smiled at him, waggling my eyebrows suggestively and chuckling.

"S'not fair," pouted Gareth.

I reached out and tenderly stroked his cheek. His pout made him look like a little boy, and that adorable, cute puppy-dog expression tore at me. I glanced down at the bulge in his jeans and was swiftly reminded that my adorable angel was waiting to release his inner devil.

"What would you like, then?"

"Suck me," he replied without hesitation.

I reached out and tweaked the nipple I'd sucked earlier, knowing it would be the more sensitive of the two. "Here?" I asked. I trailed my hand over his chest and down his torso, his muscles hard yet his skin soft and smooth beneath my touch, it was like stroking an iron girder wrapped in a duvet. "Or here?" I grabbed his solid shaft and squeezed hard.

"Oh fuck," he moaned, lifting his groin into my grip, sitting up instantly, as his abs contracted

I watched his muscles play beneath his skin in a sexy manner I hadn't seen in a while. My cock throbbed reminding me I still needed release. I licked my suddenly dry mouth. Two-thousand-odd years and a sexy, attractive man still had this effect on me.

"Mmm," moaned Gareth flopping back against the sand, narrowly avoiding the rock he'd used as a pillow.

I squeezed his hard prick again, tracing the outline through the denim, my senses on full alert as I devoured his manhood. The thump, thump of his blood throbbing through his cock called to me, enticing me, pleading with me to take him. The delicious feeling of want and need surged through my body, and for one moment, I couldn't distinguish which pull was greater – his cock or his blood.

Gareth's sexy moan filled the area as I continued to explore his groin, driving my hand deep between his thighs, stroking the seam of his jeans, which protected his most sacred of portals. With my other hand, I attacked his belt, deftly undoing the buckle, my inhuman strength and dexterity making short work of the button flies.

Yanking open the denim flaps I moaned in appreciation as my senses were assailed by the smell of man-musk; sweat, groin and an underlying tone that was Gareth himself. I licked my lips. Gareth's scent was sexy as hell, coupled with the additional aromas of his sweet blood flowing inches from me made the man irresistible.

Growling low in my throat I yanked Gareth's jeans and boxer-briefs down his legs and off, tossing them somewhere behind me, careful not to tear them straight from his body, noting again the Calvin Klein name on the waistband.

Gareth giggled. "Hey, butch," he teased, his blue eyes locking on mine, desire and need smoldering behind them.

The giggle made me pause. A man who giggled always reminded me of feminine men, and I'd never really liked them. I preferred my men to be butch men. I had nothing against feminine men per se, but to coin a modern phrase I'd recently picked up, they didn't float my boat. That said, there was something about Gareth that not only floated my boat, but also made it sprout wings and skim.

My eyes dropped to Gareth's groin and I froze, my breath catching in my throat. Such a beautiful sight. Gareth's cock, long and thick and hard lay on his flat abdomen, the head a good two inches beyond his naval, bright purple and glistening with precum. Wide veins snaked around his shaft leading the eye in all directions but unable to compete with the thick erector muscle bisecting his man-spear. His cock throbbed as I watched, his glans flaring in anticipation of what was to come.

Beneath his shaft hung a pair of large balls, heavy with unshed cum and covered in hair the same color as that on his head and chest. I licked my lips, movement slowly returning.

Shuffling backwards, I lowered myself onto the sand between Gareth's legs, settling myself comfortably. I planned to be in this position for quite a while, so I may as well be comfortable, I thought.

Leaning forward, my tongue made contact with the root of Gareth's cock and slowly licked the full length of his eight inches like a lollipop. He tasted as good as he looked and smelled. His skin was smooth and hot and slightly salty.

I wasn't sure who was moaning the loudest, Gareth or myself as the tip of my tongue massaged the sensitive spot where his glans met shaft.

Lapping up the pearl of pre-cum which appeared confirmed it was me. He tasted fantastic, sweet and salty warring for dominance in his flavor along with a hint of something I couldn't place but knew I'd never be able to get enough of and which promised a treat to my taste buds when he finally blew.

Leaning further forward I engulfed the head of Gareth's cock in my mouth, my lips, locking behind the ridge of his crown and sucked hard.

Gareth cried out, and his fingers tightened in my hair as slowly my lips made their way down his shaft. His skin was smooth and hot and delicious. My tongue swiped at his cockhead capturing more pre-cum causing me to moan anew at his flavor.

Gareth's pleading groans joined mine, echoing around the man-made cave, as my vibrations shot through his cock, kicking his pleasure into higher gear.

"Fuck me," Gareth moaned as I slurped my way down his shaft, my lips spreading wide as the thick root of his cock stretched them. His hands held my head tight against his flat belly as my throat muscles went to work massaging his sensitive head, which had slipped past my gag reflex that I'd brought under control when I was human and now no longer needed.

I loved deep -throating. It turned me on far more than anything else in my long existence with the exception of blood and as I didn't need to breathe, I could spend hours performing it – once my partner was aware of my true existence, of course.

Gareth's blood was throbbing between my lips divided only by a thin layer of skin, the smell, sweet and enticing, drove me almost as much as my desire to taste his spunk.

Reaching up, I cupped his balls and gently squeezed them, allowing them to run through my fingers like water. They were large and heavy, full of the delicious cum I was certain Gareth would produce.

"Oh, fuck me," panted Gareth as I looked up in time to see him shake his head from side to side. I grinned around his thick cock, pleased at the ecstatic feelings I was engendering in this man. Then again, after all my time, if I couldn't give a decent blowjob I had no right to call myself, in the modern idiom, gay.

Taking a chance, I increased the pressure around the base of his cock, biting. Gareth responded with a deep heartfelt moan that echoed in our enclosed space.

Allowing my fangs to descend and having perfected my technique over two-thousand years ago, I gently applied pressure and punctured the smooth skin of Gareth's penis.

His breath caught in this throat before he let out another moan but apart from that and the tightening of his grip in my hair, he showed no indication that I'd just violated his body.

I grinned around his root again as I glanced up at him, reaching up to take a nipple, rolling the bud of flesh between my thumb and forefinger.

A trickle of blood made its way over my tongue, the tingle of joy zinging over my taste buds, filling my senses, pushing out all other stimuli. He tasted healthy and clean and ... musky. Allowing his blood to slowly fill my mouth was agony and pleasure rolled together drawing me to heights I normally only experienced during orgasm.

Swallowing, I accepted his blood into my body, feeling it slip around his thick cock in my throat and down to my stomach, warming me much like a mouthful of whisky would a human. I could feel his blood come to rest in my stomach and I moaned, savoring its flavorful taste.

Sucking gently, I took another mouthful of his life-giving elixir undercover of sucking his cock. The hot liquid alive with life filled my mouth and as Gareth's fingers tensed in my hair, pulling tight, the pain a distant pleasure compared to the joy of his thick cock plugged deeply down my throat and the taste of his blood, it went the same way as the first.

The second mouthful got my body working. My stomach started to do its thing and began to distribute Gareth's blood. I could feel it creeping along my veins, warming as his blood began to bring me back to life.

Ensuring my lips were tight against his warm, silky skin I traveled back up his stiff shaft accompanied by his groans until only his head was left in my mouth. There, I reversed my direction and swallowed him again, taking more blood.

I repeated my maneuver over and over, sucking Gareth expertly each time, ensuring a steady stream of blood tricked down my throat as well as his hard meat. His blood had the warming sensation moving along my limbs, my arms and legs coming back to life.

The ecstasy zinging through my body was amazing. I felt alive again, full of strength and power, capable of doing anything I liked ... not that I couldn't usually given my supernatural existence but with Gareth's blood flooding my system it added that little extra – like showing your first love that special place that meant so much to you. I guess it's the added warmth of sharing.

A pang of loneliness engulfed me, threatening to dampen my blood-high. Ruthlessly, I quashed it not allowing anything to ruin this delightful moment.

Gareth's groans pulled me back to reality, and guiltily I checked to make sure he was okay realizing in my mental wanderings I'd forgotten about him as I took my fill. To my relief he was fine; my sucking mouthfuls of his blood hadn't adversely affected him but had served to heighten his sexual ecstasy.

He had drawn his legs up, my head bobbing merrily in the valley of his meaty thighs, his heels digging deep wells in the sand as he pushed himself into my mouth, trying to go deeper and deeper as his hands gripped handfuls of my hair and pulled my head tight against his muscular belly.

Judging by his labored breathing and incoherent mutterings it wouldn't be long before he would deposit another of his liquids in me. I intensified my sucking, both of his cock and his blood. The one I wanted to taste with an urgency, which was surprising me and the other, I needed as much of as I could safely take without hurting him.

"Oh, fuck, I'm gonna cum. So close," muttered Gareth, his grip intensifying. "Suck me, don't stop!"

As if I intended to do that, I thought, responding by increasing my tempo. I could smell his arousal increase along with the intensifying response in his blood as I sucked harder.

"Oh fuck, oh fuck," Gareth moaned with a bellow that reverberated around the enclosed area. This was likely to be the best orgasm Gareth had ever had. I knew from experience the lack of blood would make him light-headed, and coupled with the orgasm's ecstasy, it was probable the man would never reach this blissful elation again.

Gareth wrapped his arms around my head, holding me tight as his cock thickened in my mouth, stretching my lips wider still. I could feel his shaft, buried deep in my throat, pulse once before he howled, and the first blast of his orgasm shot into my stomach.

Breaking his hold, I quickly pulled back wanting to taste his offering, my lips locked tightly around his crown ensuring none of the precious liquid escaped. I gently continued to suck on his head, accepting his seed as his throbbing dick repeatedly pulsed, spurting shot after shot into my mouth.

Gareth tasted exactly as I'd imagined. Sweet and salty and musky with no hint of bitterness. His cum was thick and creamy, coating my tongue and gums as he poured forth more and more.

Gulping hard I took as much as I could each time, swallowing his seed, enjoying the intoxicating flavor almost as much as I had the taste of his blood. Six, seven, eight mouthfuls later and Gareth's bellow of his first blowing mellowed into appreciative groans as he trickled off.

Gently, I suckled his cock, milking him of every last drop of his delicious cum. Slowly, he came back to reality, regaining his senses. Wistfully, I sighed to myself as my tongue swiped around the root of Gareth's shaft, lapping at his delectable skin ensuring my saliva bathed the puncture wounds I'd made, sealing them. They would be red and sore for a few days, but they would heal and cause Gareth no problems health-wise.

Slowly, savoring every moment, I made my way back up Gareth's softening shaft, my lips tracing every millimeter of his hot skin until with an audible "plop" magnified slightly by the cool, manmade cave it slipped from between my lips.

"Thank you," Gareth whispered into the night air. "That was ..." words failed him.

I looked up at Gareth directly into his beautiful blue eyes and groaned silently, knowing I was falling for him even in this short a time. I'd not seen captivating, soul-innocent eyes like that since Douglas, a well-endowed, well-built Highlander I'd had a relationship with during the Jacobite Rebellion. He'd met his end at the ill-fated highland charge at the Battle of Culloden, and there had been nothing I could do to save him. I can clearly recall the image of six musket balls entering his body as if it were only yesterday. His death had affected me badly, and it was many decades before I allowed myself to experience those feelings again.

Now, here I was, lying before this handsome human experiencing the first stirrings of what I knew was undoubtedly a bad idea. I laid my head on his thigh wondering what I should do. Should I follow my feelings or do what I'd done countless times before and leave?

Gareth's hand gently stroked my hair, and I tensed. "Don't leave me here." he said as if he could read my mind. "Take me home with you," he whispered. "Please."

Knowing I was lost, I climbed to my feet, my face grinning broadly. Holding out a hand to pull him up I said, "Come on, then."

ELPH, VAMPIRE HUNTER
By Taurus Blue

Taurus Blue hails from Baltimore, MD, and hopes to transition part-time writing into a full-time writing career. He is occasionally surrounded by feline, human and potted-plant kind.

Sylvan Bonham was his name. We went to the same college. He was slight of build, his sandy brown, straight hair worn just past his shoulders, too long for the preference of the jocks of the school. Those cerebrally challenged oafs teased him mercilessly because of his hair. If he had shorn his locks, they'd move on to easier prey. But Syl would not. He had integrity. Heart. Soul, was that the word? The jocks could not get under his skin. I liked that in him. Unflappable. He walked straight through their line, even if he saw them coming, even if they knocked his books from his hands or flicked his hair. Syl would simply look them in the eye, pick his books up, one by one, or run his hands over his hair to bring it back in line, and keep moving. They nicknamed him Cher, because he had that distinctive curved nose and the long hair, as did she before her plastic surgery.

Syl entered into my radar on the first day of school in freshman year. We attended the North Hills University, nestled in the North Hills suburb of Baltimore City, Maryland. On that very first day, Syl got into a fistfight with Junior Goliath, a fitting name for the blond, two-hundred-sixty-pound bully. That was the beginning of Syl's hell by the hands of the jocks. But the fistfight ended in a draw. Not sure exactly why they fought, other than Junior believing he could intimidate the boy with the girly hair. But he could not fell the one-hundred-twenty-five-pound Syl, and intimidation was out, there was something under the surface with Syl, a

145

steeliness, an unspoken sense of fairness, or justice. There was something feral, too. He was a fighter and the size of his opponent mattered not. I began watching him from that fight on. He did not know I existed.

Fast forward to senior year, graduation came and went. We had some mutual friends in common. We were invited to a graduation party, held two days after the ceremony. I went to a few parties throughout the years, but never saw Syl at any, though the same friends invited him. I was pleasantly shocked when he walked through the door and was introduced to me by our hostess, Effie Shiloh. Effie was attractive, slight of build, tall at five-feet-ten, a *café au lait* complexion, dark curls, which she rarely let loose from her upswept coif and gregarious. She favored me, always invited me to her gatherings, but I remained aloof. Emotional attachments could derail my concentration. I had no choice. I relied on my concentration for survival.

Syl had gained about ten pounds since freshman year, still slight, but more filled out. His hair, up close was silky, scented of strawberries. His nose fit within the proportions of his face. His features alone were unusual, but the sum of all the parts grouped together made one attractive man.

"You boys get acquainted," Effie said. She placed red plastic cups of her famous fireball punch in our hands, no doubt laced with alcohol, then she added, "I must see to the music, 'cause a party ain't a party if no one's dancing!" She disappeared through the sea of heads to the back of the room, where the stereo was being manned.

"Hello, I'm Cher," Syl said, full of good humor. He extended his hand, and smiled with his clean, straight, white teeth. He decided to use the nickname to offset my possible teasing because I was one of the jocks.

"I know who you are, Sylvan," I offered. I wanted to say so much more, but was strangled by my awkwardness in social situations. The reason I usually attend such gatherings was in hopes of overcoming my anxiety.

146

"Oh. An intelligent jock," he said, his hazel eyes twinkled. "And you are?" He asked.

Our first conversation and I instantly liked him. He was genuine.

"I, uh, apologize, I am Elphonsious D'or, but just call me Elph," I offered.

"So you're the famous Elph. The loner. The Aloof. The 'Danger Will Robinson' dude. Nice to meet you," Syl said. He took a big swig of his fireball.

"Nice to meet you, too, Cher," I added. I risked the moniker because of his genial sense of humor. "Why do they call me 'Danger Will Robinson?'" I asked, then took a drink of the fireball and regretted it as the alcohol proceeded to strip the lining of my innards apart. How do people drink this stuff? I parked the drink on a stack of CDs.

"Oh, they used to say that you were going to go crazy one day and go berserk in school. I wouldn't pay their talk any attention, though. Think about the source of the gossip. Slutty cheerleaders who are so attracted to a jock, they're just upset because you don't give them any attention," Syl said, before he continued. "Want to know what I think? I think you know quite well that you could go all 'Hulk smash' on somebody if you wanted to, but the hard part is keeping all the anger and power under control. I get it. You wouldn't be an intelligent jock if you were as shallow as the others, working your body out just for dates or because you're in love with yourself. There's an intensity to you, Loner, I see it in your eyes, There is more to you than 'roidin' up, getting off, and bashin' fags."

The pulsing beat of music thumped from the back of the room, Effie's party was fully under way.

"Wanna dance?" Syl asked. He was more social than my from afar observations pictured him. I liked him even more.

"Together?" I asked, "What about Effie?"

"Dude, it's a party, friends are supposed to dance with each other, at least until their soul mate cuts in and in case you haven't noticed, Effie, is otherwise engaged." Effie was dancing her signature jig, curls loose, and in the company of a throng of folks. She was in her element. "What are you? One of those closeted bi-dudes? She doesn't have time for your beefy cuteness, right now. Although, by dancing with me, you might just make her jealous enough to pay you some attention. Come on, Loner."

Syl led us to the dance area. All of my observations never gave me a chance to actually know him. I liked the up-close, three-dimensional version better. I thought by his being bullied, he would be uncommonly shy. But the opposite was true, he was almost as gregarious as Effie, I was the painfully shy one, translation: brooder, loner, "Danger Will Robinson."

Impossibly, the pulse of the music got faster and more intense. I did my two-step dance that is generic enough not to be an embarrassment, but there were times when I stood in place, looking at Syl. He could dance. His hair was a silken veil encircling, caressing and protecting him. His lithe and powerful form was graceful, yet masculine in dance. His hands were attractive enough to be used in a commercial. The more I saw of him, the closer I got, the more I liked. I felt as in a trance, the strobe light flickered. The intense beat of the music overpowered the beat of my own heart, and Syl, a vision of masculinity. I shook my head. Why would they tease him? He was different. The fireball started to kick in. I felt a heaviness descend upon me. Not uncomfortable, exactly, just not right. I stood still, to gain my bearings.

Three males entered the dance area. Gatecrashers. They were not from our school, but somehow they knew about the party. They began a very popular dance. Everyone else stopped dancing. They gathered round in a circle to watch. The bald one moved in behind Syl. The heavyset one moved next to Effie. The compact, muscled one started gyrating, in slow circles, which increased in pace at each rotation. He dropped to the ground and did a Thomas Flare, and the crowd cheered. I kept my eyes on Syl, he winked at me, before he did a half turn and noticed Baldie behind him. He started dancing with Baldie, who was a little too suggestive. I crossed the floor around the edge of the crowd to Effie, my eyes still on Syl's gyrating form.

"Effie! Who are these guys? How do you know them?" I asked.

"They are the Moll brothers. Sexy flipping on the floor is Maximillian, Max for short. Hottie dancing with Syl is Muldeen, Mull for short, and Big Boy to my right is Major, but he really does go by Big Boy. They supply the secret ingredient to the fireball. Why? Do you need some of my fireball for your own shindig? Why, my dear D'or, you will have tongues flapping all over the county," Effie said.

"Effie, come with me," I said. I grabbed her by the elbow and ushered her around the edge of the crowd to where Syl was being licked on his neck by Baldie. Damn it! I was too late. I cut in between Baldie and Syl.

"I'm sorry, Syl, your soul mate would like this dance, but first some fresh air," I said, using his joke from earlier. Baldie just sneered, as if to say, he'll be mine. And if I didn't counteract the effects of that lick, Syl would be. I grabbed Syl by his elbow and ushered him and Effie both, out the back sliding glass door onto the patio.

"Dude," Syl said. "I've got to get back in there. Did you see? That bald hottie is totally into me. Why'd you bring me out here? Are we about to have a three way? You bi-dudes are so challenged. Sorry, Effie, I know you like this buff, bench pressing, boner banging, baby's daddy, but − I just can't control my thoughts, your fireball ..." and before Syl could finish the sentence, he ran to the railing and emptied his stomach: the remnants of the fireball hit the grass below.

"D'or?" Effie asked, as she brushed her curls back into her updo. Both eyebrows raised, she was about to unleash a hurricane. "Sweetie, have you not told him?" Then, she lowered her voice, "From what he just said, he TOTALLY likes you, why have you not told him?"

"Yeah, Lover – uh, Loner, why don't I know?" Syl said. His eyes began to glaze. His hearing seemed to have improved. "Uh, Effie, what is bi-buff, benchin' daddy not telling? Are y'all into orgies, 'cause I'm not? I mean, I like both of y'all, but I don't – I haven't ..." Syl's legs gave out, he planted his bottom on the patio floor.

Under different circumstances, drunk, semi-out of control Syl would be irresistible.

I reached into my back pocket and pulled out a flat square brownie. I opened Syl's mouth with the thumb and index fingers of my left hand and placed the brownie inside.

"Chew and swallow," I said, "That's an order!"

"Yes, Sir? Sire? Serious? Soul mate? Isn't that what you said in there?" Syl was losing the battle, but he didn't miss a thing, I had been underestimating him. The brownie should bring him back to sober. His glazed eyes went wide a moment, as the taste of the brownie was written on his face. He looked like a kid chewing saltwater taffy for the first time. I smiled. Effie was right; he should know. Now. But he was still too drunk.

"Effie, not now," I said, stopping her mouth just as she opened it for my lashing. "You have known me for five years, now. You know I am serious about the work I do. We've got to secure the survival of your guests and Syl, here. You must do exactly what I say. Understand?"

"D'or, you have bounded over the edge of sanity if you think ..." she stopped mid-sentence, as she looked at Syl. "What in ...?" she uttered.

I regarded Syl, whose eyes were trained on Baldie as he moved on the other side of the sliding glass door. Baldie, his arm wrapped around a cheerleader, was headed to the room behind the makeshift bar.

"See, Elphaloof, like I told ya, slutty cheerleader can't get your jock so she steals my man candy. Hey!" Syl stated, and added, in a tiny, disaffected voice, "He's mine." Then he squinted. His eyes went wide. He pointed, and I placed his hands in mine and brought them down. No need to bring unnecessary attention. "Hey, Elphie, uh, Effie, yeah, you and you combined in plural and stereo. Slutty cheerleader is in Danger, Will Robinson. Baldie's not right. His face. His mouth. Something is wro-o-o-o-ong! Mm, mmm, that brownie is so ri-i-i-i-ight!" Syl stated.

I never knew wrong and right could have so many syllables.

"Come here, you," Syl said. He tackled me to the ground and planted a kiss, demurely on my cheek.

"Why can't I ever see these monsters," Effie stated, "And you and those damn stoner boner brownies. Are you sure you didn't lace those with Love Potion Number Nine? I mean, look at him, sheesh. If that ain't an out of body experience. Really? One of my flock is about to be a liquefied zombie girl and you two play smoochies?"

Although she didn't go in as driven as I, Effie was always determined to protect those who may be caught in the fray. I appreciated her efforts. Syl was upright and inside the building, in seconds, as he followed the trail of Baldie. He stopped and took a squinty, good look at the Brothers Moll, then moved to open the door that lead to Baldie and the cheerleader. Fearless!

I moved in front of Syl, Effie was close behind me.

"Syl, you must stay here, keep the door cracked slightly open. Guard the door, do you understand?"

"Sure, Loner. Is that an order, too?" He asked. I smiled. He was close to sober.

"Yes, that is an order, Sylvan," I said, he lifted his hand in salute. Effie and I ventured into the room. Baldie was kneeling over Erica Simone's body. She was unconscious. His mouth was unusual, protruding out and flaring at the end, like a king cobra. A thick and copious fluid, red like blood but thick like snot, flowed from the tip, and dropped toward Erica's face.

"Back away, Bacchandrine," I said, as Baldie snarled. He turned from Erica and the opaque, thick liquid retracted into his strange snout as he regained his attractive visage. His tongue licked the last glob of the liquid from his lip. Baldie leveled a malevolent gaze at me, which softened, as Syl walked up behind Effie and me.

"Mull, honey," Effie said, "My fireball has proven very intense this evening. Poor Erica needs some coffee! Syl, honey, help me get Erica to the couch in the other room, please." They proceeded to lift Erica up and ushered her into the safety of the party room. Effie knew how to diffuse a crisis.

But the Bacchandrine and I had unfinished business.

"How dare you hunt amongst friends, Bacchandrine? You will leave this place, now, for you do not belong here. Find your prey elsewhere this night. These people will be protected from you and your brothers, by me," I said.

"I know you, Elphynn. And now, I know your boy, Syl. Since I have tasted him, he belongs to me. You do not belong here, either. Return to the woods and run with your kind," Baldie stated, trying to insult. But my skin was thick.

"Syl is not my boy, and he will never be yours, Bacchandrine. The day you cross his path, again, shall be your last," I said.

"Perhaps, Elphynn, perhaps," he said. He moved in close to me, his light brown eyes held my cold stare. "He is the link joining you and me together, a most, thrilling union," Mull said, as he licked his full lips. "And I look forward to tightening such a bond." He tilted his head, most seductively, eyed me sideways and exited the room. Now alone, I tried to understand why goose bumps marched across my forearms and major chills rocketed through my body at the words of Mull. I knew what he was (attractive) and what his kind did (seduce). They were the epitome of sexual lust, desire and want. They were the black widow spiders. A dalliance with one could end in death. Final.

Syl.

Mull had marked him. Tonight, Syl must learn the truth, if only for his protection. Of course, my secret heart wanted him to know, needed him to know. I hoped he could process the absurdity of the truth and would choose to tread with me through the wilds that were my life.

I ran through the door, tracked the brothers Moll, and saw them leaving the party as they entered, alone. Syl hovered on the couch with the unconscious Erica, until he saw me. He hopped up and joined Effie at the bar. She was standing beside the CD stack waiting on me, eyebrows locked and loaded. I approached with my right hand up, hoping to silence Effie before she began her verbal assault.

I examined Erica. She didn't exhibit the blue vein trace of the full on Bacchandrine love swab. She may have fainted.

"Effie, she hasn't been attacked; she may have just passed out. She'll be fine when she wakes up. Here, give her some 'Stoner Brownies' just in case. Syl and I have much to discuss," I said, knowing Effie would take care of Erica, ply her full of brownies and get her home safely. "Come," I said to Syl. I wrapped my muscular left arm about his shoulders and squeezed hard enough for him to feel my flexing bicep against his back. I liked the press of his smaller body close to mine. He fitted me.

He looked at Effie, who winked at him, and nodded, as he let out a lethargic "Help."

"Oh, Honey, you're going to be fine. Elph, I packed some special non-fireball magic for y'all," she said. She placed a small brightly colored fabric cooler over my shoulder, placed her arms about us both, before a final, "Now get!"

"Wait, I need to use the bathroom," Syl said loudly, and asked, "Mouthwash?" in a whisper to Effie, who smiled and nodded her head in the direction of the restroom while she looked at me and pushed an errant curl behind her ear. Syl joined me outside on the front porch. "Hey, do you want me to call my brother to come get us?" Syl asked. "He will, 'cause he's who dropped me off at the party. He said call when I'm ready. He won't mind taking you home. Really!" Syl emphasized as he looked at my expression, as if I didn't believe him.

"Syl," I said. I squeezed him, again, with my muscular left arm, "Let's walk, huh? A nice breeze punctuates the night, and I am in nice company. Walk with me, talk with me, and I shall bare my secret. I'll get you home safe and sound."

"Ooh, this must work with all your heterosexual dates, huh?" Syl giggled. He stopped when I removed my arm from his shoulder. "I'm sorry, Elph, that fireball is still running amok in my innards."

"I'm not offended, Syl, really. I have some heavy stuff to reveal to you. I'm just not sure you will be as friendly, or as funny, afterwards," I said.

"You think I'm funny? Cool," Syl said, as he grabbed my left hand with his warm right hand, but he avoided eye contact.

"Uh-uh, Syl, look me in the eyes," I said, so I could gauge his sincerity. I already knew I could because of his touch. My kind knew instantly in these ways, things others might never be able to discern.

He turned to me, so sincerely, his hazel eyes loosened something within my soul. For those eyes, I was forced to move beyond my debilitating shyness. His touch revealed a tenacity shown only in glimpses through actions I had witnessed involving him over the years. Something about Syl strengthened and weakened me.

We had arrived at the "Back Porch" of our development. It was a slight hill, created by the builders of our neighborhood, before acquiescing into a steep rise of hills and the forest covering those hills. The Back Porch was the term all the young people of the area had named this spot because you could view the land beyond from horizon to horizon.

"You know, most couples kiss here on the Back Porch, but since I just vomited up my guts back at Effie's, staring deep into each other's eyes will have to suffice; is that the plan?" Syl asked. He smiled. Deceptive. I already knew the truth because I felt it. He felt the pull, too, but he didn't know how to handle it. He wanted as much or more as I.

I silenced all doubt as I kissed him demurely on the lips to prove to him I felt him, too, and that the rest is irrelevant. I was rewarded with an aroma of subtle wisps of mint from the mouthwash. I smiled. Syl pleased me just by being himself.

"Eeew," he said, "You're a nasty one. I said I vomited."

"So the cooler than cool Syl is just as stymied by a kiss as I?" I said, a smile was in my voice and on my face.

"Maybe," he said, a smile brightening his features. Such a smile.

"Well, Syl, you may be wondering why I brought you here to the Back Porch. It is simply easier for me to show you than to tell you," I said, "But first, perhaps some of Effie's non fireball special magic?" I removed my leather jacket and placed it on the ground. I sat and opened the cooler from Effie. I laughed as I reached inside and pulled out some bottled beer and some fried chicken. Syl joined me on the jacket, our knees touched as he sat beside me, Indian style.

"Well," he said, biting gustily into his drumstick of chicken, "I already know, Elph, that you are something other than gay. If that is what you want to show me, you need not bother. I can handle it. Your secret's safe with me. You should know I'm gay, though. If you do not wish to be around me, I will understand. Really."

"Syl," I said, "I don't care about that. Sexuality is the least of my worries."

"Oh, good, 'cause I wasn't gonna ask for another drumstick, if gayness was a problem for you, but since it ain't, fork another piece here," he said.

"So, I'm nasty and you're greedy, huh?" I said. I handed him the food he requested.

"I know, funny, ain't it?" He asked, before we both finished the food.

We drank the beer, two bottles apiece. He leaned his strawberry scented head upon my shoulder.

"I'm glad you're not opposed to gay people, Elph," Syl said, "'cause I really like you, and you may not be interested in me sexually, and that is fine, but I like you as a person and would like to consider you a friend. I hope what I just said makes sense. Sometimes, I can get emotional and my words get kind of trippy."

I stood and reached for Syl's right hand with my left. He rose, a questioning look was on his face. "Come," I said. "You should know my secrets." I picked up the cooler and placed it over my shoulder. He dumped our refuse into the nearest of three trashcans that lined the edge of the Back Porch. Then, he picked up my jacket and wrapped himself in it.

We began to walk toward the forest edge. As we got nearer, Syl stopped.

"If I didn't trust you, Elph, I would be suspicious of where we are now. The woods. At night. With a mysterious, brooding, muscle head guy who could break me in two. Drunk on two beers. So whatever you must show me, I'm cool with it," he said.

"Good, come," I said, again, wrapping my left arm about him. I liked having him so near. "We have a ways to go, yet."

After a fifteen-minute walk and some hand holding, through the dark thick press of trees, we reached a clearing. Lit by millions of twinkling stars above in the night sky, the clearing was illuminated vividly. In the center of this space stood a huge, old petrified wood stump, carved with ancient markings. I gestured for Syl to be seated upon the stump. He complied. He could stretch out if he wanted. The stump was that wide.

"I am enamored of you, Syl. You are so cool headed. The whole way through the trees, just now, you followed me, without fear. You accept life on your terms, no matter what the situation. I admire you. I have, since that freshman year fight you had with Junior Goliath. You held your own against that human behemoth. And not once tonight, after what you have seen, have you balled up on the ground in the fetal position, sucking your thumb asking why. Tonight, a lot of questions will be answered," I said.

I knelt down in front of Syl, placed his hands in mine and looked him in the eyes.

"Elph, I'm surprised you saw that fight with Junior. Also, you should know, I don't scare easily, 'cause if I did, I wouldn't be in the dark woods with a strange man. I have never seen this clearing in the forest before and we used to explore these woods often growing up," Syl said. "Holy – Elph – this stump! I can feel a strange heat emanating from it, like heat, but like a vibration, and an emotion, too. I can't quite figure it out, and these markings are so unusual, and beautiful, like you. Are you an alien? I've seen plenty of shows and movies with similar stuff in them, and there was that one show with the cute dark haired boy from Roswell who was an alien, I really liked him and that show."

"Syl, you, too, are most unusual, but no, I am not an alien," I said. The moment had arrived. I relaxed my concentration, and allowed the vibrations about my person to change, revealing my true visage and self to Syl. I felt the burn, similar to a post exercise burn, as the length of my ears increased. I felt the curvature of my eyes change as my pupils dilated shrinking the iris. Other changes were perhaps more subtle, as my hands and feet lengthened imperceptibly. Only Syl could reveal these things to me, as he was the only human, other than Effie, who had seen my true form.

Syl's eyes went large as recognition crossed his face. His mouth mimicked his eyes. His hands ran the length of mine, a most, exhilarating sensation, subtly sensual.

"Holy Hannah, Elph, you really are – an Elf!" Syl said. He regarded my real ears, before he asked, "May I touch your ears?"

"Yes," I managed. I closed my eyes as he ever so gently ran the tips of his fingers over the edges of my elongated, nearly pointed ears. I could feel the ridges of his fingerprints moving across my sensitive elfin skin. I felt the yearning of his desire for me, magnified by my sensitivity in this form. I reached up and placed his hands in mine, partly to stop the orgiastic sensations he stirred within my body.

"Syl, you are not offended? Revolted? Afraid? Worried? You are not done with me because I am not what you thought I was?" I asked, the questions poured out of me.

"What? Elph? Do you not understand me? Dude! You are a fantasy fanatic's wet dreams come to life. Every Dungeons & Dragons game I've ever played has had an elf in it. I knew there was something more to you, some sort of magnetism, but wow. Effie knows, doesn't she?" Syl asked.

"Yes, she does."

"And what happened tonight, with Baldie, what I saw, his weird face – that was all real, wasn't it?" Syl asked.

"Yes."

"Yikes, Elph. There are other creatures, shape shifters, and beings out there, uh, out here, aren't there?" Syl asked. He eyed the clearing as if those creatures might be lurking.

"Yes, Syl, there are," I said.

"You're some kind of hunter aren't you? That's why you told Baldie I would never be his, 'cause you're hunting him. Is he some kind of vampire?" Syl asked. His sharp mind clicked along in step with the events so far.

"You heard our exchange?" I asked, surprised by his aural acuity. "I suppose I am a sort of hunter, and I suppose most might consider Baldie a vampire. He is actually one of a breed called Bacchandren. They are masters of seduction, sensuality and slaughter. The lick he gave you is one of their talents. The saliva poisons the blood, basically making the victim a slave, suggestible and compliant to whatever the Bacchandrine desires. The brownie I gave you counteracts the effects. There may be residual amounts of his spoor in you, so you are not safe from him, but I will protect you," I said. I hoped what flowed from my mouth was true. I knew all too well the effects associated with one of Baldie's tongue swabs.

"Wow, I'm glad I'm drunk 'cause that is some heavy spiel you're dropping. Listen, I'm not going to remember any of this in the morning, am I?" he asked.

"You will, Syl. What I'm telling you is the truth. You're very strong and intuitive. Besides, I tell you these things and reveal my true self for your protection. You'll be better equipped to handle what may come. I must ask. Will you, Syl, join me in this journey? I'll understand if you want nothing more to do with me. I am, as you say, something other than gay. We don't really differentiate sexuality in such a way, but I am yours. You know this on an instinctual level because I can read it in you, and I feel it, too."

"Yes, Elph. This feeling! It's an undeniable pull. I'm just glad I'm embracing it with you!" Syl said. "But I've got a lot of questions. First, what is this clearing, what is this stump with the strange markings?"

"Ah. We are in my natal forest. The stump is what remains of my crèche tree. Stand on it." I said. I stepped up behind Syl, his long hair softly caressed my left cheek. I wrapped my arms around him and was rewarded when his compact form pressed into mine. I reached around and pulled his arms out to the sides and then brought them up over our heads, our fingers laced together. I whispered into his left ear. "From this very spot I grew into being, the vibrations, heat and emotion you felt came from the stump, sort of an umbilical cord. I come here sometimes to meditate, but

159

enough talking," I said. "Now, begins the song," as I proceeded. I uttered a most ancient verse that rejoined my tree to the song of the wood and of all living things. Syl turned to face me, his arms came down, his hands framed my face, and his fingertips brushed my ears, then my lips, before his own lips enveloped mine. The markings along the stump glowed brightly as diaphanous tendrils grew up and surrounded us, caressing, connecting, cocooning.

Every experience, every nuance of my person, my being, and my spirit joined with Sylvan's at this moment. He did not resist and neither did I. We were nothing and everything; the stars in the sky, the particles of light that spread towards the earth and from the earth, the very air and wind that flowed through every leaf in every tree in every blade of grass in every meadow. Every sensation pulled and stretched and warped and magnified and realigned. From the smallest sensation to the very tips of our hair, we imploded and finally exploded, we began and we ended. Quite simply; We were. We lay naked on the stump. The glow from the embers of the carved writing matched the glow from the embers of our union.

Syl's warm, satiated, supine form lay atop me, cradled by my equally satisfied body. A thin mist generated by our sweat swirled above us both, before it dissipated, my still engorged member shifted beneath the plump gluteus muscle of Syl.

"Holy Montana, Elph. Look at my arms, I still have goose bumps, and I feel you beneath me, still frisky, huh?" he asked.

Not wanting our union to end, just yet, I kissed Syl, as if trying to devour him.

"Wow, did you see and feel and know all that transpired, Elph? The earth gives off light! I'll have to call you Earthshine or Elphshine. Awe-some! Oh, I still have questions. I don't know if I have enough words to describe the beauty of what just happened. By the way, what just happened?" he asked.

I laughed, gently. "Ha, Sylvan Bonham, I doubt you have a loss of words," I said. I kissed him on the side of his neck. "We are now joined, mated if you will, in tune with each other and the whole of the wood."

"You were a tree, Elph, I saw, no, I felt the dappled sunlight on the flesh of your bark. It felt like the bubbles splashing in the currents of a babbling brook. More awesome." Syl said, proving he picked up on the subtlest of nuances. A skill he would need to garner his survival, sooner than later because Baldie approached.

"Get dressed, quickly, now, Syl, the Bacchandrine is here!" I whispered. A few flurried gestures later, we were clothed and presentable for an audience. "Before he arrives, I want to say thank you for sharing yourself with me, I had hoped but did not expect to be wooed by you," I said.

"The moment you walked into the party, you were mine, Elph. How can you resist all of this?" Syl asked, as he moved his arms and hands downward and motioned across his body. He laughed. I laughed and then, bowed my head. I brought my hands together in a prayer motion.

Syl's eyes went wide, as the clearing, seemed to vanish as trees shifted, the stump was hidden, and we found ourselves in a thicket of sorts, seated upon an outcrop of large stones, in front of which ran a small creek.

"What the ...?" Syl asked.

"Woodland magic, "I said. I looked into those hazel eyes and away before I got lost in them. Damn! The Bacchandrine would pick this moment to slither near. He'd never have been able to sneak up on me, had I not let my guard down. But, Syl. Beautiful Syl, I had put him in danger. I should have dealt with the Bacchandrine long before this day.

"Heads up, fellas," came the ultra smooth, honey and chocolate, silken, bass voice of Baldie, the Bacchandrine, who finally emerged from the newly rearranged edge of the forest. "Sorry about the pun," he added, chuckling. "I give you credit,

Elphynn, you work fast! You knew I'd come looking for the steely one," the seductive, light-brown eyed, Muldeen Moll stated, that wistful, almost vulnerable expression he wore only for Syl, colored his face. He walked right up to the creek's edge and stopped, perhaps he contemplated what manner of defense enchanted the water. I chuckled.

"Elph, talk to me," he stated. He set his gaze upon me. "Our exchange is long overdue," the overwhelmingly seductive ravisher said. He stretched, groin forward, arms above his lick worthy baldhead, hands behind his neck, and powerful legs poised. His tight musculature was revealed through his form fitting knit shirt and low-rise jeans. A low "Unfhh" escaped him as his stretch wound down to an admirable and tantalizing abs exposing end. I looked at Syl; his smoky eyed post-loving glow was so alluring. And it was turned in the direction of the man candy. Did he care about the vision of manliness across the creek, as did I, once? More truth from which I had hoped to shield Syl, but Muldeen, true to form, was always visible, front and center, full Monty, and brazenly forced the issue.

"You play a very dangerous game, Bacchan," I said, wondering why Muldeen had taken leave of his senses. Why would he approach me in the wood, how dare he approach at all? Why would he risk death, looking for Syl in my presence? He was working on some strategy, and Syl was tantamount to his plan. I must proceed with caution because I could be playing right into those lithe, sexy hands.

"I've come to collect the steely one," Muldeen stated. "Come, Syl, I've been searching for you for a very long time."

Incredible.

Syl hopped down from atop the stone outcropping and took a step toward the water. He removed his clothes, and stood completely naked creek side, before he stepped into and immersed his beautiful body in the water, up to his chest. And I was hard, again. He beckoned Muldeen forward. The brownie must not have worked or Muldeen's spoor must be more potent than I remembered, because Syl was under some type of spell. They both must be enchanted. Or I had lost my wits.

Muldeen, with the longing for Syl clearly set on his face, also removed every stitch of clothing, except for a strange locket, eyed my engorged state quickly, his hot body had the same response and likewise, stepped into the water. Enchantments be damned! This could not be happening. The jock in me took over. I moved forward, intent on stopping the travesty about to be committed before my very eyes. As I approached, they climbed up from the creek and each grabbed one of my hands. My eyes widened as Syl's had done, so many times this night. My mind was aswirl with treasonous and venomous conspiracy theories. I pulled against them, but they would have none of my resistance. They led us to a soft patch of fragrant clover and began undressing me. I struggled as my shirt was removed. Syl's soft, wet mouth covered mine, again, and his hands moved like water over the skin of my chest, as Muldeen's face was buried in my crotch. His hands had a vice grip on my gluteus as he brushed his face against my member through the fabric of my jeans. My body was working against me because I was feeling intense and horny, when I should have been screaming. I'm sure Muldeen could feel my engorgement through my jeans. Syl removed his tongue from my mouth and looked me in the eyes. I was lost in them, as always.

"Syl, what … the …" I stuttered, feeling so many overwhelming sensations at once. Muldeen pulled my jeans and underwear down and off. His warm, wet, lithe hands touched the skin of my gluteus, ever so lightly, unhampered by the denim. He, too, fixed my gaze with his light brown eyes. My member slid easily into his mouth as Syl ran his fingers across my pectoral muscles, then, across my nipples, which caused my back to arch involuntarily. Muldeen felt amazing. Syl felt amazing. I felt amazing. And I stopped struggling because my body was aching for release, yet again. From his touch and gaze, I knew Muldeen had no ulterior motive, other than his unrequited love for me from long ago, and his more recent lust for Syl. Seems we had the same ardor. Syl's loving hazel peepers engaged my focus, and I pulled him in close and gave him a desperate hug, so tight, neither of us could breathe, but for a moment.

Muldeen unscrewed the bottom off of his odd locket and removed a condom and packet of lube. "Always be prepared," he stated, his thick lashes covered his left eye as he winked. He covered my shaft with the protection and poured the lube over me. He pumped me gently before he climbed upon my hips and plunged me deep into the heat of his innards. I gasped, and lay back, each gyration of his hips sent me reeling. Syl squatted, his ass hovered over my face, as my tongue greedily lapped at his anus, before he lowered himself and smothered me with his fragrant musk. I tried to plunge my tongue in as deep as my member was within Muldeen. The three of us were in sync, as Muldeen's hips pumped, my tongue pushed, and my right hand pumped Syl's member. My left hand pulled Syl down upon my face, deeper. The two of them caressed my hypersensitive body and sent me close to the edge. I reached up with my left hand, and Muldeen guided my fingers to his right nipple, which I pinched gently, and he gasped. All three of us pumped in earnest. My hips bucked, and my spunk erupted torrentially inside the condom inside of Muldeen. My tongue was deep inside Syl as his anus contracted and his jism splashed my belly. I gave him little kisses until his contractions subsided. Muldeen came last. He placed my hand around his thick, uncut meat and pumped my hand quickly until his dick flexed, and his warm seed spilt out over my belly, too. My fellas climbed up off me and lay down beside me, Syl on my right, Muldeen on my left, each with an arm around me. I looked from one to the other.

"That was hot guys," I said. I struggled to set the conflicted feelings rioting within loose.

"Sexy Elph, never fully understanding that our kind don't always have to fight to the death," Muldeen said. "I have always tried to wander into your orbit, Elph, but you always pushed me out, never trusting, never giving yourself a chance, never giving us a chance. But seeing your emotional attachment to the Steely one, gave me an opening, which I exploited not so subtly at the party. I'm sorry, guys, but you wouldn't have listened, otherwise. Syl, I used you to get to Elph, and I sincerely apologize."

"No need, Mull, I am indebted to you because Elph may never have told me the truth without you forcing his hand, and I truly couldn't be happier," Syl said.

"Well, look at us. The elf, the vampire, and the human, in bed with each other," I said.

"Hey, who are you calling a vampire?" Mull asked. A tender smile bloomed upon his gorgeous face.

"I-uh ..." I stuttered, again.

"And who are you calling a human?" Syl asked, most serious.

"What?" The elf and the vampire asked in unison.

"Gotchcha!" Syl said, before he succumbed to little bursts of laughter that caused us to laugh as well.

"My fellas," I stated. I hugged both so tight; they asked to stop being slowly crushed by the big old jock. I complied.

What a magical night, in many ways. My fellas lovingly teased me as Elph, Vampire Hunter, ever since.

SPOIL ME SO
A Novella
By R. W. Clinger

R. W. Clinger welcomes all naughty, hot, and nocturnal beasts inside his bedroom, among other places. The author has numerous books and stories through STARbooks Press. He can be reached at rwclinger@verizon.net and through his web site rwclinger.com.

Chapter 1 – The Chandler House

I've frequented The Chandler House numerous times, since my job requires it of me. Many artists and high-end executives do business at the establishment, fulfilling their artsy needs. Some buy paintings here while others sell their masterpieces under its three convex-structured floors. Of course I'm familiar with the business's cement floors, blinding white walls, and twenty-foot high ceilings. What journalist hasn't ventured inside its confines and enjoyed its displayed paintings, a meeting with the owners (Mr. Beverly Tandy and Mr. Brighton Marx), and the bizarre artist who occasionally pops by?

The business address is 3281 Ratshire Street in downtown Plimpton City, New York, which bumps against Niagara Falls. Those who enter its doors are welcome to enjoy a coffee at the neighboring coffee house for half off. Others can meander around the premises and take pictures, scrawl notes on their computers regarding the paintings, or feel intellectually whimsical about themselves and their splendid surroundings.

My job draws me to The Chandler House for basic reasons. A male artist is new to the business, and I'm instructed by my editor, Steven McMeredith, to interview him: Kalvin Bentley Fleet.

I've worked for the *Plimpton City Caller* for the last six years, fresh out of West End College with a degree in journalism, and have to write a brief story on the artist: his history, his work, and his future goals. The one thousand words are due on my editor's desk in one week. Steven will not take a single word late. His deadlines are strict and to the point. And his bitchy motto is simple: If a writer can't meet my deadlines, find a new job.

I discover the bathroom, building a fine piss. Here, among black-and-white tile mixed with stainless-steel, I carry out my business. While I wash my hands following my deed, I stare at myself in the mirror over the sink. Still handsome after twenty-seven years with midnight-black hair, deep blue eyes, five-ten frame, one-hundred-seventy-five pounds, black scruff on my chin and cheeks, but not a beard. My nose is tiny and somewhat pink, and my lips are cherry red, just like my deceased mother's.

Once I find myself handsome and take care of my piss, I exit the bathroom, join the gatherers and the pre-show again, mixing in with the crowd.

The Chandler House is busy for a Thursday evening in October. Queer couples move about the place in search of a perfect living room painting/print/sketch. Lesbians lurk in corners, seeking a Nigerian mask or Oriental, dragon-shaped whips to display in their apartments. Straight people come and go, the occasional queer loner visits, and columnists such as I linger slowly from one room to the next.

One-by-one, I study the pieces of art by various artists that garnish The Chandler House: clay sculptures of cocks; Kropholler-like doll houses; hand-painted plates; a priest's head carved out of jade; a hand-woven wool rug of the Mortuary Temple of Queen Hatshepsut; a Fresco painting titled Killing Birds by Banberry Feast, a local artist; faux nineteenth century porcelain vases painted with plum blossoms; basalt figurines of Shivo; lacquered wood boxes; Cambodian tapestries; bronze tea pots shaped like pregnant women.

On the first floor of The Chandler House, to the far right, is Kal Fleet's work: charcoal drawings on white or tan paper of male torsos, muscles, shoulders, bottoms, legs, and backs. Jockish bodies of young and beautiful men that he enjoys working with and finds inspiring. The show is a handsome arrangement of youthful models with smooth skin and strong frames.

His paintings have simple titles and are numbered: Torso #8; Shoulder #12; Navel #7; Lips #23; Male Bottom #48; Inner Thighs #72. Each hangs in a line on a single wall in the gallery. All are framed perfectly in mahogany. Their prices are steep, but the paintings are rare, rather sloppy with curves and sharp angles, convex shapes, and smears. Many have red dots above them, which identify the pieces as sold.

Complimentary drinks consist of a white German wine that is on the sweeter side or typical champagne. I decide on the German wine, snagging one from a nearby tray below an Incan mask called Dweller. Hors d'oeuvres are not served this evening, since this is just a preliminary fall show. Guests include professors from West End College, city architects, a banker, a novelist named Clint Shellings, a poet named Faye Worthington, artists from surrounding cities, and art dealers. The place is packed actually, brimming with people, and its straying gatherers are dressed in casual wear, since the event is not a black tie function.

A number of people speak to me: JoAnne Milford from WPSI, the local news channel; Peter Baily of Baily's Jewelry on Stuupy Street; Ty Snarr, my writing nemesis for the past six years. My conversations with these people are very short and to the point. Eventually, I just sneak away from them all, find myself at the Kal Fleet drawings, and absorb the pieces of art yet again.

# # # # #

I study Kal among a group of women and men. All of them drink champagne or glasses of wine. Since the group is too far away, approximately twenty-five feet, I cannot make out what topics of interest are currently being discussed. Mouths move in conversations, and smiles are shared, which is followed by bogus laughter. Handshakes are offered, and guests try to woo the artist. Kal doesn't seem to be amused at all and acts introverted, wanting to be alone.

My stare concentrates on the young man, whom I find rather attractive: twenty-five years old, short blond hair, aquarium-blue eyes, Greek-sloped nose, six-feet tall, and one-hundred-ninety pounds. No rings dazzle the young man's fingers. No earrings. No mustache or beard. He's dressed in a pair of jeans with holes, expensive looking loafers, and a white dress shirt, which is tucked in. A black, leather belt is wrapped around his thirty-four waist. My eyes scan the package between his legs: plump in size, bulky, and covered in denim.

To my surprise, Kal leaves the group of men and women that circle him. He makes his way up to me, checks me out from head to toe, holds out his hand for me to shake, and simply says, "I don't believe we've met as of yet."

"Cameron Temple. Most people call me Cam," I chant, grip his right hand within my right hand, and bob the two up and down in a cordial embrace.

"The columnist for our city's paper."

"That be me," I say, and smile from ear to ear. In truth, I don't try to dazzle the man, but he seems to be dazzled for some strange reason anyway. A grin forms on his handsome face, delighted to be with me at the moment.

What crosses my mind is rather sinful and alarming: I want to accomplish dirty, male-with-male things with the artist: twisting our naked bodies together in the finest rhythm; locked between his legs with my mouth coveting his stiff crank; jostling my head in a north and south manner as I push his wanker down the back of my tight throat; spanking his bottom with swift slaps from my right palm and ...

We make our way discreetly through the group of guests and end our travels outside, surrounded by slivers of blue-silver moonlight. Glass doors to The Chandler House are to our backs. We lean against a wrought-iron railing that overlooks a cobblestone walkway that is barely illuminated in what looks like a very private courtyard. The man to my right finds a Zippo lighter and cigarette in his shirt's breast pocket. When he lights the cigarette, inhales, and exhales, he explains, "I only smoke when I'm nervous."

"I didn't think I made men nervous," I respond, feel quite comfortable next to his side, and enjoy our moment together within the October evening: a wind blows through the valley, which is cool and refreshing; autumn time leaves rustle on the ready-to-sleep trees; the moon sometimes slips behind a blue-silver-gray-white cloud, but reappears almost instantly.

"You don't make me nervous," he admits. "I rather like to be around you for some unknown reason. All of the hub-bub inside makes me nervous. I'm not a big fan how they gather around me and feed me their bullshit. It's preposterous and pretentious behavior that I find maddening."

I agree with him, nod within the light breeze, and say, "I feel for you."

He chuckles, which sounds adorable, sweet, and charming for all the right reasons. Following his chuckle, he asks, "Tell me what you're writing about right now."

"I'm supposed to be writing one thousand words about you."

"Me?" he questions, seeming surprised, caught completely off guard by my confession.

"You're the city's biggest star right now."

"My fifteen minutes of fame. It will be over in a flash. I promise myself not to blink." He brushes his shoulder against my shoulder in a subtle manner, and adds, "I might lose the fame, but I won't lose the artist I am."

I tell him that I love his work: the many male torsos, chins, noses, shoulders, and inner thighs. "I like the back drawings the best."

"Cliché," he admits. "They're nothing spectacular. I'm sort of lucky people can recognize them as more, but ... really, they're not."

"Are they based on past or present boyfriends?" I ask, wanting to know.

"Victims," he replies rather quietly, takes a puff of his cigarette, exhales into the night, and laughs.

He's joking, of course. Kal has a sense of humor, and he's using it on me. Kudos to him. In truth, I'm not thrown by his comment and simply take mental notes, crafting a biographical article of his life between my temples. The moment with him is relaxing and enjoyable, and I learn to rather like him instantly.

Before our conversation has the potential to continue, the artist is pulled away by a buyer of his work. Left behind, I simply whisper to myself, "Victims," find the word strange, a bit biting, but useful no less, and now continue my evening.

# # # # #

This night, I become naked and slip between a sheet and comforter on my queen-size bed. Here, in the shadows of a post-midnight hour, I discover the nine inches of wood between my legs. Two palms become heated on the uncut shaft and work in a steady up and down motion. Panting ensues. I buck my hips upward, fall to the bed, and buck upward again. What transpires within the folds of my mind is rather stimulating: Kal talking and laughing with me; the artist smoking at the wrought-iron banister outside The Chandler House; our shoulders brushing together. Within minutes of my self-pleasure, I explode goo on my fingers, over my ripped torso and the bed's sheet. Here, I become weak, under the artist's imagined spell, captivated by his strangeness.

Victims. He said victims. It wasn't my imagination. I heard him correctly. Maybe the rumors are true about the young man. Maybe he is a vampire.

Chapter 2 – Have Your Way with Me

I establish a full history on Kal the next day at my office on Poller Street, Room 329. Notes begin to pile up on my desk about the twenty-five-year-old: son of Milton and Amelia Fleet of Rochester, New York; student at Yossner College for four years; top of his class; owner of a 2014 Ford Escape; no children; no brothers; no sisters; his income is well over two-hundred-thousand dollars a year because of his drawings; he donates a few hours of his time at the Gay & Lesbian Shelter on Mifflow Street in downtown Plimpton City; enjoys reading mysteries; regularly visits his Aunt Deidre in Tarpon Springs, Florida; enjoys horses, pinball, and Tarot cards; wants to teach young students how to paint.

A rumor suggests he kills men for their blood. Never boys. Never women. Never girls. Well-built jocks with many muscles and good looks. Does he really feed on such gentlemen? Is he really a vampire? I must know. I have to know.

Inside my office at the *Plimpton City Caller*, Steven McMeredith stands behind me at my desk, studies the Kal

Fleet notes in front of us on the desk, and replies over my right shoulder, "You're taking this article seriously, Mr. Temple."

"I'm always serious about my work." I look over my shoulder and study my editor/friend: ginger-colored crew cut with sideburns, fall-into hazel eyes, tiny teeth, handsome smile, freckles on the bridge of his nose, never wears his glasses, although he's supposed to. Steven stands over six-feet tall, works out at least five times a week, enjoys lengthy runs along the Niagara River, and adores me. The thirty-three-year-old is queer to his core, used to have a twenty-year-old male lover who looked like Liam Hemsworth, and Steven boasts that he is good in bed, being a power-top.

He reaches over my right shoulder, picks up a black-and-white glossy headshot of the artist, and admits, "The guy has a great look about him. Sexy as hell. Looks smart. I give you three days, Temple, and he'll be inside your ass."

"Actually, Steven … I want to be in his ass."

He drops the photograph where he discovered it seconds before, raises his palms in surrender, and admits in his cocky manner, "That is way too much information for the office."

I laugh.

He laughs.

When he finally escapes my side and office, I reach under my desk, push the nine-inches of shaft away within my chinos, and surrender my naughty thoughts of a skin-on-skin game with Kal Fleet.

#####

More rumors: Kal doesn't like to go out during the day, particularly when it's sunny. He's fond of a thick overcast and rain. Night is a playground for him; a place where he feels most comfortable. Sunlight is his enemy.

#####

October 24. The following day, which is cloudy and filled with rain, Kal just happens to find me at my residence: 4258 Valley Way, which sits two miles south of Plimpton City, but is still considered part of the city. I prepare an evening of writing with a bottle of red wine when the doorbell rings at the front stoop. It's a little after eight in the evening, completely dark outside, and chilly with a teasing wind.

To my surprise, the artist stands at the front of my Tudor. He holds a bottle of wine, smiles from ear to ear, which causes my heart to skip a beat, and waits patiently for my welcome.

I don't do houseguests after eight o'clock in the evening, but make an exception on this brisk and enchanting rainy night. To my own surprise, I open the front door and allow the stud to enter my world, private life, and my home ... just because I think he's a doll, a certain someone I find most interesting and appealing for my writing needs.

# # # # #

Vampires will only enter establishments when invited. Is this true? Does Kal know this? I'm really not sure.

# # # # #

He says upon his entrance, "I do hope I'm not bothering you. I realize our conversation the other night at the gallery was cut short ... and I thought perhaps we could finish it over this bottle of wine."

He politely presents the bottle to me, which I accept. The young man consumes my living room: dimly lit, one candle burning that smells of cider, two reading chairs, a sofa imported from Berlin, cuckoo clock above a mantle, no fire in an empty hearth, dry bar, television and DVD player hidden behind the far-left wall. The place is clean, small in size, and perfectly home, he possibly assumes, which he is surely right about.

175

Now, I welcome him to have a seat on the imported sofa, which he accepts, and I admit to the stranger, "I'm glad you decided to stop by. I was thinking the same thing."

"The art buyers and press are hooligans," he utters, having no inflection of rudeness in his voice regarding his opinion of my career at the *Caller*. Some will agree I'm not part of the press. Rather, they will kindly surmise me as a biographer of sorts, scavenging Plimpton City to create short pieces regarding people's interesting lives, extraordinary hobbies, and unexpected talents.

Once he says what he does about the press, he immediately realizes his goof, and apologizes. "I'm terribly sorry, Cam. My bad. Sometimes I speak before I think. No offense to your job at the press."

I shake my head and reply while opening his bottle of burgundy, "There's no reason to apologize. I'm a biographer, which really doesn't mean I'm one of the hooligans at the paper. I don't chase after ambulances and gun shots."

He laughs at my comment, takes a glass of red wine from me, swirls it around in his left hand, sniffs its contents, and says, "Speaking of your writing. I just finished your piece on Milo Dixon, Plimpton City's wealthy architect."

I now laugh, and rattle off, "He's a complete bore. That man has a stick up his ass and needs to have a little bit of fun in life."

"So I've heard. But, he buys my drawings. I can't knock his taste in art."

I toast to his confession, swallow some wine down the back of my throat, decide to sit next to him on the sofa, take in his good looks again, and add, "My God, you're a beautiful man. If you weren't an artist, you could easily be a model."

#

Can a man such as Kal Fleet possess me with his eyes? Can he have an extraordinary power over someone like me?

And if he can possess me, why exactly will he choose do so when I already like him?

How easily I can become hypnotized by the sexy immortal if he will only try. The wait for such an event is exhausting. I'm ready whenever he is, of course.

# # # # #

In the next half hour, we cover my history: parents deceased; no current boyfriend; single for the last eighteen months; working on a short novella about Marilyn Monroe; I drive an H2; collect hardback biographies; refuse to use a Kindle; enjoy Chinese food; have lived in the Tudor for the past three years; believe the attic in the Tudor is haunted by a female ghost name Benjalita; enjoy the donuts at Freshly Baked Bakery on Rodale Drive in the city; mention my best friend, Steven; enjoy swimming opposed to running; believe the masters of art were Jackson Pollack and Andy Warhol; never eat sushi; pretend I like to camp in the woods; fear spiders; and like to go to bed reading a book every night, sometimes accidentally falling asleep with it over my face.

# # # # #

I assume he enjoys biting necks after his long moments of seduction? But who am I to assume, correct? It seems such a violent game between gentlemen, yet not a game at all. If the vampire will have me, I will be his – I promise.

# # # # #

After listening to my spill, he admits, "I read your book."

"My book?" I question, raising my right eyebrow with interest. No one knows about my book, which is a love story between two men called *September Covenant*. One-hundred-forty-five pages of complete drivel. A similar tome to the short story, "Brokeback Mountain." My first attempt at fiction. A small press in Pittsburgh picked up the short and decided to publish the piece. Very little recognition was shared for the novel after its publication. When editors, professors, or everyday Joe's on Amazon did read the short piece of writing, they all bitched with incredible fury, claiming the on-hundred-forty-five pages garbage, wordy boredom, and kindling for a fire. I confess now to my new friend, "I usually don't talk about that book."

"But why? I loved it," Kal says, blowing me away. "The relationship between the two men is most powerful and lethargically brilliant. Their soul searching for love at the beginning of the piece is engrossing. I couldn't put it down. In fact, I've always wanted to know why you didn't write a continuation of their love as married men."

# # # # #

Can he love? Do vampires feel this way? If such creatures are immortal, do they wish not to discover love for eternity? I wonder. I will always wonder.

Be mine, undead of the night.

I am yours.

Come and get me ... but only if you want me.

Take my heart, soul, or whatever else you want from me.

I beg of you.

# # # # #

I laugh at his comments regarding my book, attempting not to be rude. Kindly, I shake my head and admit, "I don't do much fiction anymore. Everything that I apply to paper is usually nonfiction these days."

"Perhaps I can change that," he strongly says and consumes two swigs of his wine, swallowing them down with speed and arrogance.

"How so?" I inquire, staring into his blue-blue eyes, captivated by his Hollywood looks and charm.

"Wait and find out."

"How long do I have to wait?"

"Not long."

"Really?" I ask, curious regarding his comments.

"Really," he repeats, finishes off his glass of wine and requests a second one.

# # # # #

By dawn, I will not see him again. Or will I? Is Kal Fleet a new version of vampire? A gentleman by day and a murderer by night? This is what I want to learn. This is what I desire while in his fiery presence, under his nocturnal spell.

# # # # #

Unintentionally, we have too much to drink. One bottle of wine turns into two ... three, and both us become sloppy. We sit and chat half the night away on either ends of my sofa. Topics include: jazz, coffee shops, flea markets, running shoes, politics, lawyers, religion, and growing up queer. Both of us spill our guts regarding who we are as adult men in our twenties. There is no touching, petting, or kissing. We are complete gentlemen on the sofa with puffy, ruby-red cushions that separate our worlds, a soft material wall that so easily divides our intimate attraction; one that each of us can break within a matter of seconds, having every intention of devouring the other man on the sofa with an unstoppable hunger, which unfortunately doesn't carry out.

# # # # #

Lust is his tool, like the great vampires of past years, his fathers and grandfathers. With the power of lust he can control me ... because he wants to control me. No one can tell me otherwise.

I wish to be controlled by him, if the truth be known. My neck is his. My body. My soul. Eternity can be ours, and I will forever be his partner but only if he decides to have me for his own – honestly.

# # # # #

Because he has far too much to drink, glass after glass of red wine, I explain to him, "You cannot drive home."

He giggles in a boyish manner with much radiated charm on the sofa, "I can drive."

"I think not. Don't be irresponsible. I have a spare room upstairs where you can spend the night. I won't even charge you."

He agrees; not that he really has a choice, since I won't allow him to leave the Tudor in his inebriated state.

Following our discussion where he will spend the night for his safety, I help him off the sofa, walk him upstairs, provide a new toothbrush for his use, a Sensor razor that has never been used, fresh towels if he wishes to shower tonight or in the morning, and assist him to bed.

Here, within a room of blues and greens, masculine colors created by the famed interior decorator, Lorenzo Caulfield, I kindly help remove the artist's shirt from his torso, dropping the cotton on a nearby reading chair. Within seconds, I study his sculpted torso of deep lines, glowing muscles, and firm pecs. My eyes travel up and down his smooth looking skin in the bedroom's dim light, and absorb his flesh in a hungry manner: his crafted shoulders, nicely designed abs, a dented navel, and the blond path of narrow hair that leads magically and deliciously into his denim-tight Diesels.

Of course I help him with his jeans, because it's a ploy for me to kiss him, which I prevent from happening, since I am a gentleman. Instead, I merely unbuckle his silver buckle, undo his denim buttons, almost touch the mound of glory beneath its rugged material, and politely tell him, "The rest is your gig. If I don't stop now ... I won't be able to stop at all."

"Who says you have to stop, Cam?"

His eyes tell me he is devilish and fun, a young man who enjoys the company of another young man to the fullest, and that he is not afraid to accomplish sexual events with my skin tonight. This doesn't transpire, though. Rather, I simply step away from his chiseled body, tell him to sleep well, and that I will see him in the morning over breakfast.

He doesn't sleep tonight, or any other night, I know. Why do I think he will? What kind of fool do I make myself cut to be? Shame on me for thinking that he will close his eyes and sleep. How absurd. Ridiculous. I know he cannot accomplish such a feat because of his immortal status.

I leave his bedroom with a nine-inch staff between my legs. Drunk and horny, I escape to my own bedroom, strip out of my clothes in a heated rush, fall onto my queen-size bed, and take matters into my own hands.

Because the past twenty minutes is so spine-clenching with homoerotic niceness, four strokes on my tool causes me to blow my load. One huff and puff escapes my lips in the darkness. Here, I whisper the artist's name as strings of oozy cream twirl out of my shaft's head and decorate my sweaty and heated torso. And here, within the folds of the October night, so close to a young man, but yet so far away, I collect each drop of gooey spent from my skin and devour it with my open mouth, satisfying my hunger to the fullest, and obey my thirst in the early morning hours – man-bliss discovered at last, wholly.

He smells my cock-juice, doesn't he? A vampire of such power desires nothing less than a strong-scented masculine aroma to waft past his flared nostrils. I've done my homework on Kal Fleet, and he craves white and sticky spunk from a

181

man's cock – mine. He longs for the scent and desires nothing less, even the blood vessels at my neck or on my inner thighs.

He lusts for me, and I want to be lusted for. I won't hide this from him. I can't. Sometimes a human wants to be naughty like this. I'm one these rare humans, I guess, and I'm quite prepared for his lust, and to be naughty with him, whatever it entails, of course.

Use me up, Mr. Fleet. Take advantage of me. Spoil me so with your nightly power and have you're with me. Perhaps I long for you as much as you long for me. But only time between us will tell, won't it?

Chapter 3 – Barely Logical

Kal is gone in the morning before I wake up; just as I suspect he will be. A very brief Dear John letter sits on the two-person table in my Martha Stewart-decorated kitchen:

Cameron –

Thank you for letting me spend the night. Have to run. Meetings today. Work today. I'll take a rain check on breakfast. Of course, I'll think about you.

– Kal

I read the short letter a dozen or more times over my cup of Turkish coffee. A feeling of questionable warmness collects within my solid chest; a disruptive emotion that I am not very familiar with and haven't felt for a very long time.

Yes, I have been in love before: Darden Koleski broke my heart after dating him for two years when I was twenty-one; the man couldn't keep his shaft out of other gentlemanly asses or throats. I was head over heels in lust/love/something for the greasy and dirty mechanic, and desired nothing less to spend the rest of my life with him.

His loss, right?

Right.

Dreams shatter, though, don't they? Darden was a player, I had learned throughout our relationship. Never did he have the intention of settling down with me. Instead, I became alone, rather cold toward men, cynical, and single for a very long time. Yes, I dated and date men, and slept/sleep with them for the mere pleasure of getting off. But never have I opened my heart to their wicked games of betrayal, ongoing lies, and questionable histories of man-play.

In truth, I feel differently about Kal Fleet. His sweet and charming demeanor proves that he is maybe different than the other men in my life that I have dated. Is he a Darden Koleski? Or, is he Mr. Magic? Prince Charming? The man of my dreams? This I will discover on my own, in due time. For now, I will keep my heart closed and uninhabited. If I find Kal to be the right man, labeling him Mr. Perfect within my world, perhaps I can open my heart for his use, and find what I have always wanted to carry out with another man – boyfriendhood, intimacy, or even something more ... immortality.

Things are missing from the spare room upstairs where he spent the night. Strange things have occurred during his very short stay. The two crosses are no longer inside the room – gone. The picture of Jesus is missing from the wall. The Bible is nowhere to be found. Are these traces of Kal's immortality and his vampiric ways? I believe so. How am I to think otherwise, of course? And what did he do with the items? Where are they? Is he honestly to blame for their removal?

I write for an hour ... two hours ... three hours, and work on my article about the artist: his history, his likenesses, why he has decided to draw instead of paint. Within the Tudor, I become occupied with his inspiring and interesting world, creating three hundred words ... four hundred words ... five hundred words for the Caller.

After writing I shower, shave, and inevitably dress. I make the drive in my H2 to Poller Street, become settled within my office at the *Plimpton City Caller*, and decide to make a cold call to a popular boxer from the area; my next biographical piece for the newspaper.

Noontime arrives in a flash, and a smiling Steven appears in Room 329, my office. He declares, "Lunch is on me today, buddy. We have big things to discuss."

I lift my head from my work and ask, "What kind of big things?"

"Save it for the road, pal. Let's go."

I rise from my chair and computer, find him in the bright-white hallway, and have him escort me to a Chinese lunch buffet called Pen Palace on Third Street, which is about two blocks away from the *Caller*.

Minutes later, after walking to the restaurant, we sit across from each other at a narrow table. Gongs and a concoction of flutes play from overhead speakers. Red candlelight flickers on the table between us. A female Chinese server takes our orders and vanishes, leaving us to discuss Steven's big things.

Over hot tea, he asks me, "Is it true about you and Kal Fleet?"

"What about us? What are you talking about?" I furrow my brow with question, unsure exactly what my boss/friend is attempting to find out. I know that Steven likes his gossip like every fag in the city, and I don't want to fuel his addiction in any way whatsoever.

"Did he spend the night with you last night?"

I roll my eyes. Plimpton City is so small when it comes to the rumor mill. It's even smaller when it comes to the Caller. I'm not at all surprised that he learns of my evening with Kal. In response, I nod my head and say, "Yes, the artist spent the

184

night at my Tudor, but not in the same bed with me. We had a little too much to drink while getting to know each other. It was all talk and no play. Most of it was work for my article. Very little of it, if any, was affectionate. How did you find this out, anyway?"

"Meredith," he confesses, smiling from ear to ear; his main source for gossip in our community, inside the *Caller*, and out.

Meredith Core works in accounting at the paper and lives across the street from me on Valley Way. She is the eyes and ears of the neighborhood. I really don't talk to the woman, since I don't have to, because she knows everything about my life, including last night's events with the artist.

"That woman is fowl," I tell Steven, admitting my dislike for Core. Vehemently, I shake my head and add, "I'd like to see her get fired and kicked off my street." It sounds rather rough exiting my lips, but it's the truth; shame on me.

"She says Kal left at six this morning. Unshowered. Rumpled clothes. Hair mussed. Tell me you hooked up with him, Cameron."

I shake my head and say, "Sorry to disappoint you, but I didn't. We merely got to know each other ... with our clothes on."

He seems to wilt in his seat with my uninteresting news, and confesses, "Such a pity. I was hoping you got laid. I can't remember the last time you fucked around with a guy. When was it, 1916? During the Cold War? Was JFK president?"

"You're being absurd," I tease, finding him whimsical and at play. Now, I take a sip of my hot tea: blackberry mixed with marmalade. Once the sip is swallowed, I tell him, "When I do get laid, you'll be the first to find out. I have you on speed dial in my cell phone."

"I appreciate that, pal. Honestly, I hope to hear from you instead of Meredith in accounting, if you know what I mean."

Again, I roll my eyes, nod, and reply, "I get it."

Within seconds, the Chinese server brings our orders to the table and we eat in silence for a few minutes, which leaves me to consume my sweet and sour chicken, and think about the artist again, semi-hard underneath the table.

Between bites, I ask the friend, "Do you believe in vampires, Steven?"

He shakes his head.

"Not in the slightest?"

"Of course not."

"You're Catholic, correct?"

He nods.

"Could vampires be considered dark angels in your religion?"

He thinks about this question for a moment, contemplates his answer, and finally replies, "I imagine so, not that I would feel comfortable discussing the topic with my priest."

I consume his comments, enjoy my meal, and think to myself: Vampires exist ... and I'm attracted to one.

# # # # #

Following lunch with Steven, back in the office, I receive a text message from Kal: Stopping by tonight after dark. Eightish. Hope you don't mind. Have something for you.

A devious smile forms on my lips and I hit him back with: Sevenish works better. Clothes optional this time. (Kidding.) He he.

K: LOL. I like you're sense of humor.

Me: Some guys hate it. You're in a league of your own.

K: What kind of league is that?

Me: One of these days I might have to show you.

K: LOL. Gotta run. Meeting to attend. I'll hit you later. See you tonight.

186

Once our texting gig ends, I realize I have crossed a fine line between professional biographer and artist. I should not have mentioned to Kal that clothes are optional at our next meeting. Becoming personal like this with him only allows a new door to open between us, and one that I might just not be comfortable with. The last thing I want to do is scare the man away, since we seem to get along so well. Plus, I still have the article to finish for the *Caller*. It's better to be on my best behavior and not prove to him that I have a naughty side which surely wants to peel him out of his artist clothes and have my way with his delicious looking skin that is possibly four-hundred years old or even older.

I try to finish my day at the newspaper, but produce nothing. The only thing I accomplish is: a second meeting with the middleweight boxer is rescheduled. Mr. Carlos Santiago of Middleboro, a neighboring community to Plimpton City, postpones our engagement because he is traveling out of town, attending a funeral in Seattle. Otherwise, I sit and stare at my Dell flat-screen, produce nothing, watch the clock tick by until five o'clock finally comes, and I wrap up my unproductive day.

Before leaving for the day, Steven pops his head into my office and announces, "I have two extra tickets to the Bills tonight, you interested?"

I sit at my desk, shake my head, and say, "I already have plans."

"What are you doing, Mr. Busy?"

"The artist is stopping by my house to drop something off."

"Like his cock in your mouth or ass?" Steven can be so vulgar at times, which I have never minded. In fact, I like his humor and never know what to expect from him next. The guy is like a boy inside a man's body: fun, eccentric, and witty.

187

"I'm not really sure. He just said he had something for me."

He points at me with an outstretched index finger and warns, "Remember ... I'm the first one to find out if you get laid or not."

I smile, and find him obnoxious but loved at the same time. "I'll remember."

"Have fun with him, *amigo*. And tell me all about it tomorrow, okay?"

"Will do," I promise, nod my head, and watch him vanish from the office doorway just as quickly as he arrived.

# # # # #

Kal plays a very strange game with me, doesn't he? Something that he likes to call mortal versus immortal. I sense this and become foolish, falling for his tricks. My guard comes down so easily regarding the strange man and his nightly ways. I morph into something warm, brilliantly-colored and flighty, but I really don't know why. What or who am I changing into? Honestly, I don't know. Will I ever identify myself from this moment on?

The game continues with me. His hiding, lurking, and watching me. Kal knows where I go, who I visit, who I accidentally bump into, and everything that happens in my world. I'm his toy, I realize. A token for his use. Something he enjoys and wants to call his own. Me.

# # # # #

The drive home is nauseating because of too much traffic. Ten minutes into my travels, and a thunderstorm takes over Plimpton City. It begins to rain, thunder, and lightning. As the tempest progresses, I steer the vehicle's wheel with caution, double my time, and feel as if I'm about ready to go mad. All of this subsides, though, when a flash of the artist's naked torso surfaces between my temples. All I can do is picture his buffed body, which consists of his concave/convex set of abs, a puckered navel, mounded pecs, firm nipples, and the treasure trail that leads to an ultimate prize for my selfish taking. Driving slowly, edging my way south, outside of the city, I whisper to the rain-splattered windshield, "Kal, you're one sexy motherfucker. Just what I like in a man. It would be nice if you felt the same way about me. Only time will tell, I guess. We'll see."

Once at home, I shower, dress for tonight's planned visit with the artist, and eat dinner: leftover spaghetti and meatballs with a side salad discovered in the refrigerator. Now, feeling nervous that Kal will be arriving in less than an hour, I tidy up the place a bit: fluff pillows, sweep the kitchen floor, dust the coffee table, empty the garbage in the kitchen, and organize the remote controls on the coffee table. Once this operation is carried out, I decide to have a glass of white wine to calm my nerves, have a seat on my German sofa, cross my legs, and wait patiently for my guest to arrive.

As expected, he arrives shortly after seven this evening; it's still raining out, and he's wet from head to toe. In his arms is a flat, paper-wrapped package the size of a desk's blotter. Upon his entrance inside the Tudor, I see that he sports a pair of tight jeans, polo shirt that clings to his designed chest, and the same belt I helped him undo during his previous visit. To my surprise, the artist sets his package down, hugs me, nestles his chest to my chest, and says, "You smell great."

"Ash soap. I love it," I say, and unfortunately pull away from him, even when he feels as if he belongs against my body for the rest of our lives; such a pity how the gods play devious tricks on humans like this.

"I like it. You'll have to ..."

(What? Shower with him? Go soap shopping with him? Let me lather it all over his back, his front, and between his legs? All of these what ifs scurry throughout my mind as I imagine our bodies collected together in time; shame on me for drifting.)

" … tell me what brand it is, and I'll pick up a bar."

So much for undressing and showering together. Damn. Instead, I tell him the name of the soap, its affordable price, and where I usually purchase it. Now, I welcome him into my homey abode, listen to the October thunder and rain outside, and offer him a glass of white wine, which he kindly accepts, although I know he prefers red, since it resembles human blood.

# # # # #

His eyes. I can feel them watching me when he's not even around: peeping in on my activities; observing my movement; studying my whereabouts; observing everywhere I go. Kal is around me, yet he isn't anywhere to be seen or found.

# # # # #

Following two glasses of white wine, insisting we will not become drunk again together, he presents the flat, blotter-size, paper-wrapped package to me.

"What is this?" I stand in the living room and hold the item with both hands by its hard edges.

Thunder and lightning turn hectic and untamed outside. Inside, I feel cozy and safe in the artist's presence, exactly the way a young man might feel in the company of his boyfriend, a mysterious stalker, or blood sucker of the night.

"Open it," he instructs in a cordial manner.

I listen, glowing from ear to ear because of his kindness, good looks, and how he proves relentless regarding seeing me, infiltrating my evenings with his potent visits and hypnotizing behavior.

It's a painting of course; I know this as soon as he arrives. Carefully, I unwrap the fourteen-by-eighteen-size gift and see a pencil drawing of a man's torso under glass. The frame is

190

walnut in color. At the bottom right is Kal's signature, yesterday's date, and a title: Cameron #1.

"Thank you," I utter, studying the pencil drawing's fine lines that make up the torso's abs, shaded areas under the chest's arms, tiny sprigs of hair between its plump pecs, and sculpted navel. Half of me conceives Kal to be barely logical in gifting me such a prize. The selfish side of me, though, will cling to it for years to come, having no interest in ridding the art piece from my life.

"Of course, it's your chest, Cameron. Although I have never seen you without your shirt on, this is how I imagine it looks."

I swallow saliva down the back of my throat, study the drawing again, and confess, "It's pretty close. I love it. Thank you." I sound ridiculous, completely taken aback by his generosity and talent, and honestly have no idea what exactly to say to him in return.

He replies with a fake punch to my left shoulder in a boyish manner, and adds, "Maybe one of these days you'll take your shirt off for me, and I can sketch the real thing."

I blush. Why not? I like the guy and feel I can't hide it any longer. Besides, the comments and gift he now shares with me proves that he likes me, and my skin, crossing his own line between artist and biographer. In response to his suggestion, I carelessly rattle off, "Kal, I'd be glad to take my shirt off for you anytime you want me to."

The man removes the drawing from my hands, places it on the floor in a safe area of the living room, and kindly replies, "I was hoping you would say that."

I see his sharp and pointed teeth for the very first time: elongated white structures within the man's beautiful mouth; cutting devices that look poker-sharp and without gaps; canine-like teeth that frighten me a touch, yet I find them intoxicating, and can't pull my stare away from their jagged structures.

We celebrate his masterpiece over a last slice of chocolate-almond cheesecake that I discover in the fridge. With two forks, an onyx-colored dessert plate, and the living room's ambiance, we sit on the German sofa, face each other, and share the single slice of chilled food. Between bites, he admits, "I like hanging out here. It's like my own little club. I was hoping you would give me a yearly pass of sorts."

I laugh at this, enjoy his company, wit, and charm. I can't remember the last time I had so much fun with a guy, particularly with his clothes on while sharing cheesecake with me. Surprising him, I admit, "You're welcome on my playground anytime you want, especially if you give me drawings under glass."

He chuckles, taking another bite of the cheesecake. In doing so, a morsel of the cool dessert hangs at the right corner of his mouth. Seeing it rest against the edge of his smooth lip, I say, "Hold still."

"What?"

"You have cheesecake on your lip."

"Where?"

"Here," I say, and remove the dessert from his face with my right index finger, sliding the morsel of goodness between my own lips, savoring it like prized saliva or something more rare, like his bittersweet cock-juice.

He watches me lick my index finger and prattles with a wink, "Cam, I want to know something."

"Shoot," I say, savoring his cohabitation within my living room, his generous gift, and the soft soul that I believe he has.

"I want to know if you'll go on a date with me."

I finish licking my finger, lock eyes with him in a sultry manner, feel bubbly inside, determine that he's completely serious, nod my head, and answer, "Yes, Kal. I think I would enjoy that. Where and when?"

# # # # #

I remember how cold his skin feels at this tender moment shared between us: chilly, lifeless, and firm. When I draw my finger along his lip, my soul shutters and something shrinks within me. Darkness is touched with red light. Skin from a different world. Lips from a dank abyss. He's not human, I determine. The man is certainly immortal. He feeds like an animal in the night. He's different and of the undead. I sense this, comprehending his reality and immortality to the fullest. Really, I do.

Chapter 4 – A Victim

November 1. Kal picks me up on Valley Way in his Ford Escape on time, and tells me that we are going to have the time of our lives tonight, even if the weather is rather shitty and not on our side.

Snow is expected to fall within the next two hours. A total of eight inches is to line the streets of Plimpton City by dawn. The current temperature is a chilly twenty-nine degrees, and the ground is already starting to become hard with a pre-winter coolness. The wind is rather prickly, icy with a hunger, and will most surely keep us indoors this evening.

He's a complete gentleman, if the truth be shared. He arrives at my Tudor with a box of imported chocolates and a tiny card that he tells me to read later, which I do.

(Cameron, you're very special to me. I adore you. Shame on me for being mad about you.)

Now, I collect the items, thank him, kiss the man on his right cheek, place the small gifts on the coffee table in my living room, feel warm and fuzzy inside my stomach, nervous about our evening date, and question him in a rather fun manner, "Who says chivalry is dead?"

# # # # #

He's dead, isn't he? I know it. I sense it. He smells of death, even if he makes me feel so alive. He lives on the blood of jocks, seeking them out at night. He's my eternity, destiny

193

... something. Kal Fleet is not a human. He is not mortal. The man is something different, untamed, and seductively intense. A certain being that I learn to crave and only wish to become closer to – honestly.

Cold is found when I'm in Kal's presence. It's a frigidness that I don't fully understand. No one is as frozen as he is. No one that I know is nocturnal like him. And no one ... lusts for me more. If opposites attract, we are a match made in his dark heaven. If either of our gods align our souls in the universe, we will forever be together, inseparable, faithful, and devoted to no one except for each other, blissfully and wholly.

We dine at Padilla's on Mylo Street outside of Plimpton City. The restaurant specializes in Spanish cuisine. Ricardo, a very dapper and handsome man from Madrid, seats us at the window, claiming the November evening enchanting as it begins to snow. Here, across from each other at a two-person table, we order saffron paella with shrimp, stuffed tomatoes with quinoa and pearl onions, and yellow-orange flan for dessert.

Because Kal has to drive, he drinks one glass of sangria, claiming he will not become drunk. I follow suit, enjoy a single glass, and ask for a cup of strong coffee thereafter.

Our discussion throughout the evening entails: city artists, cubism, teaching art, writing biographies, our likeness for cats opposed to dogs, the wind that slaps against the glass where we sit, and recent vacations to Aruba (me) and Romania (him).

The dialogue between us is simple and hardly at all challenging. There is not a single moment between us that offers the sound of crickets rubbing their legs together. Silence is not discovered at the table. In fact, the complete opposite occurs. Neither of us can hold back during our

194

shared conversation, which allows the evening to zoom by, and a sad end to our dessert.

When we bundle up in our wool coats and H&M scarves, leaving Padilla's, he says to me, "I have a little surprise in store for us."

"What kind of surprise?" I'm excited and feel like a queer eighteen-year-old in a college locker room filled with football players.

"Wait and find out."

"You're up to no good," I tease him.

"Perhaps," he admits, dots my cheek with a kiss, and we exit the Spanish restaurant hand in hand, escaping into the night and its feisty cold.

Perhaps I fall for the man too quickly and need to pull back a bit. Relationships are dangerous, even the short ones. I feel safe with the artist, though, almost completely unharmed. Freely, my guard is lowered and, if he desires to, he can hurt me, which I doubt that he will. In due time, I will learn an answer regarding his strangeness: tonight, the following night, or sometime soon. I'm not really sure when the dangers of this encounter and our romantic events will harm me, but I'm well aware that they will, and that I'm always prepared for danger in the company of another man, particularly an artist who seems so suave and sweet, one who claims to be afraid of the sun, and a hardcore gentleman with the most handsome smile of sharp teeth.

Cautiously, he drives us through the building tundra, heading toward The Chandler House. Kal makes a joke that I'm a Russian princess escaping St. Petersburg at the turn of the twentieth century, which makes me laugh.

"Someone has to wear the diamond tiara in this new relationship," I admit, toying with him in return.

Once we arrive at The Chandler House, he parks his Escape, retrieves me from the passenger seat, and tells me, "How about a winter wonderland walk?"

"I'm game," I answer him and beam a smile. Crazily, I climb out of the Escape, feel his body semi-wrap around my own, comprehend that his entire frame is like ice, and we head to the snowy courtyard, behind the gallery's three-floor structure, seeking privacy and a romantic stroll in the November cold.

Why does he like me? This is what I want to know while I take in the snow-covered oaks, maples, sleeping gardens, and the cobblestone walkway of the enchanting and private courtyard that reminds me of Shakespearian scene in a tragedy. Light in this serene area is a blue-yellow hue that floats, dives, and spirals around us. Snow blows against our faces, shoulders, and covered torsos.

What exactly does he want with me? Does the artist intend on using my skin for his personal needs and have plans to ditch me? Is he building up my hopes that we are actually compatible with each other? Is the man seducing me, willed to blow his creamy load against my torso, in my face, or deep down the plunging length of my throat while he applies his sharp teeth to the veins along my neck? What is his game? What is tonight really about? This is what I want to know, desire, and contemplate as we walk hand-in-hand through the enchanting and snowy courtyard. And this is what I determine to uncover; the ultimate truth behind his questionable niceness.

We sit on a wrought-iron bench with our backs to the plundering snow, chilled to the bone. He snuggles against me, wraps one of his arms securely around my shoulder, and pulls me against his torso, attempting to keep me warm. Together, here in this magical place, an imagined czar's palace of sorts in some queer fairy tale that hovers around us, we chatter. He says, "This is amazing tonight. I'm having the time of my life."

"And I'm freezing my balls off," I admit, not really joking.

He laughs, but not in a bad way. The man insists on teasing me whenever he has the opportunity. Now, he pulls me closer to him, and confesses, "I'm beginning to like you a lot, Cam. What do you think about that?"

"You just want in my pants," I say, being quite serious. "Once this happens, you'll dump me for a new biographer."

He bursts with a hearty chuckle and says, "If I wanted your cock and ass, I would have had them by now."

He's right, raising a good point. I would have dropped my pants for him on that first night we met inside The Chandler House. How easily he could have sneaked me into a janitorial closet, yanked the fabric down that covered my private parts, and indiscreetly had his way with me; I surely wouldn't have deterred such a promiscuous action since I found him attractive, then and now.

I admit to him, "If you intend to hurt me, toying with my heart, tonight is the night to do so. Have sex with me, dump me in the morning, and forget that this nice entanglement between us never existed. What do you say?"

"You're crazy if I'm leaving you now," he confesses. "I rather find you appealing on many different levels. You're the only guy that I can really talk to. The only man that listens to me … and the only one who wants to sleep with me just for me."

It's my turn to laugh, and I add, "How do you know I don't want to sleep with you because you're just an artist?"

"The look in your eyes explains that you're not that type of guy. You have a sincere gaze in your pupils that I decipher as warm and kind."

"And an evildoer who wants to fuck you over my German sofa," I kid, and laugh out loud.

"That, too, my friend," he whispers with a sparkle of desired lust within his own eyes, a mixture of blue sapphire with the white of the falling snow.

"I know about you," I whisper.

He raises an eyebrow in an adorable manner. "What do you mean by that?"

197

"Your ways. How you feed on young men. Your immortality."

He laughs at me. "You're silly, Cam."

"Do you intend to feed on me?" I inquire, nervous and unsure of this evening's events.

He shakes his head. "If you want to know the truth, I don't. I adore you, Cam. You're very much a part of me lately. I will never hurt you. I promise. Never."

As expected, we now kiss. Neither of us is apprehensive, of course, and desire the other in full. He is the first to lean forward and connect his lips with mine. The kiss is breathtaking and rather chilly at the same time. Although he is frozen, we seem cozy on the wrought-iron bench in the courtyard. Together, we become bonded by mouths, teeth, and tongues. The kiss is sloppy but wanted, pent desire that is now expressed. It is a means of our survival in the wintry, November night on this spectacular date with a man I tend to crave. An empowering kiss that will surely change the upcoming winter season into a blistery spring of random likeness and attraction.

How long do we stay entwined on the courtyard bench? Ten minutes? Twenty minutes? I'm really not sure. Our kissing is long and heated; a combining of our stored desires finally released; a link between man and man in the freshly falling snow. It is November bliss of the night that we cannot control, carry out with greed, and fall helplessly under each other's queerly spells.

Of course, he tries to push his fingers/palms under my wool jacket and against my cashmere sweater. The artist's desire for my flesh is uncontrollable and fully uncapped. No longer do we behave ourselves on this proper date between professionals. Instead, lust is discovered, the need to become naked, and a male-with-male bond is craved between us.

I pull away from him before he removes my wool coat and unbuckles my belt. The wintry night in the courtyard is no place for our intimacy to be carried out, not when each of us have an abode to bring the other to, where it is cozy-warm and shelter from the teasing and tempestuous wind. Here, I say to him, "Your apartment is closer than my Tudor ... Why don't you take me home where we can finish this?"

He agrees, rises from the bench, and tugs me through the windswept snow. At his side, we return to his Escape in the blistery snowstorm and find safety from the November storm.

Protected by his vehicle's metal and windows, we travel through the night to his apartment and have every intention of spending the next few hours together on his bed, over his sofa, along his bathroom floor, or against his kitchen wall, minus our clothes.

I want him to bite me, I realize. Does this sound ludicrous? Am I insane? Have I lost my mind? Why do I long for his pointed teeth, which are probably razor sharp and can tear meat apart with ease? Why do I desire his mouth to sink into my skin and so easily tear open my flesh like an animal? How generous he can be, spoiling me so by plunging his teeth into one of my bare thighs, along the splay of my neck, a tender shoulder, devouring my flesh in full, and taking what he wants from me – because I will give it to him, truthfully, I will.

Men seem to take things from me, don't they? I assume Kal Fleet is no different. The bottom line is rather simple: I won't stop him if he tries anything conspicuous, yet enlightening, with my flesh. Honestly, I won't.

Chapter 5 – Lust-Motion

Apartment K-2 at 32922 Lincoln Avenue is nothing what I perceive it to be. The walls are painted a bright-white hue, bare of decorations. Pencil drawings do not garnish end tables or Kal's coffee table. The place seems vague of life; a canvas awaiting paint, the application of charcoal, or construction paper cutouts. Honestly, the abode is rather clinical looking and resembles a padded cell for a psychological defunct civilian. He does have furniture, but very little. Instead, I learn rather clearly and surprisingly that he enjoys his white space, which lacks knickknacks, anything personal, no hue, and is completely obsolete of emotion.

Without any surprise on my part whatsoever, I learn that his bedroom is decorated the exactly same way as the rest of his apartment: white on white on white on white. Color is lost. The room resembles something out of a science fiction novel or movie. A cocoon of sorts that seems eerily simple, yet breathtakingly clean and soothing at the same time.

To no avail, wherever we are, whatever remote whiteness we have entered into together, our bodies are united with yet another wholesome kiss. And soon afterward, my clothes are ripped free from my body by the artist's unstoppable hunger. My white shirt is stripped off my torso and becomes lost inside his bedroom. My jeans are pulled free from my body and dropped to the floor. My Unico briefs are ripped away from my middle and ...

Now, unable to wait a single second longer, he will apply his incisors or bicuspids to my skin and dreamily have his way with me. The stranger will pull me into his dark-dark world and consume what he wants to take from me. Every man has his desires, and my date is no exception to this rule. The important and most basic question is rather elementary, though: When will he whisk me from mortality into immortality? I wonder. Perhaps I will always wonder ... until his desirable taking of me, his spoiling of my skin finally happens between us.

My body is pushed to his all-white, king-size bed and he hungrily dives against my middle. The young artist's mouth meets my center, devouring all of my nine-inch poker with his hefty appetite. In doing so, grunts and groans escape the monster between my legs. His head bobs ferociously up and down on my post, pleasuring the both of us to our fullest capacities. Gags ensue as he eats my rod, pushing his throat over its inflated extension. Breath is lost for the two of us.

Again and again, he thrusts his throat over my stick, gags on the meat, pulls away, and continues this endless process for the next five ... eight ... thirteen minutes, until he finally comes off the shaft for air and sanity.

To no avail, our intimate connection does not stop here. His hunger for my skin continues as he flips me over, spreads my legs apart on the bed, and dives his face into my bottom. What transpires between us is nothing less than homoerotic passion: a sexual bond between his mouth and my bottom s slit. Contently, the younger man delves his tongue into my core, pulls away, and delves in again. Concurrent licks and laps to my man-crack are shared. Murmurs exit the man's mouth behind me. A slap is applied to my right butt-cheek as he grows excited at my rear, into his mouthy gig and our combined flesh.

How does he not break open my skin and mutilate it with his teeth? Doesn't my strong and masculine scent alone toy with his longing and prompt the deviant to rip my flesh to shreds? How can he hold his emotions and desire together when I am so fresh, untouched by sin, and weakly available for his needs?

I am surely one to negotiate sexual positions regarding the men I covet. This doesn't occur with the artist, though. Kal has a mind and will of his own, destined to please the both of us with his power-bottom antics. To prove such details, I am rolled over again and stare up at the white ceiling. Three hefty north and south tugs are shared with the device, which keep the stick hard.

Beneath his work, perspiring on the bed, and completely windblown by his ravenous behavior, I mutter his name with deep satisfaction. My head spins with accurate dizziness. Oxygen is lost, discovered, and lost again. Here, I become his toy, a play-thing for the man and his desire. My body is his playground for fun, a means of his superior bliss ... heated sex between our queer structures, and everything we desire to mesh our different worlds together as one.

In a matter of seconds, I become his mountain, and he climbs overtop me. The vampire stands on the bed, which leaves me to stare up at his naked goodness: thick thighs are layered in a fine blond hair; droopy balls swing between his legs; an eight-inch shaft is upright, cut, and veined with purple-blue lines of delicious beauty; rolled abs; dented navel; mounded pecs with solid nipples; broad shoulders; corded neck; a wide grin on his euphoric-induced looking face is shared.

He hisses in the night because of our connection. The monster begins to roar with pain and pleasure as our bodies align and ...

Beneath him, staring up at his beauty, I hold my shaft upright with three fingertips and a thumb for his wanted use. "Ride me," escapes my mouth, instructing the younger man. I practically beg him to carry out my petty but desired demand. "Ride me now, Kal. Do it ... I can't wait any longer."

To no avail, as if I'm in complete control, even though I realize I'm not, the artist lowers himself onto my pole, bends his knees, and pivots his tight and hairless man-hole overtop my stick, ready for its gratifying use. In doing so, he whispers down to me, grinning from ear to ear yet again, entranced by our naked union, "Here goes, Cam. Keep it hard for me, guy."

Indeed, I keep it hard for him: all nine inches of its uncut goodness, which he promptly sits on. To my utter surprise, gasping under his weight with hearty breaths, in search of an anecdote to prevent a phase of dizziness to sweep throughout my consciousness, the artist takes all of my inches on as he lowers himself down and over my tool. One ... two ... three ... five ... seven ... all nine inches enter his system, which he begins to ride up and down, which he rises and falls on, which he takes inside his system as if it nothing more than a slim finger. He becomes wicked on my rod, rides it in a brisk manner, and bucks his center with the swollen mass ... up and down ... up and down ... up and down.

Lost beneath him, tucked away in a state of confusion and numbness, I feel ripples of serenity wave throughout my core. Every nerve in my body is on full alert, absorbing his ass-pleasure, perhaps desiring the motion to never cease. I buck into his tight center with upward hip-thrusts, barely capable of moving beneath his controlling weight. Bang after bang pumps his epicenter, assisting in his rodeo-pleasure with my cock. Together, we work in synchronized motion, rising and falling, creating a compelling story of young men in lust-motion, continuously.

"Faster!" escapes his mouth in a flurry. "Harder, Cam! ... Stick me with your meat! ... Don't hold back!" He becomes a physical and eager brute above me in our sexual dance; not that I mind. He lifts off my post, falls onto it, lifts off again, and continues this aggressive action with my upright and hard gauge, willing me to blow my load.

"Ride it," I chant beneath his falling and rising torso as he stands on the bed.

He does, proceeding with his north and south motion, bucking himself with my club, pulverizing his rear, and relishing every moment of our queer rhythm.

Shockingly, he comes first. His right hand finds the stick between his legs, and he begins to stroke it up and down as he processes his manly joyride. He utters a monstrous moan ... two moans ... three moans, and plays with the puffed muscle between his legs. Feisty hand-work develops. Two fist-thrusts ... three ... four occur until the blond man's face turns a billowing red and ...

Cream bursts from his log, which covers my torso, fills my navel, and splashes against my hard-packed pecs. Long and wide splashes of the ooze flies out of his hose and covers my skin as the bloodsucker continues to ride my horse with his closed eyes, having his mouth ajar, and gasps for air. His elation is suddenly discovered, prosaically, and without holding it back a second longer. I am washed-down with his man-seed and decorated by the sticky sap.

Not even a minute later, my needs are cared for in a masculine manner. He continues to stay atop my flag, rides me until I find my orgasm, and readies me to explode in his ass.

At the very last second when my cheeks fill with air, release, and inflate again ... at the very last physical motion when a wave of man-enchantment swirls within my stomach and pecs ... at the very moment when consciousness becomes unconsciousness and I am ready to explode my pent cargo ... the artist pulls off of me with superhuman speed. He kneels on the bed. One of his palms ... no, this is not correct ... both of his palms find the veined and pulsing rod between my sweaty thighs and begin to rock it up and down with chaotic tugs. One ... two ... three hefty pulls occur and ...

I blow my load with such zeal. Cam-liquid shots out of my dick like an oil rig. White globs of the ooze ejaculate with such ease from my spike and effortlessly splat against the handy artist's cheeks, chin, and forehead, which leaves me spent, breathing hard, and semi-windblown.

# # # # #

Post-sexed, entrapped in his muscular arms, we laugh like little boys. Here, we whimsically discuss his spectacular ride, my pelvic thrusts, and both of our explosions. And here, inside his white on white on white apartment, we decide to shower together, soap each other down, kiss under the hot spray, rinse, and eventually dry each other off. Within a half hour, we are back in his white bed inside his white bedroom, side by side. Naked, facing each other on our sides, night present, our first date almost over, he rubs the base of my chin with two fingertips, and asks, "Stay the night."

"Trapped here with you," I admit.

"Only if you want to be trapped."

"I do," I confess, seal my lips to his, and decide rather unpredictably to start another sex-romp with the man, except this time we decide that he'll be fucking me.

What does he plan to do with a mortal like me? What does his sexual gig entail? Is the guy using me, and if so, why? I don't understand why he is connected to me. Why is there a magnetic bond between us? What does he really want from me? Should I know? Or like his other victims, am I to discover this answer in the future, only for myself?

Chapter 6 – Boxer of Darkness

November 6. At approximately ten-thirty in the morning, I sit with Carlos Santiago, the middleweight boxer, whom I intend to interview for the next hour, or longer, designing a biography/story for the *Caller*. Latin American men tend to be beautiful with their cocoa brown-colored skin and romantic looking eyes, I believe. Carlos is no different, of course. The man is rock-solid handsome from head to toe, a Panamanian with robust muscles and tattoos of Mary and Jesus on his biceps. I note that his right eyebrow is pierced, and gold rings decorate his fingers like a mobster. The man wears a tight T-shirt that exemplifies his buffed chest and tapered waist. Beneath the cotton is a torso to die for, which is model-perfect for *Men's Health* or *Men's Fitness*.

Of course, I thank him for seeing me and politely shake the man's firm hand while standing.

"My pleasure, sir," he replies in his thick English/Spanish, winking at me.

"Please, call me Cam."

"Yes," he says and nods his head in agreement.

"Shall we begin?" I ask, sit again, take in his handsome and rough looks, and enjoy my time with the boxer.

"Absolutely, Cam. Begin."

Before I can start my selected questions, prying into his life that the readers of the *Caller* are interested in, Steven taps on my office door, pops his head in, and apologizes for his rude entrance/interruption. When my friend/boss slips into the room, he carries two plastic bottles of Evian water with him. He passes one of the chilled bottles to the boxer and the other one to me. "To wet your whistles," he says to both of us.

"Thank you," I reply across my desk.

"Gracias," Carlos beams his rough boy-smile, which is easy to fall for and cause gay men to drop to their knees with open mouths.

I know perfectly well why Steven carries out this unannounced visit into my office: to allow the boxer to become his eye candy for the rest of the day, absorbing the man's good looks, firm body, and his rough boy-charm. Steven is a whore this way, adoring handsome and pretty men, consuming them with his eager eyes and unstoppable delight. The journalist is a pig of sorts, candid regarding his sexual longing for men, particularly chiseled athletes from Panama.

As Steven excuses himself from my office, he discreetly blows me a kiss without the boxer seeing. I begin my questioning with Carlos, carefully review notes in front of me, and choose wisely what I wish to ask him.

The boxer sips his bottle of water, leans back in his chair, spreads his legs, and shows me the mound of denim between his thighs.

My mind strays a bit because of his action, and I imagine he's huge underneath the material: eight inches soft and twelve inches hard, uncut and veined. I also imagine he sprays cock-juice like a fire hose: an unending gush of white and sticky load released from his physically fit body.

I eventually clear my throat, attempting to take control of myself and the interview. Again, I study the notes in front of me and ask, "You lived in Miami as a boy, correct?"

He nods, smiles, and admits many things to me: he's thirty years old, and happy with his life; he was a bastard child; he doesn't know his father; he lives with his mother, Rosalita, whom he protects; his younger brother was murdered in New York City while watching a Mets game; he enjoys swimming; he wants to see Spain before he dies; he has an upcoming boxing gig in January, another championship; he doesn't like to read; he taught himself to read, write, and speak English; he wants to have children, preferably three boys; never has he slapped a woman, nor treated one badly; respect regarding the people around him is his key philosophy, which is followed up with love; he goes to church every Sunday morning with his mother; he's interested in women and wants to get married in the future, but for now, he likes playing the field with both women and men.

We discuss many events in his life: how he feels about winning his middleweight class; whom he seeks out for advice regarding his moves in the ring; who is his favorite boxer; whom does he want to fight, and why; can't he tell me one of his favorite moves in the ring; how much time does he spend during his week boxing/practicing; when does he have time for himself; what are his hobbies; other questions.

Carlos is very informative, and interviews well. He never stumbles over or through my questions. He never questions me in return. His appeal and likeness is his honesty. The man is suave and a gentleman to a fault, which he admits to me. He tells me he's a flirt, and likes to be sexual. He admits that he likes lust and love, and abhors labels. The boxer clarifies with me that we are to enjoy women and men without stigmas. He doesn't consider himself bisexual. Instead, he feels he's an ambiguous lover.

Other topics are shared: he tells me his weakness is alcohol, which he stays away from because he can easily become an alcoholic; never does he swear; never does he lie; he's prompt for every meeting, hating to be late for anything; he's sort of a clean freak; he doesn't do drugs; he likes *Law & Order* reruns, but he really doesn't have any time to watch television; he's not currently dating anyone special; he likes to dance; he enjoys history; and never has he broken the law, except for two speeding tickets when he was eighteen years old.

He hints of being nocturnal, similar to Kal Fleet. The man seems apprehensive at first regarding his immortal and blood-sucking ways. I sense that he's violent and everlasting. For as innocent and kind as Kal seems, the boxer is his opposite. The man's sinewy size startles me, which proves his strength. No matter what he says about his suave and smooth personality, nothing about him makes me feel at ease. The boxer appears dangerous, without a soul, and not at all squeamish about hurting me.

He's a vampire. He eventually discloses this detail to me. From the Mal Rosa Assemblage, a gathering of young men and women from Panama who practice cult-like methods and human sacrifices by biting their victims' necks. He says he can read my mind and move quickly, darting from one place to the next with ease, without the human eye even noticing. He fears garlic, crucifixes, and cannot be seen in mirrors. A true vampire, like the rest of his people.

"Is it true?" I inquire, taking mental notes, unable to add them to my article in the future because readers will think I'm a quack.

"Every word of it is true. Do you doubt me?"

"Of course not. I wouldn't dare."

"That's a very smart move, Cameron."

The boxer flirts with me, winking occasionally. He massages one of his pecs through his tight tee. Carlos says endearments in Spanish, calling me handsome, sexy, and very nice to look at. The man says to me, "If we were lovers, I would roll the tip of my tongue along your spine, to the back of your neck, around to your ear, and whisper sweet things to you." He adds, "I would hold your naked skin to my flesh and drive my weight into you … just the way you want to be driven." Again, he shares endearments with me, whispering amorous things in his native language.

The man becomes quite ballsy with me, which sort of leaves me uncomfortable across from him. He tells me I have the most beautiful eyes and hair he has ever seen on a man. He wants to smell me and have our bare chests align with simple beauty. The boxer slides one of his palms to the center of his denim, rests it between his massive thighs, and begins to rub his protrusion of material-covered cock. He glares at me with sexual fire in his look, visually undresses me, and wants my flesh against his outstretched tongue, bare chest, naked tattoos, or his unclothed prick. Carlos desires nothing more than our bodies to meet within my office, man-pressed-against-man with our clothes off, naked, and connected by private parts and lust, fulfilling his Panamanian desire for me.

It's an utter shock for me to watch him rise from his seat with a thunderous motion. Here, upright and positioned across from my desk, he rolls both of his hands between his legs, firming up his denim-coated tool. The interviewee claims in his thick English/Spanish that my office is too hot, and he removes his skin-tight T-shirt, dropping it the floor. Here, his muscular torso is exposed with its mounded pecs and abs and many tattoos. A gold, upside down cross hangs from his neck, his faith exposed, and the semi-naked anti-Christian opens up his private and sexual and religious world to me. Within these four walls that I call my office, Room 329 at the *Plimpton City Caller*, the boxer says something about wanting to see my chest, and for me to take my shirt off. He confesses to me that he wants to take advantage of my skin, that he feels we are sexually compatible for each other.

"Never," I whisper, shaking my head. "I can't."

He winks at me, blows me a masculine kiss, pinches one of his firm nipples, continues to rub his denim V-area between his legs with his other hand, and replies, "But you want to, Cam. I can see it in your eyes."

"No," I whisper, barely able to get the word out. In truth, I'm far too nervous to have wood under my desk. This flirting and sexual act by the boxer is certainly not what the interview with him is supposed to turn into. I'm completely caught off guard by his sexual forwardness, desire, and his minor striptease act. I really don't know what to say or how to react to his verbiage or cock-rubbing. Nor do I know how to respond to his winking and kiss-blowing. Yes, the man is attractive. But no, I will not cross this sexual line with him because I fully enjoy my current company with the artist. Of course, he is well-built and a beautiful athlete with a massive tool between his legs; this doesn't mean I want to fuck him, though. Again, I say, "No," shake my head, and attempt to deter his feisty advancements.

This absurd and forward violation that he performs during his interview must come to an end, and soon. He is obviously horny, toying with me as if I am nothing more than a puppet. The man keeps looking at me with nothing less than desire and a keen sense to strip me out of my clothes. I realize I am his likeness, attraction, a meaty somebody he can play with, even if I really don't want to play with him in return.

How utterly shocking it is for me that he unzips his denim and exposes himself within my office. Inch after inch rises up and out of his middle like some one-eyed dragon. A stroke with his right hand on the flesh-stick occurs ... two strokes ... three strokes, and he says something absurd like: "It's a very nice cock, isn't it? I'm sure you want to taste it, right?"

What escapes my mouth is rather rude, but I am in no position to give a damn. I direct all of my attention to his bare chest and the extension of meat between his legs. Here, I utter to the athlete without even attempting a single smirk of approval regarding his pony show, "Carlos, what's going on here?"

Another nipple is pinched on his well-built and tattooed chest. More strokes happen with his upright prick. A smile lingers on the man's face, unembarrassed by his actions. He blows me a kiss and ... a single drop of ooze leaks out of his cock's smooth head. When this occurs, he peers into my eyes and confesses, "Mr. Temple, you know perfectly well what is happening between us."

I shake my head and plead, "You're being ridiculous. Put your dick away. I'm a taken man. Shame on you."

He laughs at me, enjoying his gig. Following his laughter, he shakes the piece of meat between his thighs to the right and left, and says, "You want this cock lodged into your ass, and you know it."

"That isn't an option. I have someone very important in my life at the moment. He's the only one I want to shove things inside my ass." I sound older and wiser and hold my ground with regards to the boxer's pushy behavior. Part of me wants to call the building's security and have him removed from my office. The greedy part of me objects to this action, since I still want an article from the man, and for the *Caller*.

As I have this ordeal within my mind, tossing it to and fro between my temples, he huffs with excitement, begins to jack himself off in front of me, releases an animal-like grunt from his lips, and replies in a bold and brazen voice, "Cameron, I think we've overdone it with the pleasantries. I highly suggest you drop your, khakis so I can fuck you."

His teeth are exposed: somewhat thin, razor sharp, glaring white, and extraordinarily long. The man's ears grow at the sides of his head, which become pointed, elongated, and begin to pulse with blue veins. His fingers look as if they stretch, bulge with more bones and massive knuckles, and become accessorized with claws that are bone-colored and quite thick. His lips turn a lush red hue and his eyes begin to transform into gold rings with flecks of piercing red. A smile grows eerily over his face and exemplifies that he is pure evil, of no goodness, and wants to hurt me. Carlos Santiago isn't a man at all, I realize. Hell has opened up, and he has stepped out of its fiery and demonic tomb. And here on Earth, he has subsequently decided to harm mortals, whatever it takes in his power to live, craving their blood, bodies, and whatnots to survive.

The dramatics of this morning meeting/interview with him become quite startling for me. Suddenly, he rises from his seat, holds his ten inches of throbbing, veined, and dark pole in his left hand, and comes around my desk. His motion is swift and rather unexpected. Here, he stands above me, looks deep into my eyes, and proves that he is hungry for my skin, sexually powerful, and not one to easily and convincingly tell no to.

Just before I finally find the courage to decide to call security, preventing a wicked scene between biographer and middleweight boxer/vampire ... just before my sanity kicks in and ...

He rips my dress shirt apart by its buttons, delighted to find no T-shirt underneath. Cotton is shredded by his claws and buttons fly in all directions throughout the office. As I try to pull away from him, his right palm grips my left pec and gives it a hearty squeeze; it feels wonderfully perfect, yet sinister at the same time, perhaps almost too rough for my sexual taste.

"Carlos," escapes my mouth, a plea to prevent him from continuing this flesh-and-fantasy show between us. I want to remind him that I have a man in my life, one that I can become serious within the recent weeks to come, if Fate and Destiny are on my side. This doesn't transpire, though. Instead, things begin to turn exceedingly ugly between us ...

Above me, having no intention of listening to my defense, the vampire growls down at me, "Perfect for my needs. Hungry for your blood."

Within seconds, my chin is cupped by his left palm and his prying fingers dig into my jaws. Angrily, I am pulled upward, forced onto the desk. Here, my back is pressed against the desk's surface. And here, my nipples are pinched and his tongue deviously finds my comma-shaped navel, rippled abs, and discovers my pulsing neck with its swollen veins.

He is not a gentleman with my skin, I learn, and prefers rough sex with his men. Biting is about to ensue. Heavy growls are heard. His grip on my jaws tightens.

Again, I want to explain that I am not at all interested in this aggressive event between us. In fact, I rather find it repulsive and physically abusive. As muttering and an awkward sound of vowels exit my lips, I become completely weak under the monster, knowing I don't stand a chance to survive during this scene of violence.

Experienced with bullying, following through with his relentless instinct, he pulls my belt open and now loosens the buttons and zipper on my khakis, only to discover no underwear and my semi-hard stick leaking male-ooze between my legs.

"Carlos," I say his name again as I attempt to push him away. One of his palms finds my throat, compresses its flesh, causes its veins to swell to his liking, and begins to squeeze air off.

I am pinned to the desk, immobile and breathless. I become the man's victim so easily, under his beastly power. The more I begin to struggle beneath his force, the more pain he applies to my throat. How easy it is for me to slip into a state of unconsciousness, but I don't. I try to hold my ground, strength ... something.

His other palm wraps around my nine inches of meaty flag at its base. As seconds tick by, his mouth begins to fall over my pulsing neck and he whispers, "What I want ... What I really came here for."

My mind travels elsewhere as I am being taken advantage of within Room 329: to a wedding between the artist and me; selecting and renting tuxedoes; leasing a limousine; purchasing yellow and off-white orchids as decorations for our special day; choosing a wedding cake and appetizers; preparing party favors for our one-hundred-fifty guests; picking out the perfect songs to dance to at our reception; lighting candles and ...

What transpires next is nothing that I expect. The door to the office opens and ... Kal appears in my blurred vision, standing behind me. The sound he makes is of disgust, a rather obnoxious huff mixed with a grunt. Or, is this Carlos at my neck, sniffing what he wants to eat for his midmorning snack, savoring my skin/blood/tissue inside his system? I'm really not sure.

I try to yell for Kal to help me, but only a weak groan escapes my mouth, which instead sounds like pleasure. My right arm thrusts backward, over my head, and reaches for the artist, expressing my entrapment by the Panamanian vampire, but Kal ignores my plea. Instead, he sees nothing more than my prick between my legs.

In the doorway, Kal exclaims, "You motherfucker, Cam!" and witnesses the boxer's head as it shifts north and south against the length of my tight neck. Outraged, Kal exits the office just as quickly as he arrives. He slams the door behind him and stomps down the hallway, exclaiming in a tantrum to my coworkers that I am a trashy whore, a slut, and someone he should have never trusted in the first place. Within seconds, he is gone, vanished from my life, history between us in the making – an ending to our wonderful something that we have so temporarily shared together.

Again, I try to mutter a plea for help under the boxer's grip. Again, I try to scream for my life. Again, I attempt to squirm on the desk's surface, unpinning myself from the middleweight's power. But to no avail, I am kept a prisoner under his wicked, vampire weight that feels like lead.

I wish Steven would enter my office at this very second and save me, but this action doesn't transpire. The office door is closed. Unlocked, but still closed, and Steven is nowhere in sight.

Now, I realize I have to save myself before ... the monster on top of me decides to take what he wants from me: my blood, soul, and mortal life. Here, he will have his way with me, savoring my veins and red blood to the fullest, unsafe and harmful with my neck; a villain at my throat who only wishes to murder me.

As this gruesome picture of forced death unfolds within my mind, I find the strength to jolt upward, lift my torso off the desk, and sit up. In doing so, strength is found in my right fist, which becomes balled. Quickly, I bash the boxer in the side of his skull, which immediately stops his tyranny.

The look on his face is of a serious nature: furrowed brows, wide eyes, and pursed lips. He rises from me, consuming what has just happened between us. The man is utterly blown away that I have actually slugged him with a fist. The middleweight boxing champion has just been struck by a light-weight faggot biographer.

As he grapples this information, consuming it to the best of his ability, allowing it to sink behind his eyes, it is my only time to escape. Quickly, I jump off the desk, rush to the office door, and yell out to my fellow employees, "Security! ... Call security!"

What follows within the next few minutes is rather daunting: security immediately arrives; Carlos is instructed to dress; an escort takes place, and he is forced to leave the building; I find an extra dress shirt within my desk that I keep on hand for unexpected measures such as this scene; Steven asks me if he should call the police, but I decline; he makes sure I'm fine, which I am; he inquires if I will press charges, which I decide not to. The dramatic explosion calms within the next few minutes. Journalists return to their desks. Steven has a meeting to attend and escapes my side.

Bottom line: I decide to head home; I refuse to write the boxer's biography, which never appears in the *Caller*; Kal escapes from my life just when I believe I emotionally have him. The vampire goes to sleep, falling dormant within

Plimpton City, avoids me, has no interest in me, and proves that our short relationship was fatal and now completely over, dissolved.

Chapter 7 – Feeding

I call Kal a dozen or more times; he ignores every single one of them. I text him; none are responded to. Two days turn into four days without any communication from him. I decide to send him an e-mail, which explains the office scene in full detail: the boxer's striptease, his seduction, and how he pushed me onto my desk, willing to forcefully take advantage of me, and started to plunge his teeth into my neck. I paint an ugly picture of predator and prey, which is the truth.

An e-mail is returned from Kal. Excitement floods through my core when I see it hanging on my flat-screen. I click on it and read his jolting admission in capital letters: I DON'T BELIEVE YOU. YOU'RE A PLAYER. LIAR. MAN-WHORE.

Anger is not discovered on my part because I like him a little too much. Instead, I'm hurt, stunned, and need a strong drink, which I find in the kitchen. Leaning against the counter with a tumbler half-full of Johnny Walker over ice, I determine that the air between us needs to be cleared. If I can only just have an hour with the man and explain what transpired in my office with the boxer … if Kal can just talk to me for a few seconds and consume the honest details of that awkward event inside Room 329 … if Kal can just open up his ears (and heart) and ingest the truth … we can become one again, in full.

I learn that Carlos Santiago is asked never to step inside the *Plimpton City Caller* again. None of the dozen journalists create his athletic history on paper and distribute an article to the newspaper's valuable readers.

I gain a new interest to write about for the paper. Molly Cobanchau, a Sioux Indian residing in the city. Her biography in the paper will entail: her family's history, significant persons of her legacy that have helped build our community, her luster for life through her historical romantic novels which are published by Berkeley.

Our meeting is planned for next Monday, November 11. Unlike the interview that wrongfully transpired within my office with the boxer, I determine that a public place of interest should be the setting. A certain coffee shop on Milner Street is the perfect place, where I will feel safe in my interviewee's company.

#####

This night, Carlos is murdered. His body is found by two queer men in a back alley in the downtown area. His neck is sliced open, as well as his chest. Some of his organs are missing. His teeth look as if they have been burned out. His eyes are no longer in their sockets. The man's penis and balls are unattached from his body.

It's Kal's work, I realize. His jealous rage. His anger for seeing Carlos with me inside my office. Carlos Santiago's murder is expected, I presume, since Kal enjoys my company and skin. In truth, the murder doesn't surprise me at all. Instead, it's a mere sign that Kal Fleet still admires me, wants to be with me, and considers my heart his. I'm taken, I know. I belong to the vampire. And I'm very much aware that we will be together for eternity because of his murderous action.

#####

The November day is chilly with a few flurries. The temperature sinks below thirty, which offers a perfect desire for a hot cup of coffee at Allister's Coffee & Pastries.

It is late in the afternoon, and the historical romance novelist is punctual. Our meeting entails her history as a

217

writer, her likeness for blue collar men, and if she plans on marrying in the near future to her current, but nameless boyfriend. The interview is swift and a rather easy process to carry out. Miss Cobanchau is witty, spry, a vixen, and will be very entertaining for those interested in picking up the *Caller* and reading about her.

Following the interview, I decide to have dinner out at The Estuary, an upscale surf and turf grill where I relentlessly and pleasurably consume shrimp scampi, twice-baked potatoes, and almond-coated green beans. The coffee is rich with half-and-half, and exactly what I need. Unfortunately, I pass on a creamy dessert, since I don't want to feel uncomfortable on my drive home, and for the rest of the evening.

Kal follows me home; I sense him around me, behind me, somewhere nearby, and watching my every move. I believe I see him at stop signs, half hidden behind buildings, and other places. A blur of his figure surfaces at the corners of my eyes. One second he is there and during the next he isn't. It's not my imagination playing tricks on me, I know. I feel his presence in my vicinity. The vampire lurks around me and studies my every move, craving my skin – everything about me.

Once at home, I shower, decide to read a current bestseller with a glass of red wine, and become comfortable on my sofa in the living room. Perhaps I carry out this pleasure for a mere twenty minutes when pounding ensues on my Tudor's front door. As the banging continues, I set the novel aside, rush to the door, and decide to unsafely confront the culprit.

Kal stands at my doorway: sinewy and smelling of blood, red-eyed and white-faced. His fingernails are three times their normal length. He has fresh blood on his cheeks, chin, lips, and teeth. The young man pushes his way into the foyer, passing me. Here, he sways left and right, and spouts, "You've been an asshole, Cameron. I just want to tell you that."

"You've been feeding," I try to rationalize with him; perhaps this being a mistake on my part since he is on a mission of discontent and being foolish.

"You've stung my heart," the man utters, heading toward the living room in a sloppy and weaving manner. Within seconds, he falls on the sofa, next to my best-seller, leans his head back, and implores, "I really liked you. When I saw you with Carlos ... something twisted inside my chest and felt as if you were sending me to hell. It was horrible to watch."

Is he crying on the sofa? I'm not really sure since his face is covered with blood and his teeth are fully grown. I close the foyer's door, cross into the living room, and decide to tell him, "Kal, you need to come off your high. Your feeding is causing you to act like you're drunk. Maybe then we can have this conversation."

He lifts his head from the back of the sofa and utters with disdain in his voice, "Maybe by then I'll find someone new who doesn't fuck around with my heart."

His comment is like fire applied to my ears and sears me. Instead of responding in a negative manner, I decide to try and help him sober up. I say to the artist, "You need a cup of coffee and rest."

"I really don't. What I need is for you to care about me more, love me, and spend the rest of your life with me. I want you to be mine. We get to choose our partners and I want you as my partner. Obviously, this isn't going to happen since your whorish scene with the boxer in your office."

I ignore his comment again. This time I escape his side and head into the kitchen, passing through the *Architectural Digest*-perfect dining room. Here, I find a Hall mug the color of cobalt blue and pour him a soothing mug of hot coffee. Before returning to his side I find a dish cloth, wet it down, and carry it with the mug of coffee into the living room.

During my entrance, the young man utters with venom in his voice, "I don't want anything more from you. Our little gig is over. I know what you're made of and find you disgusting."

I admit the words sting me. But, the man is completely intoxicated on the blood and his feeding this evening. Is it possible that he has consumed bad blood, poisoned by his own maddening travels? I believe so. Why does he act like this? How can he break me down in such an easy manner?

I place the coffee mug in front of him, tell him to have a few sips, to clean his face off with the dish cloth, and decide to sit across from him in a high-backed reading chair that I never use, finding it completely uncomfortable, such as the moment at hand with him.

His degrading, ruthless, and unappealing monologue continues, which breaks my heart. I realize the man is fully inebriated, under the stranger's blood spell, and not himself. Half of me wants to care for him, walk him up to the spare bedroom on the second floor, peel his delicious body out of their clothes, and tuck him into the queen-size bed for the night. This, unfortunately, will not transpire, though. Tonight will end rather badly and briskly between us, and he will inevitably rush out of the Tudor in a blood-drunk huff, flee into the night, and abandon my side.

He speaks: "The boxer's cock was all over you. I saw it with my own eyes. He wanted nothing more than to shove his dick inside your ass and fuck the hell out of you. The sad part about your office-gig with him is rather upsetting ... you wanted to be fucked. I could see it in your eyes, and I could smell it all over you. At first, I thought it was fear, but it wasn't. Everything about you was longing for his shaft to be rammed into your bottom. That's what you wanted. That's what you desired.

"To think I was opening up to you, allowing you closer access to my heart. To think I wanted to start something serious with you ... the artist and the biographer. To think I had every intention of calling you my boyfriend, adoring you, and emotionally caring for your needs. How foolish I was. How fucking stupid of me. You're nothing to me after what I have witnessed between you and the boxer. Nothing at all. In fact, you make me sick."

I shouldn't defend myself, but do. Perhaps this is a waste of time on my part, since the man across from me is completely intoxicated, rank with the smell of bittersweet blood, golden-eyed with flecks of burnt red, and angry to his fullest potential. I must share my side of the story with him, though, or at least what I feel he will remember regarding this evening's confrontation and his blood-stupor.

Now, I take a deep breath and provide in a soft and soothing voice, "The truth of the matter is rather easy to understand, Kal. As I have tried to explain to you in a previous e-mail and numerous voice messages, I was tossed onto the desk. My shirt was ripped open, and I was being taken advantage of. Carlos Santiago was on a mission to carry out a terrible and forceful act with my skin. I was a victim. He was going to bite my neck and take my life away from me, I believe. Those moments in my office were scary and alarming. I wanted nothing of the sort like that to transpire between us. In fact, I merely wanted to collect information from the man for my piece of writing, as my job entails."

"I know what kind of piece you wanted from him," he challenges, raising his head from the back of the sofa. "I saw it with my own eyes. You were cock-hungry. Here and now, you're lying to me. You wanted his dick inside you. You wanted his middleweight body to fuck you. You wanted to be under him."

What transpires next between us will forever be a tiny scar that we can never remove. It is a sliver of a gash along our relationship's skin that will never truly heal. It begins when I say to the artist, "This is untrue. I was being taken advantage of."

Fire enters the man's eyes across from me. A wicked grin spreads across his face and he yells at me, "You're a fucking liar!"

I shake my head, attempt to defend myself yet again, which is sort of stupid on my part since the man is high on his blood fix.

"You're a whore!" he fires off at me, pointing at me over the walnut coffee table that separates us. "You were practically begging for his boxing cock to be jammed inside you."

"It's not true," I admit, continuing to shake my head. "You're drunk, Kal. You don't know what you're saying."

"I know exactly what I'm saying," he snips at me, slurring his words. "You're a fucking man-whore, and all you want is cock."

I continue to shake my head, which I really shouldn't, adding fuel to his fire. Instead, I should merely sit with my trap shut, still and emotionless. This doesn't unfold in the way I wish it to, though. Instead, I say to him, "You've had far too much to drink this evening. Who did you suck? I think you've been poisoned. You're not yourself, Kal. Maybe you should go upstairs and lay down. Spend the night. Rest. You can sleep the rush off."

As if he finds a bolt of energy in his body, he rises from the sofa, rounds the coffee table, stands over me, and becomes face to face with me. His blood-scented breath blows against my face, grazing my lips, eyes, and nose. And here, atop me, parallel to my seated body, he growls, "I saw what I saw. You were being a whore."

Silence. Stillness. An interlude occurs during our shared confrontation. Now, unexpectedly, his right hand swings upward from his right side and its open palm swings against my left cheek, forcing my head to the left in quick motion. The sound that ensues is a hearty snap, and a humph from my lips. Two droplets of blood leak out between my lips, dripping down from my chin. Pain surfaces on my cheek and lips, a biting and stinging sensation that will not go away anytime soon, reminding me of the man's fury, his tyranny over me, and this unbelievable connection of violence between us.

He licks away the two droplets of blood with his extended tongue and says, "If I didn't love you, I'd kill you right now. Your life means too much to me, though. You mean too much to me. Do you know that? You must. I can feel it within my heavy chest that you do."

He leaves in an outrage. The artist rises from me, huffing and puffing. Blood is still smeared over his face and now decorates my face. His eyes are the size of full moons. Like a bull, he charges toward the foyer and its door, following through with his exit. In doing so, I call out to him, "Kal, don t leave! ... You can't drive like this! ... You'll kill yourself!"

Once in the foyer, looking like a monster, something out of a horror film, he erupts with more anger, "Fuck you! ... Like you give a shit about me!"

The words sting me. It feels as if my flesh is being lacerated by razors or sharp teeth, one unstoppable slash after the next. The pain is alarming, incomprehensible, and hurtful. I can't believe what I hear. I can't believe what transpires between us. I can't believe ...

Hurriedly, he opens the foyer's door and rushes out. He slams the plane of wood and glass behind him, which rattles in its frame. His exit is nothing I want to remember, more scarring tissue that will forever leave me to wonder if he can handle his required feeding, and my heart, or not.

Within seconds, I hear his Ford Escape's engine, squealing tires, and off he goes into the night, reckless, speeding, and putting his life in danger while vanishing in his intoxicated state of being blood-high.

Chapter 8 – HUNK'S

Heartbroken, confused, lost, and certainly not myself, I decide to take Steven up on his offer to have drinks at Hunk's, a college bar on Waiteford Street in downtown Plimpton City. The bar is packed with bare-chested hotties that happen to sport bugling chests, biceps of steel, and ripped tummies. Blonds, dark-haired juniors, and red-headed sweethearts dance to Lady Gaga hits on the dance floor. They gyrate together and dry-hump horny bodies with pleasure. Others lean against the walls and heavily kiss, drilling tongues into mouths and moving palms under denim.

Two bartenders in tight black tees, navigate their bar area. Beers are passed to thirsty paying clients. Whiskey, vodka, and rum are poured into shot glasses. Smiles reek on their pretty boy faces as the college boys at Hunk's flirt heavily with the two, grade-A beefy men, fulfilling their boner-hard desires.

Pedestal tables without chairs decorate the establishment. Steven and I stand at one sharing bottles of a light beer. Our shoulders practically brush together; this is how close we are. To those circulating our twosome, we look like an intimate couple, even though we aren't. Instead, we are here to discuss the artist in full, his drunken spell the night before, his outrage, and the chaos regarding Carlos, the boxer.

During my detailed spill of prior events within my office concerning Carlos, and within my Tudor regarding the angry and cheek-hitting Kal, I become a little tipsy on numerous beers. Here at Hunk's, I have too many drinks, become sloppy, and try to hold my composure intact.

Steven says to me between his own bottles of beer, "Kal will come around. Give him some space. He needs to think about his relationship with you."

I shake my head, disbelieving what my best friend says. "Kal is history. The man wants nothing to do with me.

Although I had no control of the situation in my office with the boxer ... he will never speak to me again because of it."

"Do you want me to have a private meeting with him to clarify the events at hand? Maybe he just needs to hear it from a third party that you were an innocent victim, that the boxer's intention with your skin was all one-sided."

"Kal won't hear it," I say, bummed that I admit this to myself, and Steven. "He has it set in his mind that I'm a whore, a fuck for anyone who wants to fuck around."

Steven shares a sour look with me, shakes his head, and replies, "I don't believe you. And surely, you don't believe that."

"Honestly," I admit to him, "I don't know what to believe. I only know that Kal wants nothing to do with me. Bottom line: I'm no longer a part of his life, just when we were starting to kick things off between us."

We have another beer together; Steven pays for the round. Here, we still stand at the pedestal-shaped table, and discuss my previous, but short affair with the artist. He admits, "Let me have a little chat with the guy. I can maybe clear things up between the two of you."

"You can do whatever you want, Steven, but I imagine it's not going to help the situation." I sound seriously depleted, giving up on the matter.

"How much do you like this guy, Cam?"

"A lot. I think we could have spent a few years together, perhaps even for the rest of our lives. I wanted to give it some time. He wasn't just a fuck for me, even if he thought that.'

"So you're serious about him?" It's a question more than a comment by my friend. A smile bridges on his adorable face that tells me he is up to no good.

"Of course. Why? What are you up to?"

"Don't worry about me," he confesses. "You just worry about yourself."

"I try to do that every day of my life."

"Don't we all," he admits, still grinning at me, proving to the both of us that he will surely have a private talk with the artist and explain the unfriendly and forceful events that transpired within my office between Carlos and me.

"Steven," I say his name in a serious manner, needing to release something heavy from my chest.

"Yes, my friend."

"When did you realize Kal Fleet was a vampire?"

"When you first asked me if I believed in such."

"And you told me you didn't."

"A man has a right to change his mind, don't you agree?"

"He does," I somberly reply, consuming his comments in full, absorbing them between my temples.

"I watched him closely, Cam. When an important man enters your life, I have this unfailing need to protect you."

"Me?" I question, caught completely off guard by his confession.

"Yes, you." He nods his head, simply stares at me with somewhat dead eyes. "I'm not proud to say that I have done my own personal study of Mr. Fleet."

"To protect me?" I question, disbelieving him, unsure of his admission.

"Yes, of course. Why wouldn't I want to protect you? You're very important in my world."

I become silent and motionless. My head begins to spin and I ... I can't believe what he has just shared with me. Now, I ask, "You approve of Kal, don't you?"

"I do," he says, nodding. "Believe it or not, he's not going to hurt you. I have a lot of faith in his heart and feel that he loves you to the fullest. Sometimes you have to leave bygones as bygones."

When Steven finally flutters off to the bathroom releasing his bladder after a number of light beers, I am left alone at our two-person, chest-high table. Here, a Marine with a blond buzz cut, hazel eyes, broad shoulders, and Colt-like muscles moves up to me. He leans across the table in his too-tight tank that defines every rippled muscle on his bulky torso, smiles at me, takes me in with his beautiful and enchanting eyes, and asks, "You alone tonight?"

I am. I'm not. I am. I'm not. I can't make up my mind. My affair with the artist has come full circle and is now over. We are not together. We are not coupled. Steven is simply my best friend and nothing more, someone who has my back and loves me because he just does. Here, I take in the Marine and his model-perfect looks. I absorb his confrontation with ease. And here, "Yes, I'm alone," eventually slips out of my mouth, advising the rock-hard and sexy Marine to proceed with his manly act of likeness, or whatever else he has in mind to carry out with my time and/or flesh.

"Do you want another beer?" Marine asks me, studying my bottle's label.

I shake my head and admit, "I think I've already had one too many."

"Do you want to dance?"

One of my favorite Keisha songs blares down from the overhead speakers, which causes me to nod, and reply, "I'd like to dance with you."

In a matter of seconds I am whisked to the dance floor, spun around, collapsed against his hulking chest, and feel his T-shirt against my dress shirt, which allows our nipples to touch and our biceps to glide against each other's. Now, with his face flush to my face, his breath entering my mouth with such ease, he leans into me and kisses me. My lips are separated and he slips his tongue into the gap of my mouth.

The kiss is sultry and smooth and everything I need at the moment in my state of blitzed-niceness. Together, torso locked against torso, we sway to and fro to a slow song by The Script. Here, our mouths continue to connect with a random sweetness between men who find each other attractive, and perhaps long to undress in a private room somewhere in the city where we will inevitably collide and become one – mortal with mortal.

Once our kissing and dancing ends, Marine escapes to the bathroom to piss out his beers. This gives me a sufficient amount of time to speak with Steven, who seems very impressed with my naughty-big find within the hunky bar. Steven says to me, "Go home with him. You've had a very stressful week and need to relax. Let him seduce you. Have your way with his skin. Blow him. Fuck him. Do what you do to guys that make you happy. Use him the way he wants to be used."

I agree and end up going home with the stranger. The Marine drives his fancy Mazda back to his apartment on Wessner Street, and I follow behind in my H2. In a matter of minutes, we end up at his abode, a cool little apartment consisting of four rooms (living room, kitchen, bathroom, and bedroom), tiny windows, a wall-size flat-screen, and a California king-size bed.

As expected, inside his bedroom, he strips for me. His tank is pulled free from his nicely sculpted body, which allows me to study his hairless torso: pert nipples, crafted pecs, lined abs, and a hollow navel. He removes his jeans, sports no underwear, and begins to toy with the eight inches of hard and uncut beef between his muscular thighs. One buck into his fist turns into three bucks with delighted pleasure and an intoxicating smile is spread over his adorable and youthful face.

He moves up to me and starts to undress me. My Brooks Brothers shirt is removed and dropped to the floor. My nipples are pinched, kissed, and licked with his unyielding hunger. The man is all over my torso, and has every intention of using my skin for his unlimited desire. North and south movement occurs to my pumped chest with his tongue, which navigates greedily over my swollen pecs, ladder-like stomach, and my concave-structured navel.

When the stranger decides to fall to his naked knees, he unbuttons my jeans and opens them with his busy fingertips. Now he is ready and willed to swab his tongue and mouth against my shaft. A blowjob begins that will surely knock me off my feet, but I push him away and step backward. What I say is rather jolting to the sexy beast of a man, "I can't do this."

In the shadows of the room, light caused by the streetlights outside the smallish window and decorates his bedroom, he wipes the back of his left palm across his beautiful and puffy lips, and questions, "Why?"

I'm honest with him, limp between my legs, perhaps uninterested in getting off with the stranger, and admit, "There's this guy I like. I broke his heart. He's an artist. I really want to do this with him. I'm sorry."

I learn that the Marine is a complete gentleman and understands my predicament. He finds my shirt on the floor, passes it up to me, and tells me, "I'm sorry. I didn't mean to be pushy tonight."

"It's not your fault," I confess. "I have other things on my mind."

"I get that," he says and rises to face me, still hard between his legs. The man seems satisfied with our encounter, though, proves to be a kind man, and very much unlike the evil boxer and his forceful ways. "Can I get you a drink or something?"

I shake my head and reply, "No thanks. I'm good," and slip into my shirt, buttoning it up. Once this is accomplished, I admit, "I should go. Sorry about this."

"It's fine," he says. Now, he jokes, "I'll put some Hot House on my flat-screen and jerk off to it."

I tell him I'm sorry again, find my way out of his miniscule apartment, and leave the stranger and his swollen cock behind.

# # # # #

I slowly drive home during the early hours of morning. Midnight is long gone. The city bars are closed. I think of the artist during most of the miles covered. I don't regret not fucking around with the Marine tonight. In fact, I think differently of myself, happy with my decision, yet sad at the same time, since I am now emotionally connected to a vampire who wants absolutely nothing to do with me. My mood becomes low, and I almost start to cry. The drive becomes long and tedious for me, a nuisance.

As I close in on my Tudor at 4258 Valley Way, I decide to carry out something crazy. I find my cell phone in the passenger seat, flip it open, discover the artist's cell phone number, dial it, and listen it to it ring: once ... twice ... three times.

Kal picks up. His voice is groggy, shallow, and filled with semi-sleep. He says, "Hello." Shouldn't he be feeding again, on the prowl throughout Plimpton City?

"Kal," escapes my mouth, now nothing. Silence follows. Stillness.

"Cameron, is this you?" he inquires, still half-asleep and dazed.

Unable to speak, shaking in the driver's seat behind the H2's steering wheel, I pull the phone away from my ear, close it, and toss it back into the passenger seat where I retrieved it only seconds before. Now I begin to cry, heartbroken with my chest feeling as if it has been mutilated by teeth and claws and the power of the night's intimate darkness. Aloneness discovers me. Emotional pain surfaces. Everything about my human soul is broken and begins to shatter around my feet. My heart bleeds with hurt; honestly, it does.

Once back on Valley Way, I park the H2 in its garage, find myself upstairs, and in my shower. Here, under a hot spray, I stand and absorb the artist's words yet again between my temples: Cameron, is this you?

Following the shower, I think about calling Steven, wanting to explain to my best friend that I decided not to sleep with the sexy Marine, that I'm spending the night alone, and that I called Kal on my cell phone while driving home from the Marine's uneventful company.

In truth, I fail to execute this call to Steven, since I already know what he's going to say to me: You're caught by the artist. The guy has you. You're a canvas that he's just waiting to paint. Plus, you're a little tipsy. Go to bed. Tomorrow is another day. Forget about tonight. Forget about Kal for the time being. Find some sleep and sanity. Enjoy a few healthy dreams. Tomorrow will be better, I promise.

# # # # #

He watches me, present again, almost all the time. I know he's around me. The vampire studies my every move and never leaves my side, even when I fall asleep. Although I can't see him because sometimes he's invisible, he is still a presence that is near, somewhere in my surroundings, so very attached to me, of course. No one can tell me otherwise. No one. How dare they if they even try.

Chapter 9 – The Tide Gallery (His Pretty Prey)

A week passes. Two weeks. Three weeks. Thanksgiving is here and gone, which I spend alone. Christmas is just around the corner. Winter is present, a bustling of snow, cold wind, and dramatic weather that I actually enjoy. Winter has always been one of my favorite seasons, particularly when it's July and almost a hundred degrees.

December 10. Sometime after two in the afternoon. A Thursday. Exactly fifteen days until Christmas. Steven enters my office with a copy of *Motif*, a high-end art magazine distributed to Pittsburgh, Rochester, Erie, Cleveland, and Buffalo. He plops the magazine on my desk, stands overtop me, and says, "Turn to page fifty-three."

I study the magazine's cover: red, white, and green. A painting of baby Jesus is being unwrapped by the Three Wise Men with saliva-dripping fangs. The painting is called "Pedophiles." Now, I heed my friend's advice, flip the magazine to page fifty-three, and feel my heart tremble.

Here, staring up at me, is a bare-chested shot of Kal Fleet, smiling from ear to ear with a delicious grin. He sits Indian-style on a beanbag chair and holds a cigarette between two fingers on his right hand. A caption above the picture reads: FLEET SHOWS HIS WORK AT THE TIDE GALLERY.

Steven shares, "The Tide Gallery is in Weston. I'm sure you've been there."

I nod. "I have."

"It's only a forty-minute drive from here. Kal's show is tonight. You should think about going."

I shake my head and reply, "The guy wants nothing to do with me."

"You should go anyway. I'm sure he's got some great drawings to look at."

I stare at the article about Kal Fleet, realize it's exactly what I would write about him, and close the magazine. "I have plans tonight. Remember that Marine that wanted to fuck me a few weeks ago. I think I'm going to let him tonight."

Steven huffs at me, knowing better. He utters with a sharp tone in his voice that is mixed with laughter, "You're full of shit. I know you dig the vampire. It's time you let your guard down and let him bite you.'"

I'm about to tell him he's wrong, but his cell phone jingles in one of his front pockets. The guy reaches for it, decides to take the call, and escapes my office, leaving me behind with the copy of *Motif* on my desk.

# # # # #

I go home from work early; Steven really doesn't give a flying fuck since I can write my articles on my laptop, anywhere in the city. Once in my cozy abode, I take a nap, drink a cup of hot tea with lemon, and stare out the window at the falling snow. A white blanket consisting of seven inches is supposed to fall by dawn, which I'm excited to see, since I adore the snow and foul weather.

Again, hours later, I see the picture within my mind of Kal sitting on the beanbag chair and holding his cigarette: sexy with his pointed teeth, alluring because of his raised ears, charming with his elongated fingernails that look like claws, a masculine pretty boy to the core. Within the abyss of my mind I hear his slanderous names again and again, which causes my heart to go cold within my chest.

Why couldn't things have worked out differently between us? This is what I think as I prepare for my evening at Hunk's, where I hope to find the Marine again, his strapping body, so very willed to ride his shaft until dawn, or the rest of winter. Quickly, I shower and shave, dress in a pair of fresh jeans, snug black T-shirt, and Italian loafers. Before I know it, Kal is exterminated from my mind. I hop into my H2, direct the vehicle toward the jock bar, and to a military guy I want to kiss, lick, suck, and fuck ... to accomplish something naughty that two men can derive together while being completely naked.

My H2 doesn't end up at Hunk's, though. Instead, approximately forty minutes later, having no control over my thoughts or actions, I end up in the parking lot at The Tide Gallery in a small town called Weston. Here, cars are parked all around me. The three-story building shaped like an upside-down triangle looms in the distance. Snow falls down from the sky, welcoming the seven inches that will accumulate by dawn. My windshield wipers on the H2 flick left and right in speedy motion. How long do I sit here like this, staring at the art gallery, willing myself to enter and confront Kal Fleet regarding my feelings for him? How long have I felt this way for the artist, connected to his heart, in lust/love/something ... for his skin to be aligned with my own ... for his lips to connect to my lips or neck ... for his arms to wrap about my torso and squeeze me against him ... for his endearing and soulful verbiage that states that he adores me? How long do I ...

I have never felt this way for another human being in my life. During my separation from him, which I have discovered as traumatic turmoil of my heart and its endearing feelings, I have ensnared loss. I cannot wake every morning without seeing the man behind my semi-closed eyelids. I cannot breathe in a morning's cup of freshly brewed coffee without thinking that he is enjoying a mug of java with me. I cannot shower without believing he is positioned behind me, rolling a bar of Dove over my shoulders and down the splay of my muscled back. I cannot drive the H2 without making myself believe that he is in the passenger seat next to me, and chats about his opinions regarding other artists in the area. I cannot ...

Of course I find my way into Kal's show, entering The Tide Gallery. Within seconds of my entrance, I fetch a glass of white wine from the open bar. Discreetly, perhaps smitten with the event at hand, I walk from one Fleet drawing to the next, enjoying such pieces as Man's Arm #45, Hands #4, Nipples #89, Biceps #32. These are his victims. The men he has fed upon. His pretty prey. The reason why he just happens to be handsome and flowing with their stolen and useful blood. His survival.

Slowly, sure of my steps, I consume every drawing in pencil and chalk by the sole artist. One piece of work turns into a few dozen as I make way through them on the first floor. Once this is accomplished, I climb to the second floor, enjoy three more dozen of Kal's pieces of art, consume each with needed pleasure, and enjoy them to their utter fullest.

Not once do I see the artist upon my current travels. If he does exist within The Tide Gallery, I cannot see him because of the many guests, gawkers, fellow artists, and buyers. In truth, the gallery is packed to its gills with a variety of young men and women, older relics of the art world, and artistic students with zesty talents. I become lost within the shuffle, a mere nobody or of no importance, a random spectator off the city's streets who is perhaps enjoying a glass of white wine and the expensive drawings on display.

I do find my way up to the third floor of The Tide Gallery. It is here where I become stunned ... shocked into silence ... and almost breathless. The walls are vast in size and painted a blazing white. LED light cascades down from the all-white ceiling, which is approximately twenty-four feet high. My attention is not drawn to the color of the titanic-size room or its bright-white hue. Instead, I begin to study Kal Fleet's pieces of art that accessorize the walls, analyzing their titles with utter surprise: Cameron's Arm #7, Cameron's Torso #8; Cameron's Shoulders #13, Cameron's Thighs #20, and Cameron's Navel #6.

There are over thirty drawings on the third floor inside the gallery, all of which describe my body parts by titles and visual likeness, exact mirror images of my sketched human form.

Here, I walk from one Fleet drawing to the next, seeing myself on the white walls, sketched by the artist's steady hands, a catalyst for his handy and capable pleasure, a model used for his talent. And here, I become lost within the pencil-drawn lips, chin, stomach, legs, feet, hands, and pecs. Here, on the walls of this third floor in a small town called Weston, a second Cameron Temple comes to life, perhaps a clone that is born again from my once-touched DNA by the artist's sexual fingertips. Here, I am splattered over the planes of whiteness, every body part, a life beyond my own, the vampire's subject, not only his arousal, but also his inspiration and unending longing, which is quite obvious to me.

Just before I prepare to leave, making my exit from The Tide Gallery, ending my adventures within the artist's world, having seen enough of myself on the third floor, I am pulled aside rather briskly by Kal Fleet's right arm, and tugged behind an unused wall within the gallery, completely hidden from all the guests, his high-priced drawings, and our past. Here, in the white-on-white-on-white empty room that resembles the young man's apartment, particularly his bedroom, he collides my back to one of its walls, pushes his chest to my chest, almost touches his lips to my lips, and briskly whispers to me, "Your blood, I smell it everywhere and long for it. I can't keep myself away from you. Addiction is the word. You cause a fatality to my soul. How powerful you are, Cam, yet you're extremely weak at the same time."

He grazes my neck with a long finger and his golden eyes shimmer with delight. Flecks of red twinkle within his pupils, become dull, and flicker again. "I wanted to tell you that I did these drawings of you, and that I was falling in love with you. You unintentionally became my muse, Cameron Temple, the inspiration of my life. Then I learned of your desk-affair with that boxer, and I became ruined. My inspiration was dead. I felt as if I had lost you and ... everything."

"Untruths," I whisper, nervous and still under his touch, spell, or something. "I was taken advantage of, but you didn't want to hear any of the details. Carlos was evil. You know that yourself. You only surmised that I was fucking the boxer when I wasn't. That wasn't the case, though. He was going to murder me and claim me as his own."

"I know that now," he whispers, sounds ashamed, direct, and to the point. He has elongated tears that run down and over his beautiful and enchanting cheeks that I wish only to

236

kiss or brush with my fingertips, but he wants nothing to do with me. Our affair is long over, completed, and now we are both singlelites again.

I'm weak against him, powerless, and without any strength to lean against the wall, which I begin to slide down on. My body wilts next to his, but he holds me up – somehow, without even touching me, uncannily – and peers into my deep eyes, studying my soul and the steamy-hot mortal embers that comprise my being.

My heart takes a wild leap and tumble within my chest. The room begins to swim around me, twisting to and fro, becoming a movement of mere waves that attempt to distract me. I stare at the man in front of me, concentrating on his sensitive and rounded eyes that are somewhat red and golden. Collected against the wall, pressed to it by his hefty force, I demand, "Tell me how you know." My voice is a harsh whisper that is unwavering and rather insistent.

"Steven shared everything with me. He called me a fool, unworthy of you, and a mere idiot. He told me to come to my senses before I lost you for good, before you hated me and ... could never forgive me for being wrong about you and Carlos."

"Steven?" I question, surprised to the bone, finding Kal's confession unbelievable.

"Yes," the artist whispers, exhaling carbon dioxide into my face. "It happened two days ago. He came to see me at my apartment. He forced his way inside and ... he demanded a drink from me. He called me a few nasty names, insulting me. He only did it, so I could begin to understand the situation between you and the boxer to the fullest. Steven was looking out for your best interest, and mine. He's truly your best friend, the light of your life. Someone who loves you as a friend, and will surely always love you."

"You killed Carlos," I say, holding my ground, unsure of the possibility that he will snap at any given second and sink his teeth into the splay of my neck, doing away with me.

He nods his head and replies, "I fed on Carlos. He tried to take something away from me that I thought was mine. Trust me when I say that he's in hell where he belongs."

"The drawings of me, Kal ... did Steven know about them?" I ask, having my mind race in a thousand directions at this very minute, which attempts to sort out and consume all of the vital details regarding this evening's meeting with the artist, and my discovery of Cameron Temple drawings on the third floor inside the gallery.

"No. No one knew. That is ... until Steven showed up at my apartment two days ago. Then, he knew. But not until then. I had dozens sitting around the apartment, littering the floor and walls. He couldn't miss them when he made his unexpected appearance at my apartment."

My mind flashes back to this afternoon and Steven entering my office with a copy of *Motif*. All I can picture is the man tossing the magazine on my desk and telling me to turn to page fifty-three, forcing me to read the article about the artist, a biography of Kal Fleet and his show at The Tide Gallery this evening. Steven knew I would come. He had planned this reunion between Kal and me by himself. My friend purposely pushed me here to the gallery, knowing that I would encounter the sketches of Cameron Temple (me!) on the third floor. Steven catapulted me into this event tonight, back into the vampire's life, his world – all of it was his creation and plan.

Kal pulls me out of the flashback and whispers into my mouth, "I love you, Cal Temple ... I have always loved you. Ever since our first encounter inside The Chandler House ... on our single date ... and even tonight. I couldn't get my mind off you and decided to draw a hundred or more pieces of you. All of your body parts. Things that reminded me of you. Pieces of you that were taken away from me. I wanted to keep you and couldn't, not when I believed you were with the boxer, not when I saw you with him and ..."

I kiss the artist, opening my mouth over his, quieting him. Our worlds blend together in synchronized bliss, replying to his chatter, and falling under his sexual spell yet again. My likeness for the undead man is far too strong to merely push him away from me and leave the gallery without having him at my side. My keenness of his body aligned with my own, his heart beating next to my heart, and his daily events entwined with my own daily events are all signs of my own love for him, my reality and our destiny of combined worlds. I will not deter our closeness, pushing him away from me. Instead, I decide rather instantly to forgive the man for not understanding my situation with his nemesis, Carlos Santiago, and erase our rocky past. Here and now, I collide with Kal again, and promise never to hurt the man again, intentionally or unintentionally, for as long as we choose to be together, as one.

Chapter 10 – Spoil Me So

The show comes to an end at The Tide Gallery, and we agree to meet at my house approximately a few minutes later. "No stops," he says, "I want to seduce you with all of my heart." He dabs a kiss to the tip of my nose and provides me with a hug.

"I won't stop anywhere. I'll leave the door to my Tudor open and you can find your way in."

"I really don't need a door to enter, but it sounds like a plan."

"Don't be too long."

"Never," he replies, shaking his head. "I can't wait to have you ... again."

Fifteen minutes later, we have a drink in my Tudor: two fingers of bourbon on the rocks in each glass tumbler. The wind twirls outside, whips against the house, and creates a distraught noise that I oddly find soothing. Our drinks go down smooth as the snow builds into a winter-white tempest over Plimpton City. Our heartbeats race as we crave each other. And the temperature rises within my living room by the mere act of this meeting between us.

Face to face, the artist says, "I missed you."

"You didn't," I tease him, knowing he did miss me, and that I missed him.

"I did miss you, Cam. Deep inside." He taps his chilly heart with two fingertips and drains his drink down to its ice cubes.

"It's over now. All is good between us."

We come together in silence, setting our drinks on a nearby table in the living room. Both of us are mere shadows among the arrangement of furniture. Our lips connect, fall apart, and connect again. We peel each other's clothes off with zest, clear down to our bare and muscular bodies, and drop our gear to the floor with ease, hungry for each other's skin.

He kisses my chest, one nipple at a time. His kisses turn into hyper licks as he falls on his knees to the wooden floor. His tongue lathers my abs and navel, and the top of my triangular patch of bristly man-hair. The vampire holds my hips with both palms. Our sexual romance begins as he opens his mouth and slips the head of my plump stick between his shuttering lips.

I perceive rather willingly that he truly has missed me during our time apart, and that a sliver of his pulsing heart, or a grander portion of the organ, is the landlord of my soul. As the artist covets my solid tool within his mouth, devouring the post at my winter-warm middle, I determine quite clearly that he is in love with me, proving such an endearing condition with my nine-inch long spike inside his cozy mouth. Lust, passion, and this naked connection is what we decide to process together, coupling one man with another, perhaps lost and bewildered in an upright and lips-to-cock method that we both pose no rejections to, continuing this heated sex-spell to its fullest potential. Man-enchantment is shared. Bliss between the two of us is conquered. This is what we selfishly demand and carry out during this night following his show at The Tide Gallery. This is what we long for and possess so easily.

I do believe with all my heart and soul in serendipity as the man rocks his face to and fro on my lengthy knob. Here, we carry out a homoerotic dance within my living room, perhaps exactly what we have both longed for since our last, naked encounter.

Unstoppable head-to-rod passion continues between us. An east to west current is proven to satisfy the both of us as his lips and throat cause friction to the throbbing erection at my mid-point. Slurps and slobbers turn into an audible symphony that can easily be titled Oral Satisfaction #7. And our intimate action, the motion of a vampire and mortal man – a couple who has lost something eternal but is now rediscovered again – collide ... separate ... collide ... separate ... collide ... that becomes a pencil drawing titled Spoil Me So, one that we create together, and with much tenderness.

What is this fabric of united men who have the persistent attraction to each other's bodies? What becomes of us – the artist/vampire and the biographer/mortal – when intimate fire occurs between our naked flesh? What splendidness develops as he cradles my firm cock with his narrow and tight throat?

I imagine both of us agree that this is fantastical pleasure mixed with ardent love, without any questions asked whatsoever.

I whip against the artist's face, pull away, and whip against it yet again. This brisk and sloppy motion continues for the next three ... seven ... twelve minutes, providing him with an exceptional meal of tubular meat, which slides in and out of his throat with swift motion that is mind-numbing for the pair of us.

Yes, if you should know, if you dare to even think of the sexual frenzy and likeness that occurs between us within this semi-illuminated living room during a winter's snowstorm, the vampire decides to tenderly push me over the back of my German sofa and have his greedy way with my bottom. Lick after lick transpires. His tongue circles each rump with delight. The tip of it now swirls around my taut hole, slowly delves inside, pulls away, and delves inside yet again.

I become breathless, dizzy, and unsettled on the back of the sofa. The dark room begins to swirl around me in the same pattern as the man's tongue on my man-cavern. My palms become sweaty, and I pin elongated fingers over the sofa's material, holding myself still. Moans and groans of pleasure surface from my mouth, mix with the sounds of the wind outside, and twirl within the room. Helplessly, I shake my ass in the man's face, bury my bottom against his lips, chin, and cheeks, and ride his pretty boy looks. An irrepressible need occurs and I whisper, "Deeper, Kal ... Push your face deeper inside me."

Adrift with impure lust, I practically plank the back of the sofa, allowing the artist to probe my bottom with such sufficient care. My legs are spread wide open for his amusement. And murmurs of enlightenment devour my consciousness as I fall in and out of realism. No longer are we separate. Instead, we are locked together by tongue and bottom, fulfilling each other's desires.

What happens next during this festive, flesh-act between faggots in love is nothing shocking for either of us. Rather, it is welcomed with ultimate pleas of enjoyment. Within seconds the immortal's face is replaced by his shaft, which jabs into my rump with a sudden and jarring movement. Three throbbing inches of his tool are wickedly pushed into my core, immediately tugged out, and pushed inside yet again. This action is repeated ... repeated ... repeated ... until all eight inches of his meat-sword are bucked into my system, choke my behind, bang into my organs, and provide me with the pain I so easily want to occur because of his feisty, rear-action.

"Kal!" exits my mouth within the room and bounces off its walls. "Jesus, Kal, it hurts like a motherfucker!"

His response is rather brutal, but wanted. Instead of verbally providing me with an answer, the man grapples my hips, thrusts his weight into my rear, holds his eight inches within my hub, twists his spike from left to right, and eventually pulls out.

Dramatic pounds ensue on my bottom hereafter. I become the man's toy on the sofa. In truth, it feels as if a wine barrel is being lodged inside my rump and bashes my organs. He becomes severe behind me, throttles his weight forward and backward, and builds up a fine sweat on his massive torso, which sprinkles my back and shoulders. Continuously, he dodges his post inside me, pulls out some, and presses the meat back into my crux. Bang after bang occurs; this causes me to cling to the sofa, so I don't fall to the floor. My fingers grip the cushions as his motion becomes more forceful and fluent; a to and fro action that is almost brutal, but fully enjoyed.

How shocking that the vampire decides to kick my feet apart with his own feet, and his grip on my hips becomes more powerful. The bloodsucker's bolts to my hindquarters turn into something monstrous. His east and west motion to my backside is rough and chaotic. Dart after grinding dart opens my center and pulverizes my organs. The thick shaft at his center tunnels into me, pulls away, and tunnels again, which continues for the next ten or more minutes.

Barely can I keep my weight balanced over the sofa. The undead's jolts to my posterior shove me to and fro. I'm either a little too far over the sofa's front, headfirst and stuffed into its cushions, or behind it, slipping down to the floor. Not that I'm complaining, though, since the artist's ride is memorable and pleasing. Some men such as I like a long and hard buck-game, which is exactly what he processes behind me. To complain is foolish. Instead, I relish our time spent together and this intimate act between lovers as our cock-to-ass gig continues.

Because his rump-fest is so agreeable and sends me into a torso-ripping orgasm, I cannot keep my load pent within my body. Shiver after erotic shiver waves throughout my core. Uncontrollably, I vibrate against the man, caught in his spell of lust. In a matter of sporadic seconds, a mix of time in motion, I lose my load on the back of the German sofa, ruining its expensive material. A string of cream flies out of my erect flag and splats against the sofa's back, sticking to its imported fabric with such ease. A humph escapes my mouth as this action takes place. Numbness is found and I become semi-dizzy. Utter euphoria is discovered as my cock empties white seed from my manly body.

Following my shooting jubilee, which just so happens to be a total aphrodisiac for the vampire behind me, he shares a hollow murmuring sound with me, and calls over my back, "Coming, Cameron."

One final bolt by his rammer is applied to my ass. A tug occurs as he exits my man-cavern. Now, free from my rear orifice, the man jacks his oozy cargo out of his stem. He grinds his teeth, lets out an obnoxious string of grunts, and a guttural hiss echoes within the living room. Although it is dark, I peer over my right shoulder and see the immortal swiftly tug on his beef. Hips jab at his left fist a number of times. Glowing perspiration lathers his torso. More hip-thrusts ensue and ... fire mixed with white sap shoots out of his dagger-shaped cock and lands on my spine, shoulder blades, ass cheeks, and the nape of my neck. Kal now lets out a sensual moan of gratification, proving his amusement with my flesh. Within seconds, he completely empties his undead-payload, becomes drained, and needs to feed on fresh blood because of his current state of post-sexed exhaustion.

# # # # #

Spent, heaving for breath within the chilly evening after our sex-act, he lays down on the sofa and says, "Come here."

I climb on top of him, chest to chest and cock to cock. We intimately kiss, barely capable of breathing from our man-inside-man action. Tongues entwine as the snowstorm continues to whip and twirl outside the Tudor. Here, we are cozy against each other and relish the moment together.

Beneath me, he pulls out of our kiss and begins to giggle like a little boy.

"What?" escapes my lips, curious of his laughter.

"You," he chants, staring into my azure eyes.

"What about me?"

"I want you to join me, Cam."

The surety in his voice is unsettling yet hypnotizing at the same time. I inquire, "You want to transform me?"

"I do."

"How and when?" My response poses no confrontation with the vampire. In truth, I do want to be transformed, changed into one of his kind, immortal and nocturnal, and his lover for eons to come.

"Here and now," he whispers, caught up in our passion and conversation, willing me to become his undead partner forever. "I merely graze your neck with my mouth and ... a pinch will happen. I'll drink some of your blood and then you can drink it out of my mouth."

"It sounds sinful."

"It's immortality," he whispers, glowing from ear to ear with delight, welcoming me into his dark ways.

"How long will the transformation take?"

"A few days. You'll be fine during the days. The effects happen after dark. You'll become sick with a headache for three days, but I'll take care of you. It's like having the flue, but it will pass."

"Of course," I whisper, consuming his details. Now, I turn my neck to his mouth and add, "take me, Kal. Make me yours. I'm ready to become one with you."

It happens rather swiftly and unromantically. Beside me, he applies his lips to my stretched neck, licks the length of it, opens his mouth, and ...

A pinch occurs and blood pours into his mouth. I gasp and he groans at the exact same time. He swallows some of my blood into his system, licks his lips, and eventually meets his lips with my own. Now, he kisses me with his tongue and outstretched fangs, and swirls his tongue with my own. I taste my bittersweet blood and his saliva as the two mix in a liquidy pool. The blend is hot and sizzling, and feels like fire in my mouth. I swallow the concoction down the back of my throat, feel it burn the inside of my body, and ...

He pulls away from me and says, "I love you, Cameron Temple."

"I am yours ... forever."

"Mine," he whispers, and we kiss again as immortals this time, united as one until the end of days on this planet.

After making love a second time, he says, "Shower time," and pushes me away from him and off the German sofa. "And then we go to bed. I'm spending the night here."

"Your sticky mess is all over me," I confess with my ooze-covered back and fingers. The rich smell of masculine sex lingers about the living room, wafting from one corner to the next. I feel a bit dizzy because of my transformation, windswept and somewhat drunk. My vision blurs, and my legs are weak. Every organ within my body feels as if it is on fire.

"It's my mark. I leave it wherever I go."

I laugh at this, enjoy his company yet again, realize he is the right guy for me, and that Steven's discreet plan of getting me to go to The Tide Gallery to find Kal again was pretty remarkable, and clever. I walk with my confidant to the bathroom and inquire, "Just how many marks have you left in Plimpton City, among other cities?"

"Too many to count," he provides, chuckling. "I'm quite the man-whore if you want to know the truth."

He's playing, I know. Kal is not a slut, or some racy name that describes him as easy. In truth, he's the complete opposite: careful about who ends up in bed with, and very cautious of those who he opens his heart to. This is what I surmise while following him up the stairs and to the bathroom for a quick shower and heavy-duty kissing under its hot spray. This is the immortal I have helplessly fallen for, and want to spend eternity with, however long fate and destiny will have us linked together.

Responding to his statement, I say, "You're my vampire-whore," and smack his bare ass with my right palm, coaxing him forward in a sexual manner.

"The only one," he admits, laughing as he closes in on the bathroom first.

"Exactly," I say behind him, glowing from ear to ear, excited about having him spend the night with me, and many nights to come as we feed together, enjoy sex, and whatever else he will teach me in the months and years to come as his vampire lover.

Epilogue – New Year's Day

Where are we almost three weeks later? Lost in New York City on New Year's Day, hand in hand, attempting to find Greenwich Village and one of Kal's vampire friend's apartments. It's almost dusk out, and the sky is covered in an overcast of thick gray. A snowstorm is coming, which will paralyze the massive city for a day. The two of us are here on business, a sort of solidarity trip to seal the deal of our boyfriendhood, and to have a meeting at The Luther Gallery in SoHo, where Kal will be having his next show. He is meeting Hendrich Fieldman, a high-end agent in the city that wants to take him on as a new client. The meeting is scheduled for tomorrow at lunchtime. Kal is extremely excited, and realizes this is his walk of fame. To not have the meeting with the German is foolish, the end to his career. The meeting is a must for him to attend; the true reason for our short trip and stay in the city.

As a support, I'm right here at his side. Together we become tourists in the wild city and have the time our lives. Kal finds the balls to ask a complete stranger (tall, dark, and handsome) if he can help us find the street we are looking for. The gentleman obliges, shivering in the winter's cold. He tells us where to go, wishes us luck, and vanishes among the city people.

While we walk to his friend's apartment building, some three city blocks away, I reflect on the past few months with the artist: the biographical article I was writing about him; our meeting at The Chandler House; our sexual longing for each other; his vampire identity exposed; my unexpected ordeal with the evil boxer; the tempest between us; his show at The Tide Gallery; our reunion inside the gallery; spending Christmas together; last night here in New York City and Times Square; and now ... lost somewhere in search of a street in Greenwich Village, just the two of us together among the buildings, taxis, and snow flurries. A smile surfaces on my face and a tender warmness collects within my chest. I realize two implicit things: I love the vampire and wouldn't want to be lost with anyone else in this hulking city and mad-capped world, honestly.

www.ingramcontent.com/pod-product-compliance
Lightning Source LLC
Chambersburg PA
CBHW052029020726
47501CB00004B/1323